The Saga of Kee, Book I:

Nogard

by: Robert Conard

The Saga of Kee, Book I:

Nogard

Written by: Robert Conard

Copies of this book may be purchased at Amazon.com and other online retailers, and as a Kindle or Nook ebook.

Cover image is from the 1529 painting
Alexanderschlacht (The Battle of Issus)
by Albrecht Altdorfer
(copyright expired)

ISBN: 978-1478163312

First Printing

Printed in the United States of America

Acknowledgments

This book is a work of fiction—a Saga, if you will—of a time long since passed. As to say dragons are real, I will leave that to my reader's imagination.

I wish to thank the following for their support, help and inspiration in the making of *The Saga of Kee:*

My grandfather, Wilber Lawrence, for introducing me to the *Illiad* at the age of ten, which we read by lantern light in southern Ohio. My mother, Helen Conard, an author in her own right, who encouraged me to become a writer. A special thanks to my wife Priscilla for her advice and input, and my two favorite fans, Bambi Battista and Rose Janesky. A special gratitude to Laura Ashton, my editor and layout person whose tireless work made this novel possible.

Table of Contents

Nogard

Prologue   Realm of the Dragons

A purple mist from a distant indigo sea enveloped Nogard, the Realm of the Dragons. The mist dissipated from the heat of an amber sun, revealing Nogard's rugged beauty.

A pair of dragons glided silently between the stark gray mountains. Their elliptical eyes and sharp ears searched the fingers of lush vegetation below for movement, while their nostrils searched for the scent of prey. This hunt had taken a sense of urgency, for they had young to feed.

The sound of peeping within a large nest atop a precipice broke the silence of the new morning. Within the confines of the nest six dragon hatchlings spread their wings to capture the rays of the morning sun on their skin. While the five females were different shades of green the male was black, as were all male dragons. His name was Kee, a name given to him by his father. From his parents he inherited instincts and abilities beyond all mortal creatures.

Kee was unaware a pair of sinister eyes had watched his parents leave the nest. A twig snapped revealing an alien presence. The nest shook as the hand of the intruder entered the hatchlings' sanctuary. Kee watched one of his sisters disappear from the nest, then another, until all had been taken. He was helpless.

A finger touched his wing. The hand of the intruder closed on his body. In desperation he clawed the palm with his tiny talons. The hand loosened its grip and retracted.

"I am the Sorcerer Raggnor, your Master. Do not resist me or I will destroy all of you," snarled the voice of the intruder.

Kee understood the meaning of the words and surrendered to the sorcerer. For a moment he saw a dark form with predatory eyes and long pointed ears. He was forced into a large wicker basket. The hatchlings were carried into a cave. Suddenly the basket filled with many colored lights, and they were transported through stone and space to the evil sorcerer's lair. The time of Kee and his sisters' servitude to Raggnor had begun.

Fifty years have passed since the time of the dragons' abduction. The dragons had grown to be massive, intelligent beings. During this time Kee discovered he alone was a fire breather. Kee and his sisters bonded, for all they had in this alien land was each other. They spoke and comforted one another with their thoughts.

Raggnor used his dragons and the Kreigg to control the kingdoms within three hundred leagues of his realm. The Kreigg were a race of huge man-like creatures, with horns protruding from their skulls. They feared Raggnor's magic and worshiped him as a God. The mere sight of a dragon struck fear into the hearts of the rulers below. They would pay tribute and grant the Sorcerer Raggnor all of his demands. At this time only the Mystical Realm of the Sorcerer Gaul lay beyond his grasp.

Kee detested his treatment. He was chained to his stable at night and struck by his Kreigg handlers for minor infractions. One morning when a Kreigg began to strike him, he turned, elongated his neck and grabbed the handler with his massive maw. His jaws snapped shut severing the Kreigg in half. The remaining handlers fled in terror.

Kee watched Raggnor remove his necklace of power and point his turquoise pendant towards him. A blue light emitted from the pendant and entered his body. A searing pain spread through his being. His blood started to boil. All six of his hearts swelled to twice their normal size. Kee collapsed onto the stone floor of his stable. His sisters watched in horror and shared his pain.

He lay unconscious for nearly two days. When Kee recovered, he was intimadated by his master's pendant, which could have easily destroyed him. His servitude to Raggnor continued.

A year has passed since the time of Kee's encounter with the turquoise pendant. He felt the anger coming from his master. King Burgaon of Simindor, a proud monarch, refused to bow to Raggnor's demands. He would not surrender his beautiful daughter and would no longer pay half of his kingdom's harvest in tribute.

The following morning Kee and his sisters flew in cadence to destroy the castle of Simindor. The green dragons struggled from the burden of heavy stones. Each carried a Kreigg rider. The Kreigg would strike the female dragons with an iron bar in a tender place on their neck to keep them under their control. Kee carried two riders, General Hatin, Raggnor's Dragon Master, and the Sorcerer Raggnor himself.

The green dragons dove through the volleys of arrows that deflected off their hardened scales. They saw the castle looming ever larger in their rapid descent. The Kreigg struck them three times on their necks. Kee's sisters obeyed their master's commands and hurled their heavy stones against the castle's ramparts.

The impact cracked the mortar, which bound the castle's walls. Chunks of granite began to fall as the dragons ascended to the safety of the sky. In their wake, a large cloud of dust rose from the castle, collapsing on its defenders. The Kreigg army rushed the castle to slay the survivors and take their heads.

Raggnor saw the fleeing princess and King Buagron leading the remnants of his army toward the wood. "Slay them all save the princess! She is to be mine!" screamed the sorcerer.

Kee flew over the retreating army. He felt burning plasma from deep within, as he turned to face the panic stricken army. Flames burst from his maw! He recoiled from the blast. Only the princess survived the inferno. The army of Simindor had been reduced to a column of charred bones. Kee watched the young princess with the straw colored hair continuing to run. He saw his shadow enveloping her.

For a moment his eyes entered her soul. He saw her inner beauty, her innocence and sensed her pleading. He felt the Princess of Simindor's last act of desperation, as she pulled a dagger from the sash that bound her dress. He saw her trembling hand, as it passed the blade through her throat. From this time

Kee knew he must escape the clutches of Raggnor.

Kee still feared Raggnor's turquoise pendant, which could destroy his many hearts. He waited for the time—the moment to make his escape. Over a protracted period of time, he observed Raggnor entering the cave of lights for a period of ten days on a fifty-year cycle, to retain his immortality.

He watched the sorcerer remove his necklace of power containing the deadly turquoise pendant and place it into a vault carved within the wall of stone just beyond the cave's entrance.

Kee received a vision which told him of a place of sanctuary, a glacier within the Realm of Gaul. The time had come for his escape. He snapped the shackles that bound him like straws. When three Kreigg guards blocked his path, flames from his maw set their flesh ablaze. He devoured them one at a time, being careful not to lodge their horns in his throat. He leaped into the blackness. The cold night air pushed against his wings. As he ascended, he heard the wailing sounds of his sisters, being beaten by their Kreigg handlers. "I will return to free you!!" Kee roared in the tongue of the dragons.

An icy blast from below clung to the skin of the Great Dragon. The castles beneath him appeared as tiny clusters of stones. Kee did not wish to be cold, yet he knew the glacier was his only refuge from Raggnor's turquoise pendant. His eyes beheld the snow covered twin-mountains of Gaul and the wall of ice which connected them.

For a brief time he enjoyed his freedom. He unleashed a ball of flames and passed through the inferno to remove the crystals of ice.

Kee circled over the glacier. His great wings slowed his descent. He fell gently into the soft snow. He covered his massive head with his wings before shutting down five of his six hearts, and waited for a sign—a time to rescue his five sisters.

Nearly a century has passed since Kee merged with the glacier. The snow that covered his body has turned to ice. The winters of this time have buried him ever deeper in his frozen tomb. Only a tiny cavity, which releases a wisp of steam, reveals the presence of the Black Dragon below.

𝕹ogard

Chapter 1   𝖘eeds of 𝕴nsurgency

King Rugar peered from the tower of his castle. His eyes beheld the fertile valley of Nevau spread out before him. A soft breeze caressed the hairs of his gray and white beard.

"This should be a land of plenty for all that dwell here," he said to his trusted guard. His thoughts turned to his beautiful daughter, Princess Freeya, as this would be her sixteenth harvest.

"Our Kingdom does not deserve to sink into the mire of poverty."

"Yes, Your Highness."

"The Sorcerer Raggnor is not satisfied with half the harvest that he required from my father; now he requires two thirds!"

He knew that many of his subjects would perish from starvation in the coming winter if they were forced to give more of their harvest to Raggnor. He was revolted by the many atrocities the Kreigg committed against his people.

King Rugar shed a tear. His desperation turned to anger, his anger to fear. Fear of the Black Dragon consumed his being. King Rugar had never seen the Black Dragon. He had only heard tales of its power from his grandfather. He had heard the legend of the Black Dragon's escape.

"Could the legend be true?" He said aloud.

He recalled his recent meeting with Raggnor. The sorcerer was mounted on the shoulders of a large green dragon, not the feared black beast. His father and grandfather had told him that Raggnor was only seen riding the Black Dragon, never on one of the green smaller ones. He thought for a moment, *Could it be true?* He felt his despair changing to hope.

"The legend is true! Raggnor has lost command of his greatest weapon. I am certain of this. If we can unite our forces with the Kingdom of Vall, we can purge Raggnor and his army of Kreiggs from our lands!"

King Rugar did not like the way King Copen of Vall treated his subjects. He had been told stories of King Copen having his cousin assassinated to ascend to the throne. *These were only rumors without substance,* he thought.

King Rugar knew the only way to defeat Raggnor was through an alliance. He had little to offer to seal the pact. He hoped their mutual hatred of the evil sorcerer, who took their harvest and mistreated their people, would be enough to convince him to join forces.

King Rugar outlined his proposal for an alliance.

> *To King Copen, Sovereign of Vall:*
> *The time has come to free our Kingdoms from Raggnor's tyranny. I am convinced that he no longer has control of the Black Dragon. Without this beast, his power is greatly diminished. I am confident our combined forces can defeat him and his Kreigg army. We must unite and strike now for our people's sake.*
> *King Rugar of Nevau.*

"Guard, summon my swiftest knight!"

The guard spoke to the king's general. He returned a short time later with a handsome knight of eighteen with shoulder length golden hair.

"Sire, you wish to see me?" The young Knight Skoll asked.

"Yes, I have a message of the greatest importance. This message is to be delivered to King Copen of Vall personally. If it should fall into the wrong hands, Nevau will be doomed."

"Yes, Your Highness, I understand."

Skoll knew he must ride swiftly to arrive at the Kingdom of Vall before sunrise. He opted to leave his heavy armor and shield behind. Blackness greeted him, as his horse crossed the drawbridge. He climbed the paths of the high country to avoid the Kreigg patrols. His eyes saw the spires from the castle of Vall at dawn. Upon entering the road to the castle, he heard unknown riders closing. Skoll felt his left hand clutching his sword. He knew brigands often prowled the road to Vall

"Halt knight! Lower your weapon!" shouted their leader. "We mean you no harm. We are in the service of King Copen."

Skoll saw the bear's head on their shields and knew they were, indeed, Knights of the Kingdom of Vall. He lowered his sword and followed the four knights.

"I must counsel with your king," Skoll said. "I have an important message to deliver to him personally."

As they rode to the castle, Skoll saw the ragged clothing and haggard bodies of the people they passed. Their eyes were hollow and filled with despair. He clutched the leather pouch which contained his king's message.

His escort led him to King Copen's castle. Skoll witnessed the beautiful tapestries covering the walls of the great hall and polished oak tables that supported many silver goblets. He wondered why there seemed to be an abundance of wealth on the interior of the castle and total despair beyond its walls.

He heard the voice of King Copen shout from above the hall. "Come to my chamber, Knight of Nevau!"

Skoll climbed the stone stairs and entered King Copen's chamber. He observed two men. King Copen had dark menacing eyes and a naked face. To the king's right stood his portly son, Prince Luffin.

"What brings you to my Kingdom, Knight of Nevau?"

"I bring a message from my King, Your Highness," Skoll replied.

"Dine in my hall and then take your rest. I will send my reply in the middle of the night."

When Skoll left the chamber for the great hall, King Copen motioned to his guard. "Send for my scribe and tell my cook to give the knight from Nevau a goblet of special mead."

Within the galley of the great hall the cook followed his king's orders. He added a special potion to the drink to be served to the young knight. To test its potency, he poured a small portion into his cat's bowl. The cat drank the tainted mead, curled into a ball and collapsed.

The cook poured the mead into a golden goblet and placed it onto a silver tray filled with meat and bread.

"Mlia, take this meal to our guest," ordered the cook.

"Guard, did the knight from Nevau drink the special mead?"

"Yes, Sire. He will not awaken until the time of darkness."

King Copen opened the pouch and peered at its content.

"Guard, signal the Kreigg envoy."

A thick spire of black smoke ascended from the tower of the Castle of Vall.

"What does the message say, Father?" Prince Luffin asked.

"King Rugar has proposed an alliance. He wishes for our armies to unite and drive Raggnor and the Kreigg from our lands." King Copen thought for a moment. He knew the King of Nevau had a young daughter. "Do you wish to have Princess Freeya as your bride?"

Prince Luffin's thoughts turned to Princess Freeya, the beautiful maiden. He had only seen her once, when she came to Vall with her father, yet her image remained in a special place within him. "Yes! Oh yes, father! I desire Princess Freeya for my bride."

Copen's scribe entered his chamber. "Scribe, I have two important messages. The first is to King Rugar of Nevau."

The scribe wrote as his sovereign spoke.

To King Rugar of Nevau:

I am confident our combined forces can drive Raggnor and the Kreigg army from our lands. As you are aware my son, Prince Luffin, is unwed. To seal this alliance, I will need you to promise to him your daughter, Princess Freeya, to unite our Kingdoms. The marriage will take place once we have defeated Raggnor. If you accept my terms, light the signal fire from your tower. When I see your fire, I will need two days to prepare my army. My army will join with you at your castle.

King Copen of Vall

The treacherous king drank a goblet of mead before he started the draft to his master the Sorcerer Raggnor.

Master Sorcerer Raggnor:
It pains me, exalted one, to report an act of treachery by King Rugar of Nevau. As you can see by the proposal he sent to me, he plans a revolt against you. I will remain loyal to you and await your orders. His Knight has told me, they will attack your army in three days, with or without my support.

Your Humble Regent,
King Copen

King Copen placed the message with the one he received from King Rugar into a large leather pouch with a long leather strap. He gave the pouch to his guard.

"Go to the tower!" King Copen commanded. "Deliver this message to the Kreigg courier when he arrives."

Prince Luffin was puzzled by his father's actions. Father, why did you tell the Sorcerer Raggnor of King Rugar's rebellion and send a message to King Rugar telling him you agree to his alliance?"

King Copen shook his head. He told of his plan to rule Nevau. "My dear son, I wish for this war to take place. When Raggnor destroys King Rugar's army, I will be made Regent over the Kingdom of Nevau as well as Vall."

"What if King Rugar wins, Father?"

"If by some slight chance King Rugar is about to become victorious, I will join forces with him. You will marry his daughter and in time, we will rule both kingdoms."

Skoll's limp body had been carried to a room deep within the walls of the castle to prevent him from hearing the sound of the approaching dragon. King Copen did not want the knight from Nevau to suspect he was communicating with the Sorcerer Raggnor.

Even in his drug induced sleep, Skoll heard what sounded like a huge windmill sail. Vibrations shook his bed. When he tried to rise, the drug took control. His mind became a black void.

A large green dragon hovered near the tower, as the guard passed the pouch to its Kreigg rider. The Kreigg placed the strap over his shoulder and commanded his dragon to return to Raggnor's fortress.

Darkness greeted Skoll when he awakened. He felt his head spinning.

"Mead can be a potent drink," spoke the voice of a young woman.

"Who speaks?" he asked.

"I am called Mlia, and you are called?"

"My name is Skoll."

"Come, Skoll. My King summons you."

He felt her hand clutching his, as they walked through the dimly lighted passageway. Mlia pushed against a heavy door. The door swung open to the large hall of Vall. Mlia entered first. She strolled through the hall with her head held high. Skoll watched her for a moment, and then followed. He felt an impulsive attraction to the young woman. Mlia climbed the stairs to King Copen's chamber and halted at the door. A guard opened the door to allow Skoll entry.

"Knight, your steed has been made ready," King Copen said. "This is my reply to King Rugar. Guard it with your life. It must not fall into Raggnor's hands."

"Yes, Sire. I shall guard it with my life."

As Skoll guided his horse toward the drawbridge, Mlia approached him. He starred into her blue eyes reflecting in the torchlight. He beheld her yellow hair and slim frame. Mlia's gentle voice beckoned across the night air. "Be careful. Will I see you again?"

"Yes, Mlia. I will see you again."

Skoll guided his horse down from the path of the high country. In the distance, he saw the torches of Nevau. A fire roared beside the road leading to the castle. The firelight revealed two creatures. He knew they were Kreigg warriors by the horns that protruded from their helmets.

At first, he considered trying to avoid them in the darkness. The glow of the moon changed his mind. His only chance was to attack the enemy on the narrow road. Skoll's weapons were a short lance and a broad sword. A cold mist kissed his face. Steam exited from the nostrils of his horse.

He guided his horse onto the road. First, he approached his enemy slowly; then, he urged his mount into a gallop. Horse and rider became a single force as they charged.

His only chance was to impale the Kreigg to his right and break through. Closing rapidly on his enemy, he saw fear in the red eyes staring at him, an instant before impact. He felt resistance against the point of his lance, as it penetrated Kreigg armor, and heard the blood-curdling screams as it sliced into flesh.

The second Kreigg stepped aside, to thrust its spear into his side. The impact drove him from his horse.

Skoll did not think of his wound, he knew he must complete his mission. Blood gushed from the gaping hole in his side, as he pulled out the spear. Staggering to his feet, he clasped both of his hands onto his broadsword. He blocked out his pain to turn and face his closing enemy. The Kreigg screamed a savage war cry then wielded his weapon.

Skoll reacted instinctively. The blade of his sword pierced flesh and bone. He heard the iron headed axe of his enemy strike the earth and saw the Kreigg's hand still clutching its handle. When the Kreigg bent to grab his weapon with his remaining hand, he struck a fatal blow across the back of his neck.

Skoll felt the strap of the blood soaked pouch, still attached to his shoulder. He tried desperately to mount his horse. Falling upon the bloodied ground, he closed his eyes. His last thoughts were of a young woman in the Kingdom of Vall.

𝔑ogard

Chapter 2 Sisters of the Sword

At first light, the creaking sound of massive chains of iron broke the silence of the new morning. The hooves of the four knights' war horses thundered across the wooden planks of the bridge that surrounded Nevau. The rays of the morning sun glinted off the knights' armor. Their leader raised his hand to halt their advance.

"Proceed with caution. Beware of a Kreigg ambush," said General Jal.

General Jal, a military strategist, was truly a 'Black Knight' with dark eyes. His armor concealed his ebony colored body. A short gray beard masked the scars of life that covered his face. The general was a Nubian prince who had come to Nevau fifteen years before, with his infant daughter, to escape the desert raiders who had conquered his African Kingdom.

King Rugar's Queen, Rachel, raised his daughter, Princess Jasmine, as her own, with her daughter Princess Freeya. When the Kreigg slew Queen Rachel, Jal trained both princesses in the arts of war. He was proud of Princess Jasmine whose skill on horseback was unmatched by all the knights. He was equally pleased with Princess Freeya's skill as a master archer. The young women were known as *'Sisters of the Sword'*.

Jal smelled a rancid odor drifting over a mist covered knoll in the road. The general motioned for two of his knights to come forward. "Draw your swords, follow the rise; if you are attacked, retreat." Jal saw the upper bodies of his knights and the heads of their horses, as they proceeded through a thick caldron of white mist.

Both knights were nearly overcome by the stench of death.

Jal saw the fog dissipating from the heat of the rising sun. He heard his first knight yell, "I see Skoll's horse!" As the knight approached, his horse stepped onto the headless body of a Kreigg warrior.

The second knight discovered the body of another Kreigg, with a lance still protruding from its chest. Both knights approached Skoll's body. They saw the blood soaked pouch still hanging over his shoulder.

"Come, General! We have found the body of Skoll. He has killed two Kreiggs!"

Jal removed the pouch. With tears in his eyes, he touched Skolls face. "'I love you, my brave young knight. Your death will not have been in vain. Take my brave knight to his home."

"What of the Kreiggs?" the first knight asked.

"Burn them!" Jal responded defiantly.

While his men attended to their fallen comrade, Jal raced to Nevau with the message from King Copen. A guard met him at the drawbridge and escorted him to King Rugar's chamber.

"I have the reply from King Copen, Your Majesty."

"Where is my brave knight?" asked King Rugar.

At first Jal did not speak, only his eyes broke the silence. "He was slain by the Kreigg, Sire; we found two of their bodies near his. Skoll gave his life to protect this packet."

King Rugar opened the blood stained pouch to remove the parchment. He read King Copen's reply to himself then turned to his guard. "Light the signal fire in the tower!"

"Yes, Your Majesty."

"Jal, prepare our knights for war! King Copen has accepted my proposal for an alliance against Raggnor. His force will join ours in three days."

"Yes, Your Highness!" Jal responded. "Will that be all, Sire?"

"Send my daughter Freeya to me!"

In a special place above the knights' quarters, lay the chamber of the two princesses. Unlike the daughters of richer monarchs, they did not possess a bevy of beautiful gowns, or bounty of jewels. Each owned a silver crown and a single dress to be worn only at affairs of state. They usually wore tunics and woolen stocking hose, like the male knights living below. Each of the young women possessed a suit of chain armor. Beside Jasmine's bed stood her lance and shield. Next to Freeya's rested her long and short bow. Each of the princesses possessed a large double-edged broadsword. A shaft of sunlight penetrated the narrow space between the shutters of the single window. Freeya rose from her bed and pushed the shutters aside, Jasmine squinted her brown eyes.

"Freeya, close those shutters now!"

"Rise Princess Jasmine, we must join our knights for our morning meal," Freeya said trying to be cheerful.

"Must we? They are so boring. All they speak of is horses, weapons and the Kreigg. They practice for war and do nothing to protect our people."

"What of Skoll?"

Jasmine's eyes twinkled, as an impish grin broke across her face. "He speaks like the rest, but he is a beautiful young man. I think I would like to spend some time with him."

"Jasmine!" responded Freeya.

Jasmine rose from her bed and started to braid her hair. Freeya admired her sister's beauty, with her high cheekbones and dark hair. She admired her brown skin and slim frame. Mostly she admired the way she carried herself with an air of aristocracy.

Jasmine loved her sister Freeya. She admired her long frosty white hair and her green enchanting eyes. Though she was not as tall or slim as herself, Jasmine recognized her sister's special beauty.

"Freeya, what kind of man do you desire for a husband?"

Freeya's eyes twinkled. "I wish for a beautiful young man. He would be strong and compassionate."

"Should he possess great wealth?"

"No! Well, I hope he could provide me with more than one dress."

Both of the young women laughed. The princesses descended the stone stairway to Nevau's hall. They saw twenty knights and squires. Jasmine looked at the empty table in the center.

"Where is my father?" she demanded.

"General Jal goes with his three knights to search for Skoll," replied a squire. "Skoll is overdue from his mission to Vall."

"What mission!"

"I do not know, Princess Jasmine," responded the squire.

When Jal entered the knight's hall his defiant daughter Jasmine confronted him. "Father, why did you choose Skoll to be King Rugar's courier when you know I was a far better rider?"

Jal appreciated Jasmine's spirit, but he did not like having it directed toward him, especially in front of his men. He spoke in a stern voice. He knew his words would strike his daughter like a lance.

"Jasmine, Skoll is dead. He was slain by the Kreigg. He died protecting an important message for our king. After me, you are the rightful ruler of Nubia. Someday you will return to our kingdom."

Tears streamed from Jasmine's eyes. "Forgive me, Father." For a moment Jal held his daughter's head against his chest.

"Freeya, your father wishes to see you in his chamber," Jal said.

As Freeya turned to leave the hall, she heard General Jal's proclamation.

"Knights of Nevau we are at war with the Sorcerer Raggnor and his Kreigg army! We will no longer pay him tribute or standby while his army commits atrocities against our people."

"Death to Raggnor! Death to the Kreigg army," chanted the Knights of Nevau.

Freeya entered her father's chamber. "You wish to see me, Father?"

"Yes, Freeya. We are at war with Raggnor."

"I know, Father. I heard General Jal speaking to our knights."

"Freeya, we must make sacrifices to free our kingdom from Raggnor's tyranny."

King Rugar looked into his beautiful daughter's eyes. His words came hesitantly. A tear slid over his right cheek. "King Copen, ruler of the Kingdom of Vall, has agreed to form an alliance with us against our common foe. To seal the pact, I have promised you to his son Prince Luffin. You will marry him once we have purged Raggnor from our Kingdoms."

"No! Father you have no right."

"Freeya, it must be done for our people's sake. This marriage will unite our Kingdoms," King Rugar pleaded.

Freeya fled her father's chamber in a state of panic. She had been betrothed to the heir of Vall without her permission. She entered her chamber.

"Freeya, what did your father say?" asked Jasmine.

Freeya responded in anger. "My father has betrothed me to Prince Luffin of Vall. He said it will be good for our people and it will form an alliance against Raggnor."

"He promised you to that swine! We must not allow this," Jasmine said in an effort to support her sister.

"Jasmine, what can I do? We are at war. I am the Princess of Nevau. My sworn duty is to my people."

Nogard

Chapter 3　　Raggnor

Raggnor paced within a room in his fortress. His pacing ceased beside a large oak table. He stared intently at the message from King Copen. Raggnor did not trust his regent in the Kingdom of Vall, whom he considered to be a mortal version of himself. The parchment read of a plot against him and it contained King Rugar's signature.

"King Rugar has a beautiful daughter and of course she is of royal blood," Raggnor mused to himself. Raggnor made plans to have Princess Freeya for his queen. He would have her brought to him after the destruction of Nevau. Then he would cast a spell over her and she would belong to him.

Raggnor summoned his generals. "General Tog, General Hatin."

The Kreigg generals bowed before the evil sorcerer. "Yes, Master."

"Prepare my dragons! Prepare my army! We march on the Kingdom of Nevau. General Tog, do not slay Princess Freeya. I wish to have her brought to me."

"Yes, Master. What of Princess Jasmine?"

"Do with her as you wish, General. She will be your victory prize."

Raggnor knew his forces could defeat King Rugar's army, but he wasn't as confident he could defeat a combined army of the two kingdoms without his greatest weapon, the Black Dragon. He would have to make certain his regent, King Copen, would remain loyal to him.

The Kreigg withdrew from both Nevau and Vall to join with their main force. The dragons where fitted with special harnesses by their Kreigg handlers. Their riders forced them to carry huge stones and bags of smaller stones to great heights. When the great beasts bellowed from their heavy burdens, they were struck by an iron bar in a sensitive place in their neck. The stones where released over targets far below.

Raggnor knew he had to strike quickly. He knew in a short time he would be forced to return to the cave of lights to rejuvenate his life. Even now when he used his necklace of magic crystals to cast a spell, he felt a sense of fatigue overcoming his being.

Raggnor prepared an elixir to maintain his strength until he could enter the cave of lights. He sensed his dark magic would be needed to subdue the rebellious Kingdom of Nevau. He knew even with this potion his powers would be limited. He felt a searing pain in his throat, as the potent brew passed into his being. His body glowed for an instant before he fell into a state of unconsciousness.

Later, when he recovered, Raggnor wrote an order to his Regent in the Kingdom of Vall.

> *To my Regent King Copen:*
> *You must obey my following commands.*
> *Tomorrow at first light bring your forces to the hill overlooking the castle of Nevau. You will witness the destruction of those that dare to oppose me. Do not permit any of these rebellious fools to escape.*
> *Your Lord and Master,*
> *Raggnor*

He would send his message by a dragon rider when the sun emerged to form a new day. Raggnor closed his eyes. He pictured the fair Princess Freeya. *It would be good to have a young queen,* he thought, *especially after his body had recaptured its strength from the cave of lights.*

𝔑ogard

Chapter 4   𝔇efenders of 𝔏und

The Kingdom of Nevau prepared for war. The air in the armory filled with sparks, as swords and lances where ground to a killing edge. Hundreds of spears where fitted with iron points designed to penetrate Kreigg armor.

General Jal sent scouts to all points in the kingdom to monitor the Kreigg movements. Word of the pending rebellion spread to all parts of the kingdom. The villagers armed themselves with pitchforks, picks, and whatever weapons they could find. In one village, two drunken Kreigg where slain by an angry mob.

King Rugar counseled with General Jal in his chamber.

"My scouts report the Kreigg are retreating to Raggnor's Realm, Majesty."

"General, can we defeat the Kreigg Army?" King Rugar inquired.

"Yes, Sire. With King Copen's help we can defeat them," Jal replied.

"Without his help?" the King asked.

"We will die fighting them, Sire," Jal responded defiantly.

"General, I fear the King of Vall will not join with us until he is assured we can be victorious," spoke King Rugar, while a look of concern crossed his face.

"We will strike the Kreigg when they are most vulnerable."

"What is your plan, General?" King Rugar asked.

"My scouts tell me they are massing near Raggnor's fortress. I believe they will cross our border at dawn the day after tomorrow. We will attack during the dim light of the new day."

Jal knew his enemy well. He knew their strength lay in their numbers, their great size and their brute strength. Jal knew that even with their crude brains, they presented a formidable force. He knew the Kreigg had very poor night vision, and in the dim light of the new day, they would be easy prey for his knights.

"I need sixty more men, Sire, to hold the Kreigg at bay," Jal said, "while my knights regroup."

Jal was interrupted by the loud rapping of a staff against the oak door of the King's chamber. He heard the voices of two men.

"We must speak to you, Your Majesty." King Rugar recognized the voices of the two men. The first was that of the Village Elder from the hamlet beneath the castle. The second belonged to the headman of the village that lay on the frontier with Raggnor.

"Guard, open the door and escort the village leaders into my chamber."

Jal saw the elder with his long gray beard and thin hair. He saw his bent frame being supported by a crooked staff. Jal felt the passion and the resolve of the old man. He was glad to have him as an ally. He turned his attention from the elder, to the headman of the village on the frontier. He saw the huge hands of the large peasant leader. *Such hands could crush the head of a Kreigg,* thought the general.

The younger man spoke first. "Sire, I am Stom, the leader of Lund. We have fifty young men and women who wish to join forces with the Knights of Nevau."

King Rugar spoke to Stom, "My general wishes to speak with you, Stom."

"Stom, I need to form a human shield at the narrow pass which guards our border. We desperately need your assistance."

"I know this place well, General," Stom responded. "We will fight and die for our kingdom."

"You must stop the Kreigg when my knights regroup between assaults." Jal embraced the leader of Lund. "We will slay many Kreigg on this day."

The elder spoke. "Our people wish to defend our castle."

"Thank you, my friend," King Rugar replied.

"Elder, assign your people to the Captain of the Castle Guard," spoke Jal.

"Yes, General," the elder replied.

"Stom, are your people in need of arms?" Jal asked.

"Yes, General. We have but a few picks and our bare hands."

"We have enough iron tipped spears for all that march with us. Gather your force, tell your people to feast with us this night. Tell them that tomorrow we prepare for war. Soon we will march against the Kreigg."

After the village leaders departed, King Rugar spoke to Jal. "The brave people of Lund will be sacrificed, General."

"Yes, Your Highness, as will many of our knights." Jal paused then spoke once more. "The dragons are my main concern, Sire."

The king replied. "We have no weapons that can bring them down."

Jal spoke of a possible solution. "If we could but slay their riders, Sire, they would be out of control."

King Rugar spoke to his general more as a father than a king. "Jal, is the plan in place for our daughters escape?"

"Yes, if the Kreigg breach the outer wall, they should be able to escape the castle through the hidden passage. I have made arrangements to have their horses waiting for them, at the opposite end."

King Rugar's eyes looked into his general's. "Thank you, my friend."

When the sun disappeared into the western mountains, the people of Nevau gathered in the castle's large courtyard. King Rugar watched his subjects from atop the inner wall. Soon a large fire glowed within a sunken pit in the middle of the enclosure. The carcass of a large bullock was skewered onto a large spit, to roast over the open fire. As the meat started to roast, minstrels played their lutes and sang songs of knights and kings. They told of the Legend of the Black Dragon, Kee.

The King spoke to his people. "Feast well, my friends. Tomorrow at first light all women with small children must leave the castle. They must seek refuge in the wood near the Kingdom of Vall. Citizens of Nevau, tomorrow you will make our castle a bastion of strength against Raggnor and the Kreiggs. Defenders of Lund, tomorrow you will join with our knights and train for battle."

Nogard

Chapter 5   Touched by a Princess

General Jal had just released his knights to join in the festivities in the courtyard. He heard the sounds of two pair of running feet approaching from behind, and turned to face the closing forms of Freeya and Jasmine.

"Father, Freeya and I wish to ride with you to Lund to fight the Kreigg!" Jasmine shouted.

Jal spoke to his daughter more as a general than as a father. "No! You will not be riding with me! Both of you have been assigned to the Castle Guard. Captain Daron needs you to defend the outer wall."

"No, Father, our place is with you," Jasmine pleaded.

"Freeya, take your sister with you; report to Captain Daron after he has counseled with your father."

Freeya waited with her sister outside of King Rugar's chamber. The princesses pressed their heads against the heavy oak door, but they could only hear a few fragments of King Rugar and Captain Daron's conversation. King Rugar motioned for his guard to open the door. Jasmine sprang back, while Freeya tumbled through the doorway.

"Freeya, Jasmine! What a surprise," King Rugar said. The king paused to give the princesses a moment to regain their composure. "Captain Daron wishes to speak with you."

Freeya beheld the blue eyes of steel possessed by Captain Daron. She saw a heavy scar on the face of the man, running from the top of his right eye to the left side of his chin.

The captain turned from Freeya to address Jasmine. "Princess Jasmine, I have given you the command of the outer wall. Your task will be to hold the wall as long as possible. If you can repel the Kreigg until the Knights of Vall arrive, we will be victorious."

"Thank you, Captain Daron," Jasmine said in a state of bewilderment.

Captain Daron continued. "Jasmine, you will be in charge of twenty men from Nevau, six of my archers, and a four man crew to man the catapult. All of your men will be armed with spears for close combat."

Suddenly, Jasmine realized the seriousness of her situation. She had been charged with defending the outer wall of Nevau with a force of thirty-two including herself and Freeya. She knew if Raggnor broke through the pass of Lund, he would attack the wall with over a thousand Kreigg assault troops and five of his dragons.

Jasmine wondered why she had been chosen for such an important position. The captain did not tell her that she had been chosen because all of his officers would be riding to Lund with her farther.

The captain turned his attention to Freeya. "Princess Freeya, I have heard of your skill with the longbow. Are you able to slay the dragon riders when they approach our castle?"

"Yes, Captain. I will slay them when they come into my range."

"Good. I am confident you will."

"Thank you."

"I will meet with the two of you at first light on the outer wall."

"I have many tasks ahead of me, Majesty."

"I will counsel with you again tomorrow," King Rugar said.

Captain Daron knew his castle well and the best way to defend her. He planed more than one surprise for Raggnor.

Once Captain Daron had departed, King Rugar beckoned to Freeya and Jasmine. He clasped Jasmine's hand with his left and Freeya's with his right. "Tomorrow we prepare for war; tonight I wish for the two of you to be princesses." He hesitated for a moment, and then continued. "Dress in your finest gowns and wear your crowns. Now go enjoy the feasting and dancing."

Exhausted, King Rugar lay across his bed. He worried for the safety of his people. He wondered if he had made the right decision.

Within their chamber, Freeya and Jasmine helped one another dress for the festive occasion. Though Jasmine felt at ease in her gown, Freeya felt awkward.

"You are beautiful, Jasmine. You walk and speak like royalty," Freeya said.

Jasmine placed her comb into Freeya's tresses. "My sister, we are different in many ways and yet we are the same. Now let me comb your hair and take off your old boots and wear your slippers." Jasmine placed her silver crown atop Freeya's head.

"You are a beautiful princess, my sister."

Freeya placed her crown on to Jasmine's head. "Thank you, Jasmine; you are truly a beautiful princess."

As Jasmine descended the stone stairway to the courtyard, she tasted the aroma of the roasting bullock. She saw several young knights beckoning to her. Jasmine loved their attention and tonight she would be conquering one of their hearts. Freeya was shy. She liked the young men but they made her feel uncomfortable. A youth of her age with red hair and a face masked by freckles approached her.

"I must go to fight the Kreigg in Lund, My Princess." The youth looked into Freeya's eyes. "I am afraid. I do not wish to die alone."

Freeya's innocence departed. The youth's words had transformed her into a position of royalty. Suddenly she became aware of her authority and responsibilities. Freeya read the sincerity of the youth's words in his eyes. She knew though he feared for his life, he would fight for her and her beloved kingdom. Princess Freeya touched the youth on his right cheek. She had become a captive of the moment. She embraced the youth.

"May I have a lock of your hair to carry into battle, My Princess?"

Freeya pulled a dagger from a sheath beneath the sash that bound her dress. She severed two locks of her snow colored hair and handed them to the youth, then pressed her lips against his.

She barely heard her sister's voice.

"Freeya, bring your friend; the bullock is ready."

"By what name are you called, young soldier?" Freeya asked.

"Vass, My Princess," replied the astonished youth. This had been the first time anyone had addressed him as a soldier and he had never dreamed a princess would ask for his name. Vass felt the princess's hand clasping his own.

"Come Vass, you will be my escort this night," Freeya said.

Jasmine had chosen Joran, a young Nordic knight with blonde hair and sparkling blue eyes for her escort. The two couples entered the courtyard to join in the festivities.

"Freeya, you know Joran, my father's aide," Jasmine said. "Tell me of your new friend."

Freeya placed her arm around Vass' waist.

"Jasmine, Joran, I wish to introduce Vass from the Village of Lund. He is one of the soldiers who will join our knights," Freeya, said proudly.

Joran stared at the young peasant soldier. He appreciated the youth being willing to fight against the Kreigg, and yet he did not consider him to be his equal. He turned his head from the young peasant and spoke to him, as if he were a beast of burden.

"I am confident you will be a decent soldier once you have shaken the mud off your boots," Joran said.

Vass felt the arrogance in Joran's words. He pushed Freeya's arm from his waist and turned to face her. With his head bowed he spoke. "I do not belong with you, My Princess. I go now to join my own kind."

"No! Vass you are my escort this night! As your Princess, I command you to stay with me." She lifted Vass's head and kissed his lips in front of her astonished sister. Jasmine responded to Freeya's impetuous behavior by kissing Joran. Soon both couples were immersed in the merriment of the evening. They danced to the music of flutes, and lutes, and watched a stumbling juggler.

The cooks began to carve the bullock, while the royal bakers brought forth loaves of bread. One of General Jal's officers asked the two princesses to give a speech. Freeya and Jasmine stood on a large table in the center of the square. Freeya looked at the faces of her people. She knew many of them would perish in the coming battle.

Freeya spoke from the heart. "I thank you for your courage. I love all of you. Tomorrow we prepare for war. This night is for feasting and dancing."

Jasmine was at a loss for words. She looked at the people of Nevau and though she had come from a faraway land, she too loved Nevau and its people. Jasmine spoke the words everyone had been waiting for. "I am hungry. The bullock is ready. Let the feasting begin." While the musicians played, everyone formed in line behind the princesses and their escorts.

As they feasted on the royal bounty, Jasmine sensed the growing tension between Joran and her sister's escort. She spoke to Vass. "Defender of Lund, tell us of your village." Vass looked into Freeya's eyes then turned to face the beautiful dark princess.

"Lund lies in a fertile valley on the eastern border of Nevau. A cold swift river separates my village from Raggnor's Realm. During the first light of the new day, deer and wild horses drink from the pure water of the river. At the time of harvest our valley turns amber from its bounty of grain."

"Tell us of your family," Freeya asked.

"My father was slain by the Kreigg, when he tried to protect my mother. The Kreigg took my mother to Raggnor; she was never seen again."

Freeya and Jasmine struggled to hold back their tears while Joran remained cool. Though he felt some compassion for Vass, he still had not accepted the peasant soldier. The night passed swiftly. Joran kissed Jasmine on her cheek. "I must take leave, Princess, and rest before I prepare for battle."

Joran bowed to Freeya before speaking to Vass. "You must know when to rest young soldier. Tomorrow we train for war then we march against the Kreigg." Vass did not respond to Joran, but he deeply resented his rude behavior. He did not wish for the evening to end, yet he knew Joran was right. This evening had been the most wonderful event of his life. He looked deep into Freeya's eyes.

"I must join my people and prepare for battle, My Princess.

I will think of you and this night until the time of my death," he said emotionally. Freeya embraced the young man, she saw his tears and felt her own cascading over her cheeks. In her heart, she knew this would be the last time she would be with this brave young soldier. Freeya watched Vass disappear into the darkness.

The princesses entered their chamber.

"Freeya, why would you choose a mere peasant to be your escort?" Jasmine demanded.

"Better a peasant than a spoiled knight who probably sleeps in his armor!" Freeya responded angrily.

Jasmine started to laugh. "You are probably right, Freeya. He wouldn't be much of a lover if he slept in his armor."

"Jasmine!" Freeya responded in laughter.

Suddenly Jasmine faced reality. "I fear they will both perish in battle."

"As could we, my sister. I do not wish to die."

Jasmine embraced her sister. "We must rest for the remainder of this night, Freeya. The new day will soon be upon us."

While the defenders of Nevau slept a thick mist shrouded the castle, protecting it from the prying eyes of the dawn patrol of the dragon riders.

Nogard

Chapter 6   The Intruder

As the early sun dissipated the mist that enveloped Nevau, Jal and Captain Daron counseled with King Rugar in his chamber.

"Should I awaken our men, Sire?" Jal asked.

King Rugar thought for a moment. "Not at this time, General. I wish for them to rest for now. I do not want the dragon rider to see the strength of our force."

"I agree, Sire."

"Captain Daron, do you think it wise to give my daughter command of the outer wall?" Jal asked.

"General, you give me little choice. As you know, my officers ride to Lund with you. Do you not trust your daughter?"

"Of course I trust Jasmine!" Jal responded sharply.

"Please do not be angry, General! My men will follow her commands," the captain reassured. "You should be proud of her. You have trained her well. She has become a true 'Warrior Princess'."

Jal listened with pride as the captain spoke, while in his heart he feared for his daughter's safety. Though King Rugar did not speak of it, he shared concern for his daughter's safety as well.

"Dragon!" screamed an alarmed sentry. Within moments a shadow fell upon the castle. From his perch on the shoulder of the dragon, the Kreigg rider peered below. He did not witness the knights still sleeping in their chambers, or the peasant army that had found shelter with the villagers of Nevau. He only saw a handful of guards manning the outer wall. The Kreigg turned the dragon toward the fortress of his master.

King Rugar watched as the dragon flew from his sight.

"Sound the trumpet! Awaken our men! General, prepare our army! Captain, prepare for war!"

Suddenly, the once sleepy castle transformed into a domain of activity. Joran had been given the task of training the peasant army. Upon entering the courtyard, he saw the peasants leaning against their spears. Joran approached the new army with General Jal and Stom, the Headman of Lund.

"Joran, teach them to march and hold their ground," Jal commanded.

"Yes, General."

"Do you feel there will be enough time, General?" Stom asked.

Jal spoke to the headman of Lund. "Yes, Stom. Joran is my finest knight. Your people must follow his instructions. Remember, my friend, you will be in command of your force when we reach Lund."

Jal addressed the peasant army. "Defenders of Lund, soon we march to your village. Knight Joran will teach you to march and use your weapons to stop the Kreigg."

Stom spoke to his command. "People of Lund, tomorrow we fight the Kreigg in the pass that leads to our village. Raggnor thinks we will flee before his army. He is wrong! We will make his army bleed and die!"

"Stom! Stom!" shouted the defenders of Lund.

Stom paused for a moment. "We have little time to prepare. We must listen to the instructions of Knight Joran."

Joran spoke. "This morning I will teach you how to march and the use of the spear in combat. Later you will be joined by our knights." Joran looked at this army whose only experience had been walking behind a plow. He knew if he tried to march them with their spears, half of them would be impaled before they left the courtyard. Joran pointed to two ox carts he had left at the end of the courtyard.

"Leave your spear in the empty cart. Take a broom from the one beside it."

The peasants obeyed Joran's first command reluctantly and awaited his next.

"Form two lines!"

Joran saw Vass and motioned for him to come forward. Though he still felt superior to the peasant, he sensed promise in the youth, and of course he was the only member of the peasant army he knew. Joran gave him an assignment.

"Vass, from this time forward you are to lead the left column."

"Yes, Knight Joran."

"Vass, I need your assistance."

Joran struck Vass's left leg with a stick. "This is your left leg the other is your right. To march, you lead with your left leg then your right leg." Next Joran placed a broom over Vass's right shoulder and placed the handle in his right hand.

"Defenders of Lund, hold your brooms as I have shown Vass."

"When can we train with our spears?" shouted a peasant soldier.

"When I think you are ready," Joran responded. "It is far better to feel the straw of a broom against your face than the point of a spear."

With Stom at the front of the right column and Vass leading the left, Joran guided his army over the drawbridge, to a field beyond the castle's moat.

Unlike Joran's untrained army, many of the soldiers under Jasmine's were professionals. As Jasmine ascended the stairway to the outer wall, Captain Daron approached her.

"Jasmine, I must speak to you of our plan."

"Yes, Captain."

"Look to the field which stands before the approach to the castle's main gate."

Jasmine peered at the field from the top of the stairs. From her vantage point on the entry to the outer wall, she saw the merchants of Nevau spreading a layer of a black substance over the field.

"What are they doing, Captain?"

"They are spreading pitch onto the field. When the Kreigg mass to attack, you must hurl firebrands to the far side of the field to ignite the pitch and straw beneath it. Your archers will torch the pitch in front of the Kreigg."

"It is a good plan, Captain. Do you think it will stop them?"

"I do not know this. I only know many of them will perish in the flames. Jasmine, be careful. I fear there may be an intruder amongst us. Go now. Join your men."

Jasmine approached the catapult. She recognized three members of the crew. The fourth was much larger than any of the others. She noticed he kept his face from view by hiding it beneath a shroud. Jasmine called aside Russk, the leader of the crew.

"Russk, who is this large one, who hides his face?"

"I do not know his name. He is a mute; I think he covers his face to hide the scars from a fire."

"Has he been with you long?" Jasmine asked.

"He has been with us for only a short time, Princess."

The intruder sensed he was about to be exposed. He knew only the eyes of the princess from the distant African kingdom could pierce the illusion his master Raggnor created to mask his appearance. He slipped down the stairs and overcame a young knight and took his horse.

Jasmine and Russk drew their swords and approached the catapult. As they pursued the intruder they nearly ran over Freeya climbing the stairs with her bow. Jasmine halted for a moment to speak with her sister.

"Go quickly to the tower. A Kreigg intruder has infiltrated Nevau. I fear he knows the plans for the castle's defense. Stop him when he climbs the hill overlooking the castle."

Freeya hurried to the tower to give her a vantage point over the road leading to Raggnor's Realm. Jasmine mounted her horse quickly. She knew she must slay this Kreigg, though he was nearly twice her size. She passed a wounded guard with a lance imbedded in his chest lying at the entrance to the drawbridge. The guard gasped, then pointed to the rising column of dust.

The Kreigg knew once he had made it past the summit of the hill, he would be safe. The horse beneath him struggled from his weight. It slowed to a walk, as it ascended the hill. Suddenly, the spinning feathers of an arrow kissed the chest of the Kreigg's mount. Instinctively the frightened horse reared, throwing its rider. The Kreigg's body struck the earth, while his panic stricken mount fled. He heard the galloping of a single horse closing. He planned to slay the knight and take his horse. He saw a cliff beside the road which presented a perfect place for an ambush.

Jasmine's horse slowed as it began to climb the steep hill. She stopped to listen and heard only the sound of silence. Her eyes scanned the terrain around her. Before her were the hoofprints of the Kreigg's horse. She saw the feathers and the shaft of Freeya's arrow. Jasmine approached the arrow and saw the place where the horse had thrown the Kreigg. She dismounted and drew her sword. Turning slowly she sensed the lurking presence of her enemy.

From the corner of her left eye, she saw a large stone hurling towards her. It was too late to avoid the projectile. Her body recoiled from the shock of the blow. Jasmine fell backwards from the force of the impact. She clutched her right shoulder with her left hand and lay helpless on the hard ground.

Jasmine heard the approach of her enemy. The presence of his shadow covered her. She felt the handle of her broadsword touching her left leg. She watched the Kreigg lifting a large stone with both of his massive hands over her head and heard his savage roar. In an instant she sprang forward, grasping her sword with both of her hands, plunging the flat of her blade between the surprised Kreigg's ribs. She felt resistance as the steel sword severed his heart and spine. The forward motion of the Kreigg carried his body into hers. She fell backwards and was trapped by the heavy body lying on top of her.

Jasmine felt the pressure from the weight of the Kreigg. The handle of her own sword pushed into her chest and she was overcome by the oozing foul blood of her slain enemy. She heard the faint sound of distant hoofbeats a moment before fainting.

Joran had seen a rider coming from the castle. Within a few moments he saw a second rider pursuing the first. He did not recognize the first, but he knew the pursuer to be Jasmine. He mounted his horse to join her.

Joran ascended the hill and saw Jasmine's horse. He was overcome by the stench of the dead Kreigg. He approached the body to see Jasmine's lifeless form lying beneath it. Joran fell to his knees. He had known her since they were small children. He admired her enchanting beauty and skills. When her lips had touched his at the feast, he knew his feelings for her were far more than mere admiration. Tears cascaded from his eyes.

"Oh, Jasmine, I love you. Why did you have to die?"

His grief was short lived when he heard a muffled sound coming from beneath the Kreigg.

"And I love you, Joran. Now please remove this rancid Kreigg from my body."

Joran struggled and finally rolled the Kreigg away.

"You are free, Princess."

"Thank you, Knight Joran."

Jasmine found a stream where she could wash the blood and stench of the Kreigg from her body.

"Knight Joran, while I clean myself you may remove my sword from the Kreigg."

"Yes, Princess."

"Joran, I heard your words. Tell me, do you really love me?"

"Oh yes!"

"I have feelings for you as well. Now I need my sword."

Joran struggled until he was able to free Jasmine's sword from the Kreiggs rib cage.

"Do you wish me to take his head, Princess?"

"Yes, then clean my sword!"

Jasmine heard a chopping sound, followed by the thump of the Kreigg's head striking the earth. She felt a shudder throughout her, then took a deep breath to regain her composure.

Joran approached the stream and saw Jasmine standing in the water. He saw the smile on her face and felt the beckoning of her dark eyes. "We must return, Princess; my men are waiting for me."

Jasmine saw the embarrassment encompassing her young knight. She slipped into her tunic and mused to herself, *Perhaps Knight Joran does sleep in his armor.*

Jasmine and Joran returned victorious. Joran placed the head of the intruder atop a pole beside the entrance to the drawbridge. "I must return to my men, Princess."

"And I must return to my command." She looked into his eyes. The young knight nearly fell from his horse, when he felt the lips of his princess pressing into his own.

Nogard

Chapter 7   Prelude to War

Jasmine did not proceed to her command at the wall. First she went to her chamber to make herself presentable for her men. Once she had entered her room, she began to cry and shake and the fears within her surfaced. She struggled to remove her blood-soaked tunic and replace it with a fresh one.

A large hand rapped against the oak door, which guarded her chamber.

"Jasmine, may I come in."

"Please enter, Father."

Jasmine opened the heavy door. She immediately embraced Jal. He comforted his daughter, as she spoke of her ordeal. She told of how she slew the Kreigg and how Joran had rescued her.

"I am so very proud of you. You risked your life for the people of Nevau." Jasmine listened to her father's words and her fears subsided. A brave smile crossed her face.

"Father, Joran said he loves me...," Jasmine paused, "and I think I love him."

Jal was at a loss for words. He hesitated for a moment and spoke the first words that entered his mind. "Joran is my favorite knight."

"Thank you for coming, Father. I love you."

Jasmine kissed her father as he departed. She pulled her sword from its scabbard and ran her hand down the edge of the blade. She watched a tiny stream of crimson flow through her fingers to join with the steel weapon.

"You have served me well, my friend," spoke the Nubian

Princess. "I fear I will have much need of you in the coming days." She placed her companion once more into its protective sheath, before proceeding to her command.

Russk greeted Jasmine at the top of the wall. "We welcome your return, Princess. What is your command?"

"Do you see the barren ground on the far side of the field?"

"Yes, Princess."

"You must be able to strike it with a firebrand!"

"Princess, we would have to realign the catapult and even then...."

"Do whatever is necessary! There is no choice. We must be able to strike that target before the sun disappears."

While the catapult crew worked at a frantic pace, Jasmine addressed her archers. "At my command you will launch fire arrows to the near side of the field. Do you understand me?"

"Yes, Princess," the archers answered in unison.

Freeya waited for her sister to approach her tower.

"Jasmine, I feared for you."

"I have something which belongs to you."

Jasmine handed Freeya the arrow that caused the horse to throw its Kreigg rider.

"I saw you and Joran returning together. Did he kill the Kreigg?"

"No, I slew the Kreigg alone. He pulled its body from mine."

"Are you wounded?"

"No." A broad smile crossed Jasmine's face. "Freeya, Joran said he loves me."

"Did you and Joran make love?"

"No. I think you are right about Knight Joran."

"What do you mean, my sister?"

An impish smile crossed Jasmine's face.

Joran continued to train the peasant army.

"Vass, spear me with your broom!" Joran commanded.

Joran charged Vass. The peasant lunged forward to impale Joran with the straw bristles. The knight stepped aside and with a single motion wrenched the broom from Vass.

"Did everyone see what I did? The Kreigg are much stronger than are we! Place the butt of your weapon into the earth. Let them face a forest of iron tipped spears!"

"Yes, Knight Joran," the peasant soldiers responded.

"Vass, charge me as if you are a Kreigg soldier."

When Vass closed within a few paces, Joran thrust the butt of the broom's handle into the ground. Joran pivoted slightly to align his straw tipped weapon. Vass could not react in time and felt sharp straw bristles against his throat.

"Thank you, Vass. Your men will be the attacking force. Stom, your men will be the defenders."

Joran watched the two sides skirmish. He watched the two sides reverse their roles. In his heart he knew they were not hardened soldiers, but at least they were learning the basics. He knew all too well his time for training was fleeting. He called his army together and sent a man to the castle. In a short time the man returned with a pair of oxen pulling a cart filled with iron tipped spears.

"These spears are designed to penetrate Kreigg armor. Use them well my friends. There are two important commands. The first is 'Form'. At this command you will quickly form two lines across the pass of Lund. You must hold the pass and stop the advance of the Kreigg, while our knights regroup to assault them. The second command is 'Break'. At this command those men assigned to Stom will go to the right. The men assigned to Vass will go to the left. You must do this rapidly, or you will be trampled by our own knights."

The new army formed two lines leading to the cart. Each man placed his broom into the cart and took an iron tipped spear. The soldiers felt an air of confidence as they brandished their new weapons.

"The first time I give you the command 'Form', you will form two lines slowly. The next time you will form at a faster pace. Each time you will be quicker until I have decided you are ready for combat. The same will be for the command 'Break'. Do you understand me?"

"Yes, Knight Joran!"

Joran shouted the command 'Form'. He was not impressed. His army struggled with their new weapons. While most of his men managed to plant the butt of their spears into the earth, some still held them at their sides. He was even less impressed after his second command. Two of his soldiers received minor flesh wounds, when they struggled to form a large breach in their lines.

He shouted words of encouragement. "Do not be dismayed! We will form and break again, only walk faster." After each command the soldiers became more familiar with their task. By mid-afternoon they had become a force to be reckoned with.

"Stom, the time has come for you to train your men. When you see my sword raised, give the command 'Form'. When I point my sword forward, give the command 'Break'. Vass, you must do the same from the opposite side. Only I, General Jal and two other knights can give you this signal. We will be wearing red sashes over our armor."

"What if one of our knights is left behind?" Stom asked.

"It is the way of war, my dear Stom."

Stom gave the command 'Form'. Within moments the soldiers formed two lines. They planted the butt of their spears into the earth and pointed the sharp iron spear heads menacingly forward. Stom saw a horse galloping towards his line of defense. Joran pointed his sword forward. Stom shouted the command 'Break'. He heard his counterpart shouting the same command from the opposite side. As rapidly as the lines had formed the two sides folded, creating a large breach.

Joran turned his horse and rode back through the breach. As he passed through he signaled to Stom with his sword held high. He heard the thunder of fifty warhorses approaching the rear of their lines. Without hesitation he gave his command. He felt the ground tremble when the knights galloped ten abreast through his army's ranks and saw them turning. The earth shook once more when they passed through the breach. He shouted the command 'Form' when the last knight wearing a red sash signaled him with his sword as he passed.

"You have done well, Joran," Jal said.

"Thank you, General."

"I wish to thank you for helping my daughter."

"I would do anything for Princess Jasmine. I care for her very much."

Jal paused for a moment and twisted his beard. "Yes, I know you care for her. We will speak of this another time. Now we must prepare for battle."

As the men spoke they heard the sound of the catapult launching a large stone. A loud cheer rose from the eastern wall when the stone struck the opposite side of the field.

"I see my daughter prepares for war!"

"Yes, General," Joran replied.

ᥦogard

Chapter 8   Vanguard of the Kreigg

Two nights had passed before Raggnor regained consciousness. When he recovered from his elixir he summoned his two generals.

"General Hatin, have your dragon riders seen any of Nevau's force beyond the walls of their castle?"

"Only a few poorly armed peasants guarding the pass of Lund, Great One."

Raggnor flushed with anger. He pivoted to face General Tog. "General, you incompetent fool! Must I think of everything? If the rebels control the pass, we will not be able to march against Nevau. Do you wish to be fed to my dragons?"

"No Master," replied General Tog in a fearful voice.

"Take the pass at sunrise!" Raggnor demanded.

"Yes, Master."

General Tog did not like being humiliated in front of his counterpart. He would have preferred to march with his entire force in daylight, but he feared his master's wrath more than the forces of Nevau.

"Lieutenant Raum, assemble a vanguard to take the pass of Lund at first light."

"Yes, General."

"Raum, take Lt. Hardoc with you. He needs experience in the taking of heads."

The Kreigg smiled revealing his crushing teeth. Raum began assembling an army of three hundred Kreigg. The soldiers put on their armor and tucked their double bladed axes into their leather belts. They held their iron-headed spears over their shoulders. To part the blackness, every fourth Kreigg held a torch.

General Tog was confident of an easy victory at Lund. His only concern was the darkness. He knew his army would be nearly blind if they attacked before sunrise.

"Lieutenant Raum, do not enter the pass of Lund before sunrise!"

"Do not be concerned, General. I will obey your order. We face a mere handful of peasants. If they do not flee before us we will take their heads."

The Kreigg vanguard began to march four abreast toward the frontier of the border with Nevau.

Nogard

Chapter 9 March into Darkness

"Joran, return command of the defenders of Lund to Stom. Tell him we march soon, when the sun returns to its cradle. Tell him we march into darkness. You are to ride with me. I need you at my side," Jal ordered.

"Yes, General."

When Nevau became cloaked in blackness and hidden from the eyes of the dragon riders, the army of Nevau began to leave the relative safety of the castle. King Rugar had gone to the tower to watch his brave army marching toward their desperate battle. In the blackness he could only see his men in his mind, as they trod over the bridge. He heard the sounds of his knights' horses with their ironclad hoofs clattering over the wooden planks. He pictured Jal leading the procession of knights. Following the knights he heard the sounds of marching feet. The king felt a solitary tear departing his left eye. "I love you, defenders of Lund, as I do my knights." He spoke softly and yet his words where felt by his entire army. He heard the chains pulling the bridge into its upright defensive position.

Jal saw the light of a half moon when he reached the summit of the knoll overlooking Nevau.

"Joran, we shall have no need of torches this night."

General Jal knew the element of surprise would be his. He knew the Kreigg would not be alerted of their presence by a column of flames.

Vass felt a cool breeze kissing his face. His legs and feet moved in a rhythm with his fellow soldiers. He clutched his spear and felt its weight against his shoulder. He saw the glint of moonlight reflecting from the knights armor that rode before him. He heard the sound of oxen pulling heavy carts at the end of the procession. To mask his fears, Vass thought of the beautiful princess who had befriended him. His feet felt the surface of a slippery wooden plank. He had come to the first of the three bridges that led to the Pass of Lund.

"Prepare the bridge for our retreat," ordered Vass. Six men under his command unloaded one of the carts filled with hay and spread it over the bridge.

"Soak the hay with pitch!" Vass placed a hidden torch a short distance from the bridge. He felt a sense of pride. He had just made his first real command. The night march continued. The column crossed the second and third bridge. Vass and his men prepared both bridges as the first.

Jal and Joran rode into the pass and surveyed the place where they would bring the fight to their enemy. Joran saw a band of men armed with pitchforks running towards them. He drew his sword then rode between his general and the approaching band. Their leader, an older man with a slim frame and long white hair, addressed Jal.

"General, we are pleased you came."

"By what name are you called?" Jal asked.

"I am called Kal, General. My men and I know this pass well. We wish to serve with you."

Jal desired the help of these men, yet he knew in time of war one must be careful when choosing allies.

"Kal, stay in this place until I return!"

"Yes, General."

As they rode to their column, Jal spoke to his aide. "Joran, bring Stom to me."

In a short time Joran found Stom and delivered him to Jal. "Stom, I must know if the men in the center of the pass are with us."

Stom walked briskly toward the vague images standing in the center of the pass. He recognized the leader and ran towards him. Kal opened his arms to embrace his son.

"Joran, provide my new scouts with their weapons."

"Kal, we must council," Jal said.

"Yes, General."

Jal spoke to his new ally. "Kal, you and your men will take position atop the cliffs overlooking the pass. You will be our eyes. When you see the Kreigg approaching wave your torches to alert us, than run to give the impression you are fleeing from the cliff. Return in silence to your positions to hold the high ground. You must keep the Kreigg from attacking us from above."

"We will hold the high ground to our last man," Kal assured.

Jal held the man for a brief moment knowing he would never see him again in this lifetime.

The knights watered their horses and drank from the water of the cold, spring fed stream. Stom returned to his men who where refreshing themselves in a clear pool above the knights. Joran rode to the edge of the pool. "Stom, the time has come. Bring your army into the pass."

The defenders of Lund marched silently into the narrowest point of the pass. Stom and his men took up their position on the right side, while Vass and his took their position to the left. In the moonlight Stom saw his companions. He heard the murmur of a clear stream to his rear, knowing it would soon become a torrent of blood. The night had become cold and silent. Stom saw the shadow of an owl and heard the squeal of a rodent within the grasp of its talons. He felt time had become an eternity with seemingly no end.

Suddenly Stom heard the sound of men running on the precipice above. He knew his father had signaled the approach of the Kreigg. Instinctively he gave the command 'Form', and heard the same command from the opposite side of the pass. The lines formed together, creating a human barricade. The butts of the defenders of Lund's weapons dug into the earth while their spear points glinted in the half-light.

From atop his horse Jal saw the ever-closing Kreigg. From the number of torches he determined they where a large force, but not the main body of his enemy. He knew the Kreigg where nearly blind in the predawn. When the invaders neared the pass, he gave his command.

"Knights of Nevau, mount your steeds! Ready your lances!"

Nogard

Chapter 10   Lund

The horses of war pranced in anticipation, heat from their massive bodies rising in the frigid air. The knights did not feel the cold. The time for thinking and feeling had passed. They guided their horses in a canter toward the narrow place being held by the defenders of Lund.

"Slay the invaders! Take no prisoners!" Jal shouted.

"Slay the Kreigg!" responded his knights.

Stom and Vass heard the thunder of hoofs coming from behind and the savage battle cries of the Kreigg army rushing towards them. They each took a breath and screamed the critical command, "Break!" The defenders of Lund reacted as a seasoned force, falling to the sides of the pass in a fluid motion.

Vass felt the tremors from the approaching horses. As the knights passed he saw only their heads and the tips of their long lances pointed skyward. When the last of the knights had passed, he and Stom shouted the command, "Form!"

The surging Kreigg army flooded the far end of the pass. Their lieutenants believed the defenders had fled at their approach.

Joran's eyes joined momentarily with Jal's. Both men knew they had the element of surprise. The Kreigg army had marched into their trap. Jal signaled with his sword. A thin line of fifty knights, mounted on their warhorses became a thundering entity. With every hoofbeat the momentum of their force increased. In a single motion fifty lances dropped to killing range.

Joran was the first to make contact. He felt the impact of his lance penetrating a Kreigg soldier's armor, and heard his screams when the head of his lance penetrated flesh. To his right and left he heard the thud of lances striking Kreigg armor. In the corner of his left eye, Joran saw a Kreigg charging towards him wielding its large axe. He turned his horse to face the threat. The impact of the horse felled the Kreigg. Joran heard a crunching sound from below, when the hooves of his horse crushed the skull of his enemy. He saw a Kreigg fleeing from the carnage. In the faint light he detected the glint of horns and knew he was not wearing a helmet. Joran felt his broadsword in his hand, as he pursued his quarry. He closed rapidly and swung his weapon. The body of the Kreigg continued to run without direction from its severed head.

Jal saw the Kreigg army fleeing. He had driven his enemy from the pass. He did not wish for his knights to go beyond the pass, where they would be spread too thin and become prey for the Kreigg. He signaled for a retreat to regroup his force. The knights rode in small groups toward the defenders of Lund's position. Jal saw his soldiers separate, as he neared their human barricade.

Stom beheld the blood covered knights and horses. Some of the horses limped from their wounds; one horse still had a broken spear imbedded in its flank. He gave the command to form when the knight with the red armband gave his signal.

The sun rose from behind the knights, as they dismounted to give their horses a brief respite. The horses drank from the cool spring fed river, as their knights tended to their wounds. Jal was confident they had inflicted heavy casualties upon the Kreigg. He believed over half of their force where dead or dying. He knew as well they no longer had the element of surprise. He surveyed the damage inflicted upon his own force. Though none of his men had perished, six of his horses and four of his knights would be unable to continue, due to their wounds.

The Kreigg lieutenants had watched the knights withdraw and made a decision to take the pass at all cost. They marched their army past the foul bodies of their fallen comrades. With the light of the new morning, the Kreigg were no longer blind. One lieutenant sent thirty of his soldiers to scale the cliffs, to attack the knights from above.

Stom saw the massive size of the approaching Kreigg soldiers, some carrying their large double-headed axes, while the rest held iron tipped spears. He saw some wearing helmets, while most bared their horns and hideous faces. Stom heard the sounds of combat from above and saw a Kreigg body hurling from the cliff. *My father has returned,* he mused to himself. He watched the Kreigg approaching slowly, then rapidly as they charged.

The first wave engaged the defenders of Lund. As a single unit the soldiers of the front line pivoted to deflect the weapons of the attackers. In a rapid motion they turned their spears to impale the Kreigg.

Vass felt the thrashing body of a Kreigg at the end of his spear. He wondered if this was the one who slew his father and took his mother. He heard the snapping sound when the shaft broke, and saw the lifeless stare of his enemy crumpling to the earth.

The first line of the defenders fell behind the second, to take spears from the ox cart to the rear of their position, then formed a new row behind their comrades. The rotation continued, as fatigue began to take its toll.

The enemy force withdrew to regroup for a massive assault. They no longer charged blindly. They marched slowly, methodically toward the defenders of Lund.

Stom knew his men could not repel another attack. They were exhausted and their supply of spears had diminished. Suddenly he heard the thunder of horses coming from behind. He gave the command "Break!" Jal led the charge into the remaining enemy ranks. The Kreigg army crumpled from the onslaught of the knights.

Vass saw three Kreigg surrounding Joran. Sensing his peril, he broke ranks and grasped an iron tipped spear from the hand of a wounded Kreigg. He heard the din of combat surrounding him. Vass closed with one of the Kreigg fighting Joran. The Kreigg charged. Vass reacted as he had on the line.

Suddenly he realized he no longer had the support of his fellow soldiers. He faced an enemy far greater in size than himself. The Kreigg attacked using his brute force to wield his axe. Vass planted the butt of his spear into the ground to deflect the axe's deadly blow. In an instant he turned to aim the iron head of the long spear into the Kreigg's chest. Vass released his weapon and vaulted to his right to avoid the massive falling body. The head of his enemy struck the earth, snapping off one of its horns.

Vass did not sense the approach of the second Kreigg. He heard the sound of the blade of the axe severing his spine. Pain wracked his body and mind. He clutched the lock of hair given to him by Princess Freeya and cried out her name. Vass's spirit departed his being before the shell of his body struck the hardened earth.

Joran slew the Kreigg before him. When he turned his horse he saw another standing over Vass. Instinctively he reacted. Clutching his sword he charged the one who slew his comrade. The impact of his horse knocked his enemy to the ground. Joran held on to his horse, as its hooves crushed the life from the Kreigg.

Nogard

Chapter 11   Retreat and Betrayal

Jal had ordered his knights to regroup at the river. Joran placed the body of the one who had given his life to protect him over the back of his horse. He no longer heard the din of combat as his horse trod through the place of conflict. Only the sound of Stom's soldiers scavenging weapons from the corpses of the Kreigg broke the eerie silence. Joran wept when he took the body of Vass from his horse and carried him to the back of the stream. He joined the remainder of the knights, tending their wounds and those inflicted upon their horses.

General Jal touched the fingers of his right hand to his beard. He knew their hard fought victory would only be a brief respite from the battle that would soon be upon them. He feared his small army could not hold the pass against the Kreigg's main army and Raggnor's dragons.

Jal approached his aide. "Joran, ride to Nevau, tell our King of our victory, then ride to the King of Vall and ask him to help us defend the pass. Tell him together with his army, I am confident we can defeat Raggnor.

"Yes, General."

"Joran, tell my daughter I love her."

"Yes, General, I will," Joran promised.

Jal looked deep into his knight's eyes. "Joran, if I do not return, watch over Jasmine."

"I will, Jal."

Joran mounted his horse and urged it forward. He heard the loud cry of a sentry on the summit of the pass.

"Dragon! A dragon is coming!"

The dragon rider peered at the carnage below. He saw the bodies of the Kreigg Vanguard strewn throughout the pass. He turned his dragon toward the lair of his master.

From the eastern tower of his castle, King Rugar watched the Army of Vall assembling on a nearby hilltop. He estimated over a hundred knights with as many or more foot soldiers, along with a compliment of archers. He wondered why his counterpart did not confer with him at his castle. King Rugar feared King Copen would not fulfill his commitment to their alliance.

Without warning Freeya screamed and began to weep uncontrollably. Jasmine rushed to her sister and tried to comfort her.

"He is dead! I felt Vass's pain, Jasmine."

"Are you certain he has been slain?"

"Yes, I heard him call out my name."

Slowly Freeya regained her composure. She realized this was not the time for mourning. Jasmine touched Freeya's shoulder then returned to her command. She did not reveal her anxiousness for her father and Joran.

Joran urged his exhausted horse forward. He heard the sounds of its hooves striking the timbers of the last of the three bridges. From the summit of the knoll, he saw the spires of Nevau. His horse faltered when he approached the castle. When he dismounted, he saw a large bleeding wound on its side. The large warhorse took but a few more steps than collapsed.

Joran saw several riders crossing the drawbridge. Two guards led the procession, followed by both princesses and King Rugar. Jasmine raced to Joran. She alighted from her horse to embrace him. Before he could speak, she pressed her lips into his. After a brief moment of bliss, she stepped aside. Joran looked deep into to her eyes.

Jasmine spoke in a serious tone. "Tell me of my father."

"Your father, the general, remains in command."

Joran turned to Freeya, "Vass has been slain, Princess; he

was killed saving my life." Joran did not see the pain and sorrow buried within the princess.

"He will be missed, as will all that died for our cause," Freeya responded.

"Yes, Princess," Joran acknowledged.

King Rugar spoke to his knight. "Joran, what news do you bring from Lund?"

"Your Majesty, we slew the Kreigg vanguard. We killed hundreds of their soldiers. General Jal believes with the army of Vall we can hold the pass."

"I will send a message to King Copen of Vall. Guard, bring a fresh mount for Knight Joran!" King Rugar commanded. Freeya returned to the castle with the king.

"Joran, do not ride to the King of Vall. I do not trust his intentions," Jasmine said.

"I must, Jasmine. Without his help we cannot hold the pass and the Kreigg will march on Nevau."

"No, Joran. I will send one of the men from my command!"

Joran paused for a moment. He thought of Vass and the sacrifice he had made.

"Jasmine, I will not risk another. I must deliver our king's message to the King of Vall and bring his army to the pass of Lund."

Jasmine's words came slowly. "You must complete your mission. I love you for the noble man that you are."

"I love you, Jasmine."

King Rugar's guard crossed the drawbridge leading a second horse. He approached Joran and handed him a pouch that contained the message for King Copen. Joran mounted the fresh horse.

"I wish to ride with you, Joran."

"No, your duty remains with your command."

"Joran, bring home my father."

"Yes, Princess."

As her horse entered the outer wall of Nevau, Jasmine felt empty and alone. She sensed this would be the final time she would behold her beloved Joran. She dismounted then hurried up the stone stairs. She saw her beautiful young knight riding to the east and sighed when he turned toward Nevau for a brief moment.

Joran entered a great forest. He felt the presence of many soldiers as he followed the winding path through the trees.

"Halt!" demanded a knight from the Army of Vall. Joran made out the images of two knights, several foot soldiers and archers surrounding him.

"I am Knight Joran of Nevau. I carry a message of great importance from my king to King Copen of Vall."

"*We* will escort you to Our Majesty," the first Knight of Vall insisted. Though he sensed treachery, Joran followed the first knight. The second followed him as they ascended the path. When he reached the hilltop, King Copen's personal guard surrounded him. Joran saw King Copen standing by a large elm.

"Dismount, Knight. Bring me the message from your king." Joran obeyed the command and handed King Copen the message and bowed before him.

"This will be all the proof I need. Bind this rebellious fool!"

"No! No!" Joran shouted as he struggled with his captors. He was silenced by a blow to the back of his skull.

"Take him from me. Do not slay him now I may have use for him later," King Copen commanded.

The King of Nevau watched and waited from his tower for the Army of Vall to ride towards the pass of Lund. He did not know Joran's plight; he only knew without reinforcements his army would soon be overwhelmed.

Jal heard the sounds of the approaching horde. He watched the bulk of the huge army halting at the far end of the pass. A hundred Kreigg soldiers entered the pass. They moved slowly forward then took a defensive position. The defenders of Lund took their position at the neck of the pass. Stom's men had stripped the fallen Kreigg of their weapons and prepared to make a final stand. Jal rallied his knights for a final charge.

"Where are the Knights of Vall?" asked a squire.

"I fear the King of Vall does not wish to join us in our victory," Jal responded.

Jal planned to make one final charge in the pass, then fall back to the bridge. He turned to his knights and pointed his sword forward.

"Slay the invaders!" Jal screamed.

"Long live Nevau!" shouted his knights.

"Break!" shouted Stom a moment before forty horses of war thundered past.

Jal could see this was not the same Kreigg army he had routed earlier. He saw two rows of iron tipped spears.

"Dragons! Dragons!" screamed the sentry from the cliff.

The rider of the first dragon targeted the foot soldiers. Swooping over the defenders below, he released hundreds of fist-sized stones. Stom did not have time to react. The projectiles crashed to the earth striking his men. He heard their screams, as they were felled from the impact. Within in moments ten of his men had been slain.

Jal saw the Kreigg falling back. He heard the beating of huge wings above him. "To the cover of the trees!" shouted Jal.

The dragon riders pursued the fleeing knights. Eleven knights were caught in the open. Jal heard the sounds of stones smashing against their armor. He saw his knights and their horses being felled by the onslaught. He reached the safety of the trees and heard the stones crashing on the branches above and falling harmlessly to the ground around him. As quickly as the attack of the dragons had begun—it was over. The Kreigg gave a savage battle cry and surged forward. Over a thousand strong they flooded the pass of Lund.

Jal ordered a retreat. "Stom, take your men across the bridge! We will give you some time. The pass is lost!"

On the cliffs above, Kal and his scouts made their final stand. One by one they were slaughtered by the overwhelming force and thrown from the precipice. Jal's knights fought a holding action against the advancing horde. They rode to the bridge then turned to charge. Though they where vastly outnumbered, their assault momentarily halted the Kreigg advance. When Stom's men had crossed the river, they broke off the attack.

Jal and his twenty-nine remaining knights thundered across the narrow bridge in pairs. The Kreigg surged forward in an effort to take the bridge.

"Torch the bridge!" Stom commanded.

Flames raced across the pitch-covered planks of the structure, sending a plume of blackened smoke skyward. Several Kreigg tried to breach the wall of fire and were felled by the blast of its heat. Their burning bodies added fuel to the inferno.

"The flames will not stop them for long!"

"What is your command, General?"

"How many of your men remain?"

"Twenty five, General," Stom replied.

"We must ride to defend Nevau! Every knight must carry one of our brave defenders on his horse. Stom you will ride behind me. We must destroy the two remaining bridges!"

The Kreigg forded the river upstream from the burning bridge, while their dragons were loaded with stones for another attack.

Jal and Stom crossed the middle bridge. From a knoll near the bridge, Jal saw his army spread out over the exposed plain leading to the bridge. Behind his men he saw a rising cloud of dust from the advancing horde of Raggnor's Army. Jal saw a wooded area at the base of the knoll, which could provide cover from the dragons and their lethal stones. The knights and soldiers rode across the bridge. They dismounted from their exhausted horses to give them a brief respite. Jal saw his worst fears winging towards him.

"Take cover in the wood. The dragons have returned!" He saw three of his knights being cut off from the bridge by one of the dragons. A second dragon was winging toward the bridge. He had little choice; six of his men and three of his horses had to be sacrificed. Jal gave his painful command. "Burn the bridge!"

The second dragon hovered over the bridge. Stom ran to the bridge with a torch. The down draft from the dragon's wings nearly extinguished the torch's flames. A volley of stones struck Stom he crashed onto the planks. Struggling to his feet he hurled his torch on to the pitch. Rising flames and thick black smoke forced the dragon skyward. Stom fell forward and was consumed.

Jal urged his horse into the shelter of the trees, where he and the rest of his dwindling force were spared from the dragons' deadly stones. He was confident the Kreigg could not ford the deep river. Jal's Army reached the last of the bridges without incident. As with the first and second, they torched the last bridge leading to Nevau. Jal thought it would take many days to rebuild and traverse the two bridges.

From the tower of Nevau King Rugar saw the rising plumes that signaled the retreat of his army. He saw a single dragon winging toward the army of Vall. The green dragon hovered over the hilltop to the east.

"King Copen!" boomed the voice of the Sorcerer Raggnor from atop his dragon.

"I am your servant, Master!" King Copen replied.

"Bring the knight from Nevau!" commanded King Copen to his captain.

"As your Regent, I have come to remind you of your task!"

"I am but your humble servant, Master."

"Do not interfere with my army when it attacks Nevau! Slay any of Nevau's army that tries to escape me!"

"Yes, My Master," King Copen replied.

"Princess Freeya is to be my new queen, and I have promised Princess Jasmine to General Tog. If they escape from Nevau, you are to search for them."

Joran was still dazed from the blow. His hands had been bound behind him and a gag prevented him from crying out. He was dragged in front of the King of Vall and forced to kneel. He heard King Copen speaking to Raggnor.

"Master, I wish to demonstrate my loyalty to you."

Joran closed his eyes. His last thoughts were of Jasmine. He pictured her standing in the stream revealing her beauty. He felt her lips touching his.

King Copen held his broad sword above the back of Joran. With a single blow he severed his neck. The King of Vall held Joran's head skyward to present it to his Master.

"I am pleased, My Regent!" boomed Raggnor's voice. The dragon beat its wings leaving a great cloud of dust in its wake.

From his tower King Rugar had seen the King of Vall holding an object up to the Sorcerer Raggnor. A tear fell from his eye when he surmised it to be the head of his knight.

Nogard

Chapter 12   Battle for Nevau

From her position atop the wall, Freeya was the first to see the retreating army of Nevau. She hurried across the wall to give her sister the news.

"Jasmine, your father is safe. I saw him leading our army."

Jasmine did not reply. She could no longer speak and her body trembled as she collapsed onto the stone battlement. Her loss was far greater than Freeya's. Jasmine had hoped to marry Joran and one day bear his children, now he was gone—murdered by the King of Vall. Freeya knelt by her sister. Jasmine began to speak.

"Freeya, I hate this terrible war! Joran has been slain. I felt his death. His last thoughts were of me."

Freeya touched Jasmine's cheek. Though she shared her sister's pain, she knew the seriousness of their situation. She spoke in a commanding voice.

"Rise, Princess Jasmine! Be the leader Joran would want you to be! You are in command of this wall and we must defend our home!"

Jasmine rose to her feet. A new resolve filled her being. She marched to the catapult.

"Are we ready? Can we strike the target with our firebrand?"

"Yes, Princess Jasmine! We await your command!" responded Russk, the leader of the crew.

"Archers, are we prepared to strike?"

"Yes, Princess!" responded the archers in unison.

King Rugar saw the approach of his army. He spoke to his guard. "Tell General Jal to counsel with me in my tower once he has taken care of his men."

"Yes, Sire."

After the guard delivered the king's message to him, Jal had the horses taken to the stable to be fed and watered. The knights and soldiers washed the blood and sweat from their bodies before entering Nevau's hall. Jal climbed the winding stairs leading to the king's tower.

"Enter, General Jal."

Jal lowered his head and slipped through the narrow passageway leading into the tower. King Rugar extended his right arm and pointed his finger toward the last bridge his army had set ablaze. "General, before you speak I must show you something."

Jal looked in the direction of the bridge. He saw two dragons that appeared to be connected by a large beam. He watched as they hovered over the river then lowered the beam to form the framework of a new bridge. Beyond the bridge, a rising dust cloud told him the Kreigg had crossed the second river.

"I fear Raggnor's army marches on Nevau," King Rugar said.

Jal looked upon the hill to the east and saw the army of Vall.

"Will King Copen join us, Majesty?"

"King Copen's allegiance is not with us. I fear he has sacrificed your aide, Knight Joran, to his master Raggnor," King Rugar said bitterly.

"We will fight to the last man, Majesty. I will speak with Captain Daron. We will defend Nevau together."

Jal met with Captain Daron near the drawbridge. "Captain, I have need of your men at the gate."

"Yes, General. We are under your command."

"Captain, I wish to address my men and spend some time with my daughter."

Jal entered the hall to a rousing cheer from his army. He saw they had become an army of one, no longer were they divided into knights and peasants. They had bonded into kin with a single purpose. Though this army had suffered from the blows of the dragons and felt the wrath of the invading Kreiggs, they were still a potent force.

Jal spoke to his army. "My friends, we have fought bravely together. We destroyed the vanguard of our enemy. Many of our comrades have been slain by the Kreigg and Raggnor's dragons. I must ask you now to fight what may be our last battle."

"We are prepared to fight and die for Nevau!" shouted his army.

Jal continued. "The Kreigg and their dragons are building bridges beside the ones we destroyed. They will soon be assaulting Nevau. Captain Daron has asked that we defend the main gate. We will no longer have need of our horses, they will be set free before the Kreigg arrive. Eat, drink and rest while you may, my brave friends."

Jal left the hall. He knew in his heart they would face the jaws of death before the sun fell into its cradle. He met with his daughter at the place of her command.

"Joran is dead, Father! The cursed King of Vall took his head!" Jasmine said defiantly.

"Yes, Jasmine. I know of this!"

Jal held his daughter's hands. He saw the lines of grief covering her face.

"The Kreigg will pay a heavy price for Nevau, Father. We will slay hundreds of them when they mass in the field." Jal saw the catapult awaiting the firebrand. He saw the arrows that would soon be flying torches.

"You have done well, Jasmine."

"Where will you be when they come, Father?"

"Captain Daron has asked me to defend the main gate. I will be below you," spoke Jal as he looked into his daughter's eyes.

Jasmine embraced Jal. "I love you, Father."

"I love you, my Princess Jasmine."

Jal joined his men at the front gate. They lowered the bridge and herded their horses across. Jal's steed, a large black stallion, led the herd to a high pasture.

"Secure the bridge!" Jal shouted. The drawbridge was pulled into its upright position. Spiked poles were loaded into a trench filled with pitch to form a second line of defense.

The distant sound of a drumming cadence and marching feet drifted toward the king's tower. "They are crossing the last bridge to Nevau," King Rugar murmured to himself.

Freeya saw the advancing column marching with the tips of their spears pointed skyward. She saw a part of the column pulling carts filled with large stones. The carts separated from the main column and pulled to the summit of a small mound. Freeya surmised this to be the place where the Kreigg would load the dragons.

From atop his dragon, Raggnor saw his plan taking place. The Black Dragon was the only missing ingredient. His Kreigg army would be forced to fight. He could no longer depend on the Black Dragon's flames to consume his enemy. The Kreigg army would mass in the field across from the main gate of Nevau and wait for his dragons to fill the moat with large stones to create a causeway. Once the moat was filled they would smash great stones into the weakest point in the castle's wall above the main gate. His army would rush across the moat. Once inside the castle, his overwhelming force could easily slaughter the defenders of Nevau.

The sounds of the Kreigg became louder, as they approached the field. Their growling and war chants joined with the cadence of their marching. Four dragons circled over the carts on the mound. Row upon row of the invaders filed into the staging area across from the castle. Soon the pitch covered field became a mass of Kreigg soldiers.

Jasmine's opportunity for vengeance had arrived.

"Catapult, load the firebrand!" Russk set the oil soaked wood into the basket of the catapult. Jasmine ignited it with a torch.

"Launch the fire brand!" Jasmine commanded. The entire wall vibrated when the catapult hurled the flaming missile towards its distant target. The firebrand was nearly spent when it fell beyond the Kreigg army. Only glimmers of the embers touched the straw. Wisps of smoke, then tiny flames spread to the pitch. Suddenly, an inferno erupted behind the Kreigg.

"Archers, torch your arrows!" The archers took aim with their flaming arrows in front of the Kreigg lines. The flaming arrows set ablaze the field in front of the Kreigg. The rising firestorm consumed all within its path. Kreigg soldiers screamed as their flesh blistered from the intense heat, joining with the rising column of thick black smoke.

From his position on the hilltop, King Copen considered changing his allegiance. He began to wonder if King Rugar could defeat Raggnor.

Raggnor had seen the firebrand hurling towards the opposite side of his army. He ordered his Dragon Master to return him to his fortress, where he could counter its effect.

Jasmine saw Raggnor atop his dragon being followed by a massive black cloud. Suddenly, she heard a volley of thunderbolts, announcing a cascade of water from the blackened firmament. She watched torrents of rain striking the earth. Pillars of steam formed as the deluge smothered the flames. Jasmine felt her heart sink when more Kreigg soldiers filled the ranks of the ones who had perished.

"Dragons!" shouted the sentry.

"Freeya be ready! The dragons are attacking!" Jasmine screamed.

Freeya looked down the shaft of her arrow. She took aim on the first of the dragon riders closing with the wall. Her fingers released the spinning arrow. The impact of the iron arrow head severed the heart of the Kreigg. His lifeless form fell from the back of the green dragon. The female dragon spiraled out of control and crashed into the ranks of the Kreigg Army. She lashed out against her tormenters. Her talons ripped through the Kreigg's armor and tore into their flesh, while her jaws ripped their heads from their bodies. In a short time she slew over twenty of Raggnor's army.

Raggnor had little choice. He had to destroy one of his prize dragons of war. He removed the necklace of gems from his neck. General Hatin guided his dragon over the thrashing one below. Raggnor aimed the light of the turquoise pendant into the crazed dragon.

"Draco be domma! Draco be domma!" chanted the Sorcerer Raggnor. The light of the pendant intensified, when it struck the inner being of the dragon. A bluish hue emitted from her body. She felt her blood bubbling and the explosions of each of her six hearts. Her suffering and time of torment ceased forever.

Raggnor had lost over five hundred of his army and now one

of his Dragons of War. He felt fatigue from the spell he cast over the firmament.

"General Hatin take me to my fortress. I must prepare for my journey to the cave of lights."

"Yes, My Master."

The dragons ascended to a height beyond the range of Freeya's bow. Their first target was the moat encircling the castle. They dropped huge stones to displace the water of the moat until they formed a causeway leading to the main gate. Then the dragon riders turned their attention to the wall. Huge stones fell relentlessly against the rampart. Cracks formed and grew with each onslaught. Two large breaches formed on both sides of the drawbridge. The Kreigg surged forward. They forded the moat through a volley of arrows from Jasmine's archers. Stones crashing into the courtyard forced Jal's men to retreat. The Kreigg screamed a hideous battle cry, when they swarmed through the breaches in the wall.

Jal heard the drawbridge falling across the moat and heard the Kreigg charging across.

"Jasmine retreat to the inner wall," Jal shouted.

The Kreigg army flooded the courtyard. Jasmine led her men in a desperate battle to reach the inner wall. Her archers sent a volley of arrows into the Kreigg ranks to make a path to her father's men. For a brief moment the Kreigg halted their advance.

"Jasmine, Freeya, come with me quickly!" Jal yelled.

With the remaining defenders of the castle, Freeya and Jasmine passed swiftly through the inner gate. They heard the door slam shut, followed by the sound of Kreigg battleaxes beating against it. From atop the inner wall Jasmine saw the bodies of the defenders of Nevau strewn over the courtyard. She saw many men being led away in chains.

"What will become of the prisoners father?"

"They will be forced to toil as slaves in Raggnor's mines," Jal responded.

"Freeya!"

"Father!"

King Rugar spoke to his daughter, "Freeya, you must follow General Jal's command. Nevau has been taken you and your sister must escape."

"Father, escape with us," pleaded Freeya.

"No! I must stay with our people. Remember I will always love you."

The King of Nevau embraced his daughter and turned to direct his army. He took but a few steps when a great stone hurled from the sky crushed out his life. Freeya was in shock. When she tried to run to her father, Jal's large hands restrained her.

"Freeya, Jasmine! You must escape now. The Kreigg are breaking through!" Jal yelled urgently.

Jal guided the princesses to an oxcart covering a deep hole. He lowered Freeya into the opening then his daughter. "Jasmine, Freeya, follow the walls of the passage. When you are beyond the moat you will see a burning torch where the passage joins a tunnel. The tunnel leads to a cave. Follow it to its entrance. You will find your horses and weapons there. Travel beneath the cover of darkness to the Realm of the Sorcerer Gaul and he will protect you. Go now, while you can."

"Come with us, Father," Jasmine pleaded.

"No! Now go. I will cover your escape."

Jal covered the portal with a large stone then pushed the oxcart over it. He rejoined his men in their desperate struggle. Two Kreigg soldiers attacked him. Jal slew the first with his sword, the second delivered a glancing blow to his temple.

The once beautiful castle of Nevau lay in ruins. Half of her brave defenders had been slain. The survivors had been taken to become forced labors, in the mines that lay below Raggnor's fortress. The taking of Nevau had been complete.

Raggnor sat on his throne in the bowels of his fortress. He knew his Regent King Copen would not dare to oppose him at this time, yet he still did not trust him.

Nogard

Chapter 13   Escape From Nevau

The Kreigg soldiers searched in vain for Princess Freeya and her sister. They did not realize both princesses where but a few feet below them, working their way through the blackness of the narrow passageway. Jasmine led the way, followed by Freeya. She heard the squeaking sounds of rodents scurrying before her.

"I don't like it here, Freeya! I hear rats and I can't see a thing!"

"Keep moving Jasmine. We must escape before the Kreigg find us."

"I see a small flame ahead. I think it comes from a lamp."

Jasmine held the oil-burning lamp and saw a torch hanging next to the entrance to a tunnel. She touched the flame of the lamp to the torch and its glow revealed a large tunnel. She entered with her torch held high. Freeya followed clinging to her bow, as they waded through waist-high ground water. Freeya saw two more passageways joining with the tunnel.

A foul odor filled their nostrils when they left the tunnel and entered the vastness of a massive cave. A winged creature alighted on Jasmine's shoulder and inserted its long sticky tongue into her ear. She shrieked in horror. Suddenly, the cave came alive with hundreds of flying, screaming bats. Jasmine dropped her torch and clasped both of her hands over her ears. Freeya dropped her bow and did the same as her sister. Neither one heard the hissing sound of the torch being snuffed out by the water on the cave's floor. Once the commotion had ceased, Freeya found her bow.

Freeya starred into the blackness and beheld a form floating in the void. Though she had never seen him before, she knew he was indeed the Sorcerer Gaul. He lifted his staff to become the image of the Black Dragon. He gave Freeya a vision of herself mounted on the Great Dragon leading an army of dragons and men against Raggnor's Army.

"Jasmine, I have seen the Sorcerer Gaul and the Black Dragon! The Sorcerer Gaul will support us. The Black Dragon will be our ally against Raggnor."

"I saw nothing, Freeya."

"Jasmine, please help me in my quest. We must find the Black Dragon and form an alliance with him."

"I go with you, my sister. Your quest shall be my quest."

Jasmine did not share her sister's vision. At the moment she was more concerned about leaving the foul smelling cave and escaping to a place of sanctuary. She pondered how does one speak to a dragon let alone form an alliance with one. She found the torch and blew on the embers to bring light once more into the cave. Glimmers of pink glanced off the damp walls of the cave. A brilliant light over came the princesses from the funneled radiance of the setting sun.

"Do you see our horses, Jasmine?"

"No! The light is too bright. Wait—I think I can hear them."

"We must approach our horses with caution, Jasmine. I fear a Kreigg ambush."

Freeya notched an arrow to her bow, while Jasmine drew her sword. Both princesses moved with stealth from the relative safety of the cave toward their horses. Jasmine approached the animals, while Freeya stood guard with her bow. Jasmine discovered two saddles, a pair of lances and a short bow adjacent to the tree anchoring the horses. In a short time she readied both horses for their quest.

Freeya heard the sound of snapping twigs behind her. She pulled her bow to a full draw to feel the feathers of her arrow touching her cheek. Freeya aimed instinctively and released. She heard a loud squeal from her prey. The charging boar fell a mere ten paces in front of her.

"We have meat for our journey," Freeya said proudly.

"Our horses are ready," Jasmine replied.

Working as a team the princesses skinned and quartered the wild pig and cooked enough meat for subsistence over a small fire. They waited for the cover of darkness before beginning their journey. Freeya stowed both her long and short bow behind her saddle. Suddenly, she began to sob and shake uncontrollably.

"Freeya, what is wrong with you?"

"Our fathers made our escape possible and now they are gone."

Jasmine struggled to fight back her own feelings. She looked into her sister's eyes and spoke. "Freeya, we must complete your quest or their sacrifice will be for nothing."

Freeya regained her composure and mounted her horse. "You are right. We must travel toward the cradle of the sun to the Realm of Gaul and find the Black Dragon."

Freeya took the lead, she steered her horse over an ancient trail ascending into the high country. At the summit of the first ridge she looked back to see what had been her home. The once beautiful castle had become a hulk, reflecting its death in the moonlight.

As they descended the ridge they saw a fire where the trail crossed the road.

"Kreigg. They guard the road," Freeya whispered.

Jasmine clutched her lance. Her desire for revenge dominated her being. "I want their blood," she whispered defiantly.

"No, Jasmine, we must try to avoid them."

Jasmine's mind took control of her emotions and her anger subsided for the moment. They dismounted and fastened pieces of boars-hide to their horses' hooves to mask their sound. Freeya motioned to go forward when a large cloud shrouded the moon. Jasmine led her horse behind her sister's. Though it seemed an eternity, the princesses crossed the road swiftly. The Kreigg never left the comfort of their fire. Jasmine heard their hideous laughter, as her feet trod on the narrow trail.

"Laugh while you may, you vile beast. When we return we will slay you and your master," she mumbled defiantly.

They journeyed through the darkness. A lone fox escorted them over two ridges. Owls flew silently over their heads then made haunting cries when they alighted on the pine brows. A silent chorus of stars illuminated the heavens. The princesses heard the muffled sounds of their horses treading over a myriad of pine needles as they ascended into the evergreen wood. For a brief time they were absorbed by the beauty surrounding them.

The third ridge became steeper than the two previous ones. They dismounted to lead their horses toward the summit. At the time of dawn, they searched for a place to hide from the dragon riders and rest before continuing their quest. Jasmine saw a large outcropping near the summit.

"We can stay here, Freeya."

Near the outcropping a tiny waterfall cascaded into a large pool at the base of a precipice. Freeya and Jasmine removed the gear from their exhausted horses, and led them to the pool and the lush grasses surrounding it. The young women felt safe for the moment. They cooked boar meat for their morning meal over a small hidden fire. After eating, they climbed to the summit. In the distance, Princess Freeya and her sister beheld two snow-covered peaks connected by a massive glacier reflecting the radiance of the morning sun.

Nogard

Chapter 14   Dragon Quest

After tethering their horses to a large pine in the evergreen forest, the exhausted princesses slept beneath the cover of the precipice. While they slumbered, a gentle rain joined with the cascading water. Jasmine awakened to a warm sun.

"Freeya, you smell worse than the wild pig you slew!"

"Princess Jasmine, you look worse than any wild boar!"

Simultaneously they looked at the pool and each other. Within moments their tunics lay on the floor of the outcropping. With a resounding splash both leaped feet first into the deep cool water. They scrubbed their bodies to remove the soil and sweat. Jasmine lay on her back immersed in her cool refreshing bath. She looked skyward and froze in fear of the shadow passing over the pool.

"Freeya, I see a dragon," she whispered.

"Where?"

"It is flying directly over us."

They had become vulnerable. The princesses were naked and defenseless. Their weapons lay some distance away at the base of the precipice. Their only hope was if the reflection of the sun on the pool would mask their presence. They held their breath and slipped beneath the surface.

The dragon passed, its rider guided it in an arc toward the east. Jasmine surfaced to hear her sister gasping for air.

"Did he see us, Freeya?"

"I don't know."

"We must leave this place now," Jasmine said.

They dried themselves and dressed for battle. Within a short time their horses where made ready to continue their trek to Gaul's Realm. The warmth of the day dissipated, replaced by a cold biting wind from the glacier. The incline of the trail became ever steeper. Once more they dismounted to lead their horses. Snow and Ice crystals pelted their faces as they approached the summit. Jasmine slipped on the cold, slippery surface then crashed onto the hard frozen ground. She cried from the pain in her chest, her tears froze to her cheek. When Freeya helped her sister to her feet, Jasmine pushed her aside.

"Freeya, forget your stupid quest! I am going back to die fighting the Kreigg."

"Jasmine, we must continue for our fathers' sake. If we return now, we will die for nothing. Please help me. We are near the summit and soon we will be safe in the Realm of Gaul," Freeya pleaded. Jasmine's words trembled from her partially frozen lips, "I will continue with you on your quest." She paused for a moment. "Freeya, I am cold—so very cold."

Freeya held her sister in an embrace to warm her. She felt the bond between them growing ever stronger. Though Jasmine did not witness her sister's vision of the Sorcerer Gaul and the Black Dragon, she had placed her fate in her hands.

The Sorcerer Gaul sensed their plight and sent forth a warm flow of air to replace the cold biting wind. Jasmine felt warmth returning to her body. A lunar radiance replaced the dark snow clouds. They continued their ascent. Upon reaching the summit they saw a broad plain stretching to the Realm of Gaul.

"We must find shelter, Freeya.We cannot cross this plain tonight."

Freeya saw a wisp of white smoke. Her eyes followed the smoke to its source.

"Jasmine, I see a house."

They approached the small house cautiously. Freeya felt the presence of eyes. She drew her sword while her sister readied her lance. They heard the snapping of a branch. Suddenly—like an apparition—an old man appeared, clutching a pitchfork.

"Who are you?" he asked.

"We are travelers," Jasmine replied.

"I know who you are! You are Princess Jasmine and you are the one they seek—Princess Freeya," the old man replied.

Jasmine aimed the point of her lance toward the old man. "Who seeks Princess Freeya?"

"The Knights of King Copen, my cursed king," replied the old man.

"We seek shelter," Freeya said.

"You are welcome to stay in my humble home."

"Where are we?" Jasmine asked.

"You have crossed into the Kingdom of Vall."

Jasmine lowered her lance. "Can we trust you not to reveal us?"

"I would die before betraying you. You can leave your horses in my shed. Please follow me."

Once the horses were sheltered and unloaded, the old man fed them grain he had hidden from his king and the Kreigg. Upon entering his house, he added kindling to the small fire in his hearth.

The old man watched the princesses remove their armor. "I am pleased you have come to my home."

"Thank you," Jasmine said.

"I am truly sorry about the fate of your kingdom."

"What is your name, kind sir?" Freeya asked.

"I am called Erain."

"Erain, we travel to the Realm of Gaul. What dangers do we face?" Freeya asked.

"By day dragon riders, the Kreigg Army, and the Knights of Vall, by night, wolves, and as you near the Realm of Gaul, Brigands," Erain responded.

The exhausted princesses slept through the remainder of the night and well into the next morning. They did not hear the rumbling thunder and the torrents of rain cascading on the Kingdom of Vall.

Freeya awoke to the aroma of fresh bread and a chicken roasting over the hearth.

"Rise, my Princesses. Feast while you may," Erain said.

As the storm waned, Freeya knew there would be little daylight left to descend the trail to the plain. After dining on Erain's meal they readied their horses to continue their quest.

"Thank you Erain," Freeya said.

Jasmine embraced the old man.

"I will think of you often," he said.

At dusk they entered the broad plain. Though it was not as difficult to cross as the high country, the terrain was not as flat like it appeared from the summit of the ridge. The rolling hills of the plain consisted of a scattering of trees within a sea of tall grasses. As they reached the summit of each rise they saw the twin peaks of Gaul looming ever larger in the moonlight.

They crossed nearly half the distance of the plain when Jasmine heard the piercing cry of a wolf. She heard the sounds of many wolves running towards them through the tall grass.

"Freeya, I hear wolves!"

"Jasmine! Ride to the clearing on the top of the hill."

When they reached the hilltop they dismounted to start a fire. Jasmine quickly made a pile of dry grass and twigs. Freeya struck a spark with flint and steel she had stored beneath her saddle. The pile burst into flames she added larger sticks to feed the fire.

"They want our horses!" Freeya shouted.

The yellow eyes of the predators glistened in the firelight. Freeya counted twelve wolves and she knew there were many more in the darkness. The wolves kept their distance from the flames.

"We are trapped," Jasmine said.

"Perhaps they will let us pass," Freeya said confidently.

She saw the leader, a large black male. She took the remainder of the boar meat from behind her saddle and approached the leader of the wolf pack. Somehow, the fierce eyes of the large predator began to soften, as she approached.

"I have a meal for you if you let us pass." Freeya placed the meat in front of her feet then stepped back a single pace. She took a deep breath and waited, showing no fear. The wolf approached, she felt his cold nose touching her hand. The predator turned, grabbed the boar meat then disappeared into the night, followed by his pack.

When she returned to the fire, she found Jasmine trembling.

"I thought he would kill you," Jasmine cried.

"They are truly beautiful. We can pass through their realm now," Freeya said confidently.

The princesses extinguished the fire and continued their quest. The time spent with the wolves meant they would have to cross the remainder of the plain in daylight. Jasmine enjoyed the warmth of the morning sun. She heard the chorus of songbirds greeting the new day. Suddenly, silence dominated the plain. Jasmine heard the sound of huge wings behind her. She turned her head and saw a pair of dragons closing. Beneath them she saw dust rising from the plain and knew it could only be a patrol of the Knights of Vall.

"Freeya, ride for the trees! It is our only chance!"

The trees became larger and closer, as they raced towards the forest. Jasmine reached the safety of the trees with Freeya close behind. The canopy of elms and evergreens blocked the sun, creating a maze of blackened tunnels. They heard the snapping of dead branches, as they rode ever deeper into the thick wooded land.

Nogard

Chapter 15   Brigands

Freeya heard a voice coming from the blackness. "Stop there is a trap ahead!" She saw the form of a young man motioning to her with his hands. "Come towards me quickly," the young man's voice commanded. Freeya had little choice. She drew her sword and obeyed the voice in the shadows. Jasmine clutched her sword. Like Freeya she did not trust these men, but she had little choice. She saw ten, perhaps more men advancing toward her. One man grabbed her horse's bridle, another grabbed Freeya's. "Be silent pilgrims, they are coming to our trap," the leader of the band whispered.

The Knights of Vall galloped into the dark forest. Without warning, the two lead knights crashed into a deep pit. The leader of the band signaled to his archer. An arrow struck a tree beside the captain of the patrol. "You are surrounded! Yield, drop your weapons or we will slay the lot of you!" the leader of the brigands demanded. The captain of the patrol heard the sounds of men coming from every direction. He did not wish to die for his ruthless king.

"Who asks for my surrender?"

"I do not ask—I *demand* your surrender! I am Prince Khrom, the rightful heir to the Kingdom of Vall." Prince Khrom continued. "Leave your horses, your weapons, your armor and boots."

"Not our boots!"

"Do you wish to die for your boots?"

Freeya saw the leader of the band, a handsome young Norseman, standing with a young man of Asian heritage. The knights began their long trek across the broad plain clad only in their tunics.

"Prince Khrom! Prince Khrom!" shouted the youngest knight. "I wish to serve you!"

"Manchu, bring this noisy knight and the two pilgrims to our camp," Khrom ordered to his second in command.

"Yes, Sire!" Manchu said obediently.

"These pilgrims must be of great value, to be pursued by dragons and a patrol of Copen's knights," Khrom said.

"Sire, did you know they are females?"

"Yes, Manchu. I noticed."

Manchu approached Freeya and Jasmine. "Lower your weapons, pilgrims, you are safe now. You will come with me to our camp."

As they rode they heard the cry of wolves on the plain.

"I think the Knights of Vall are going to have a difficult journey home," Khrom said.

"Yes, Sire," replied a smiling Manchu.

Freeya watched the poorly armed band as they crossed a clearing. "Jasmine, they only have one bow between them."

They tread slowly through a maze of vines and bogs. Freeya felt a tingling sensation, as she passed through a blanket of light. She looked in disbelief at a beautiful creature prancing on the far side of a lush clearing. The creature appeared to be a sparkling white horse with a large horn mounted on its forehead.

"Jasmine, I see a unicorn," she said softly.

"Freeya, we have entered the Realm of Gaul."

𝔑ogard

ℭhapter 16   ℚueen of 𝔜all

A cool clean breeze kissed Freeya's face. She saw hundreds of small colored birds flying between the branches of the evergreens. When the band forded a cold stream, she saw wisps of smoke spiraling from two cottages. She did not see the eyes of a woman following her every movement.

The leader signaled for his band to halt. "Manchu, bring the knight to me!" Khrom ordered.

"Yes, Khrom."

"Young knight, by what name are you called? Do you wish to be in my service?" Khrom asked.

"I am called Orin, Sire. Yes, I wish to be in your service."

"Orin, tell me. Why are these two pilgrims so important?"

The knight pointed toward the white haired princess. "This one is Princess Freeya, the one Sorcerer Raggnor has chosen for his bride. The other is Princess Jasmine. She has been promised to General Tog of the Kreigg."

Freeya shook in fear. She would rather die than become the bride of Raggnor. Jasmine was so revolted by the thought of belonging to the Kreigg General she started to vomit.

"Pilgrims, dismount!" Khrom commanded. Freeya and Jasmine reluctantly obeyed his order. Freeya did not care for the arrogance of this one whom she considered to be little more than a common criminal.

"Bow before me, wench!" Khrom said in a demanding tone.

Before he could speak again, he felt the point of a steel sword against his throat. Freeya felt the back of her sister against her own. Manchu drew his weapon to face Jasmine.

"Now, *Prince of Brigands*, fall to your knees!" demanded Freeya.

Khrom did not wish to grovel before this woman, especially in front of his men. He felt a prick of his skin and a trickle of blood flowing along the right side of his throat. Suddenly, a brilliant light dominated the field. Freeya dropped her weapon, as did Jasmine and Manchu. The light transformed and became a large image of the Sorcerer Gaul.

"Acts of violence are not permitted within my realm," boomed the voice of the sorcerer. "Princess Freeya, Princess Jasmine, welcome to my realm. I am sure Prince Khrom will be at your service. Khrom, you and Manchu will escort our guests to my hall this night. We have much to discuss."

"Yes, Great Sorcerer!" Khrom replied.

Khrom bent forward and handed Freeya her sword. "I am at your service, Princess. I apologize for my behavior."

"You should apologize!" Freeya responded. "I do thank you for saving my sister and myself from the Knights of Vall."

"I am glad we were able to help, Princess."

Khrom did not tell Freeya that they did not ambush the Knights of Vall with her in mind. In truth, they had used the princesses as a lure to obtain the Knights of Vall's horses and weapons. Khrom touched the dried blood on his throat. "Tell me, Princess Freeya, do you make a habit of slaying your rescuers?"

Freeya smiled. "Tell me, Prince Khrom of Vall, what brings you to the Realm of Gaul?"

Before Khrom could respond two riders raced past. "My Mongol brother wishes to show your sister his skill on horseback," Khrom said proudly.

"My sister is the finest rider in the Kingdom of Nevau," Freeya responded.

They watched the horses come to a halt at the far end of a lush pasture. "I think they wish to be alone," Khrom said.

Freeya saw a middle aged warrior with a flowing brown beard standing in front of a cottage.The man stepped forward to embrace Khrom then looked at Freeya.

"I see you were successful in your raid."

"Yes, Captain. We took four horses, many weapons and suits of armor. Captain, I wish to introduce Princess Freeya. We rescued her and her sister from the Knights of Vall. Captain, we have come to speak to my mother."

"Enter, Khrom. I wish to meet your guest," spoke a regal voice.

Freeya entered the cottage. Her eyes met the sparkling eyes of a beautiful mature woman. The tall woman stood revealing her slim frame her long silver hair fell to the center of her back.

"Princess Freeya of Nevau, allow me to present you to Queen Dora of Vall, my mother," Khrom announced.

Freeya attempted to curtsy. She stumbled and nearly fell to the floor. Queen Dora smiled, as she fought to restrain her laughter.

"Forgive me, Your Highness, for I have not been trained in the ways of court," said Freeya, trying to hide her embarrassment.

Queen Dora held out her arms and embraced Freeya for a moment. "Welcome to my home."

"Thank you, Queen Dora."

"Call me Dora. Khrom, have the second cottage made ready for Freeya and her sister."

"Mother, Freeya wishes to know how we came to the Realm of Gaul."

"Freeya, please sit by my table," Dora said.

Queen Dora began to speak: "It was so long ago, and yet it seems so recent. I was a young queen not much older then you are now. My husband, King Handamar, was a just and noble ruler. He hated to pay the tribute to Sorcerer Raggnor that kept his people in poverty. He sent a message to your father, King Rugar, asking him to join in a rebellion against Raggnor and his Kreigg army.

"His cousin Prince Copen, who desired to be the King of Vall, intercepted his message. Prince Copen plotted with Raggnor to assassinate my husband and become Raggnor's Regent. I had given birth to my son a mere three months before. He was a beautiful infant, who gave me comfort when I suckled him."

"Mother!" interrupted Khrom.

"May I continue?"

"Yes, Your Highness."

"Prince Copen gathered members of the castle guard who were more loyal to their greed than their king. My husband was slain at first light by Copen's assassins when he entered the tower of Vall. I awoke to the sound of battle outside my chamber. I heard the young captain of our guard cry out. 'The King has been slain, My Queen! You and the young prince must escape!' I dressed quickly and wrapped Khrom in several blankets.

"The castle had become a place of chaos. I held Khrom and ran behind the captain. When we reached the courtyard, I heard screaming. Two dragons had cast their shadow over the castle.

"'We must hurry, My Queen, the Kreigg will soon be here!' the captain shouted. He placed me onto a large black horse and handed me my child, then mounted his horse while two of his men lowered the drawbridge. I held Khrom in one arm and the reins to my horse with the other. A Kreigg soldier blocked our escape. The captain slew him with his sword.

"'We must take the high road,' spoke the captain. We entered the forest and hid in a wood cutters hut, while waiting for the cover of darkness. The captain maintained guard, while I fed and cared for my boy child. It was there I saw my first image of the Sorcerer Gaul. He spoke to me through a ball of blue light. 'I grant you sanctuary within my realm. Follow the trail over the hills and across the broad plain and look for the glacier that joins two mountain peaks.' Then his image vanished.

"We traveled by night to avoid the dragon riders and hid beneath the forest canopy by day. By the third night I was weak from lack of food and feared I would not be able to feed my child. 'We shall feast this night My Queen.' I heard the captain slaying his horse with his sword. He made a small fire to cook its flesh. I heard the howling of wolves and knew we had but a brief time before they would come to feed.

"'Captain, what is your name,' I asked?

"'Eric, My Queen,' he responded.

"'Eric, why do you protect me and my son?'

"He spoke with his eyes and I knew it was not out of loyalty to my husband, or the Kingdom of Vall.

"'We must leave now, My Queen. The wolves will soon be here.'

"'Yes, Captain Eric,' I said.

"Eric led my horse through high drifts of snow. I held my child to my chest to protect him from the bitter cold. I watched Eric fall only to stand once more and continue the trek toward the Realm of Gaul. After the fourth night and well into the fifth morning we passed through the barrier of light and entered this place of sanctuary.

"As time passed, Eric and I grew close. He made this cottage, and as Khrom grew he trained him in the ways of combat, while I gave him a formal education."

"Mother, Father said we have a guest!" shouted an excited young girl with long brown hair.

"Freeya, allow me to introduce you to my daughter Sharonn."

"I hear riders outside," Khrom said. "I think your sister has returned."

Freeya met her sister in the doorway to the cottage. "Jasmine, come inside. I wish to introduce you to Queen Dora."

While Freeya introduced Jasmine to Queen Dora, Khrom stepped outside to be with Manchu.

"Captain, where does my mother expect Manchu and me to sleep? She has given our cottage to the princesses."

A broad smile crossed the captain's face. "You might try the stable. Manchu tells me he loves his horse."

Queen Dora spoke at length with the two young women, while her daughter listened intently. She had not spoken with other women since she had entered the sanctuary. They spoke at length of men and court. The princesses told of the fall of Nevau and their desperate journey.

"We are to meet with the Sorcerer Gaul tonight, Queen Dora. I wish we had something better to wear," Jasmine said.

"Many things are possible within the Realm of Gaul, Princess. Behind my cottage you will find a hot spring to remove the journey from your body," Dora said.

The young women felt the warmth of the water caressing their skin in a pool beneath the hot spring.

"Freeya, what are your feelings towards Prince Khrom?" Jasmine asked.

"He is really quite nice," Freeya blushed, "and quite handsome."

"Freeya, a short time ago you were about to slay him, now you say he is quite nice!"

"Well that was before I knew him and met his mother. Tell me, Jasmine, of this one called Manchu."

"He is the finest rider I have ever seen. He spoke to me of his land, a vast plain to the east. His people lived in a sea of grass. They were nomads who followed their horses and goats. The land was in constant conflict. The warlords of the south and the north each sought the rich plain for their own.

"One day the southern warlord attacked his people. His mother placed him on his horse and told him to flee. He does not know the fate of his family. As a young boy he traveled in fear for many days until he came to this place. Queen Dora and the captain raised him with Khrom."

"Do you like him, Jasmine?"

"I enjoy his companionship." A look of sadness spread across Jasmine's face. "It will be a long time before I can be as close to any man as I was to Joran."

The young women felt a chill when they left the warm pool. They removed the beads of water from their skin with cloths provided by Queen Dora. Jasmine was the first to see the gowns hanging from the pine boughs. She beheld a shimmering pink gown made from an unknown material. Beneath the gown, sitting atop the pine needles, rested a pair of knee length pants to be worn beneath the dress, and a pair of new boots for riding.

"Freeya! Freeya! We have been given a beautiful gift!" Jasmine squealed.

Freeya's dress was shimmering blue made from the same material as her sister's. She had matching slippers and a crown of silver. Queen Dora approached the young princesses. She wore a beautiful white gown with a crown of gold.

"Many things are possible. Your gowns are a gift from the Sorcerer Gaul. Will you ladies please help me with my hair?"

Khrom and his brother Manchu followed Queen Dora's orders. They removed their gear from the cottage and swept the floor free of dirt and cobwebs.

"What do you think of the white haired princess, my brother?"

"She will be my queen when I take back the Kingdom of Vall!"

"What! Did I hear you say 'she will be my queen'? Khrom, I don't understand you. A few hours ago the girl nearly kills you, and now you wish to have her as your queen!"

"Yes, I have never met any girl quite like her."

Manchu started to laugh. "My dear brother, she is the only girl you have met."

Khrom did not care for his brother's comments. He did not know why he felt the way he did for the Princess of Nevau.

"What say you of the Princess Jasmine?"

"She is a good person. I wish to be her friend and...."

"And what? Go on!"

Manchu hesitated for a moment. "I think she is quite beautiful."

"We are finished here Manchu. We should ready ourselves for the meeting with the sorcerer."

𝔑𝔬𝔤𝔞𝔯𝔡

𝔠𝔥𝔞𝔭𝔱𝔢𝔯 17   𝔠𝔞𝔳𝔢 𝔬𝔣 𝔏𝔦𝔤𝔥𝔱𝔰

The Sorcerer Raggnor walked slowly through his fortress. He wore a flowing black robe with his head encased within its hood. He held his staff, which he used to support his weakened body. Raggnor felt the stone surface beneath his feet, as he walked past the shackled dragons and their Kreigg Handlers.

Raggnor entered the tunnel that led to the cave of lights. Once inside the passage, he removed the necklace of power from his neck. He knew the pulsating vibrations at the cave's entrance would shatter his precious gems. The sorcerer removed a stone from the wall of the passage that revealed a small hidden chamber. With great care he placed the necklace of power into the chamber and replaced the stone.

The sorcerer waited patiently at the end of the passage for a portal to appear. His mind reflected to the time in his youth, when he discovered the mysterious cave of lights and how he was transported to the Realm of the Dragons. He recalled the awesome world of the great flying beasts, with its stark mountains and lush valleys. He had observed six dragon hatchlings in a nest. He remembered plotting to take the tiny dragons to his own world and raise them to do his bidding and provide him with great power. Raggnor lamented his prize male, The Black Dragon, had escaped and he was forced to destroy one of his females.

Raggnor saw a tiny sliver of light penetrating the solid stone wall at the end of the passage. The light grew in size and intensity as it expanded the opening to create a portal into the cave. The sorcerer dropped his robe and shielded his eyes as he entered the portal. He felt the vibrations as the light transported his body to the place of rejuvenation. He lay suspended, as lights of many colors encircled his being. He would lie in this state for ten days as fifty years of his age were removed from his body, and he would emerge as a man in his prime. The process of immorality had begun.

The lights had no concept of good or evil. No one knew how or why the mysterious lights preformed their service, as only a few knew of their existence.

The Sorcerer Gaul monitored Raggnor's progress. He knew there was little time to set in motion his plan to end the evil sorcerer's tyrannical rule.

Nogard

Chapter 18   Hall of Gaul

Khrom and Manchu bathed in the warm water beneath the hot spring after the princesses had joined Queen Dora in her cottage. The captain joined the youths that had become his sons.

"What is this place called The Hall of Gaul, Captain?" Khrom asked.

"I am sure it will be a place of beauty, Khrom," the captain responded. "I have never seen the Great Hall. This is the first time I have been invited. Our meeting with the sorcerer must be of great importance."

When the men emerged from the water, Manchu saw new uniforms lying beside the evergreens.

"Khrom, we have been given new clothes," Manchu said.

Khrom wept when he saw a crown of silver resting beside his new boots. "Captain, the sorcerer wishes me to be the King of Vall."

The captain did not speak, as he embraced this one who he had raised from a child. After the three men dressed, they walked to the front of the cottage. Captain Eric knocked on the door and was met by his daughter Sharonn.

"They are not ready, Father. Mother and Jasmine are working on Freeya's hair."

"Tell them to wait outside. We will be with them soon," Dora shouted.

"Yes, My Queen."

Sharonn stepped outside and twirled her new dress in front of her father. He saw the shimmering yellow gown, with its matching slippers. The captain lifted his daughter and kissed her on the cheek. Jasmine was the first to step through the doorway, followed by Freeya and Queen Dora. The men were spellbound by their beauty. Jasmine still loved attention from young men. Tiny ringlets of her hair dangled in front of her flashing brown eyes. Manchu tried to speak. His words stumbled from his mouth.

"You are the most beautiful woman I have ever seen."

"Thank you, young warrior. You shall be my escort this night," Jasmine replied.

Khrom felt drawn to Jasmine's exotic beauty, then he became captivated by Freeya's presence. He desired the white haired princess above all things.

"May I take your hand, Freeya?" Khrom asked.

Freeya was a bit hesitant. She still felt uncomfortable around men, but she placed her hand into Khrom's. She did not speak as they walked toward their mounts.

The captain looked into Dora's eyes. "I love you now more than ever, My Queen."

"I love you, Eric," Queen Dora responded.

Eric lifted his queen on to her horse then placed his daughter into her mother's arms. The princesses mounted their horses.

"Freeya, did you bring your slippers?" Jasmine asked.

"Yes, Jasmine. I have them tucked away."

"As do I," said a smiling Jasmine.

Captain Eric led the procession. Though he had never been to the Great Hall of Gaul, he did know the way to the sorcerer's castle. Queen Dora and Sharonn rode close behind, followed by Khrom and Freeya. Jasmine and her escort lagged a distance behind. Manchu tried to steal a kiss. "Not now. You could mess my gown," Jasmine said.

She urged her horse forward to be with her sister. Suddenly, she realized the attention from Manchu was helping her recover from the loss of Joran. She decided to live for the moment. She turned her mount and raced back to Manchu. Jasmine pressed her lips against those of the Asian Warrior. Manchu nearly fell from his steed.

The procession passed through the camp of Khrom's band. His men were spellbound, for they had never seen women of such radiance.

"Hail, Queen Dora! Hail, Prince Khrom!" shouted Khrom's men.

While most of the men gave homage to Khrom and his mother, the young knight from Vall became fixated with his younger sister. Captain Eric halted their progress until they where once more joined by Jasmine and Manchu.

"We must make haste, Manchu. The sorcerer awaits."

"Yes, Captain," Manchu acknowledged.

They continued their journey through the Realm of Gaul. Their procession passed through a beautiful forest, where exotic creatures flourished. They ascended a steep hill. From the summit, Freeya beheld the towers of the sorcerer's castle shimmering in the setting sun. As they descended, a village of small thatched huts appeared. The serpentine road passed through the heart of the hamlet. Freeya realized this place was now home to those who had been granted sanctuary by the Sorcerer Gaul. She saw many faces from Nevau. Queen Dora knew many of the people were from her own kingdom. She halted her horse for a brief moment.

"We cannot tarry, My Queen."

"Yes, Captain," Dora responded.

Beyond the village rose the Castle of Gaul, appearing as an apparition and blending into the mountain. The horses trod over small white stones as they neared the castle's gate. Captain Eric saw no outward signs of defense for the castle and wondered why there was no moat or drawbridge. He saw two guards about his age standing by a huge door. As their party approached, he recognized the men from a long time past.

"These are my men, Dora. They are the loyal guards who helped us escape."

"Your Highness, Captain, we feared you had perished," spoke the stout bearded guard.

The thinner guard could not speak; when he beheld his queen he began to weep.

The great door opened slowly, releasing the scent of freshly baking bread.

"Enter, my friends. You shall be my guests this night. My guards will care for your mounts," boomed a voice from the interior.

They proceeded through a torch-lit passage for a brief distance to an inner door. The castle was but a façade, when the inner door opened they stepped into a massive cavity within the sorcerer's mountain. The interior glowed from an unknown light reflecting from a wall face of amber. The beauty of the palace overwhelmed the sorcerer's guests.

Dora saw a small room adjacent to the main chamber. She held her daughter's hand and motioned for Freeya and Jasmine to join her. The women used the guest facilities and removed their riding boots, and took their slippers from beneath their gowns.

"Oh, that Manchu," Jasmine cried.

"What did he do?" Queen Dora asked.

"He messed my beautiful gown."

Freeya and Dora both laughed. Jasmine suddenly felt herself spinning. In a twinkling her gown regained its elegance. The women used a large silver mirror to primp themselves.

"We are beautiful, are we not?" Jasmine asked.

"Yes, we are," Queen Dora responded.

The women joined their escorts. They passed many beautiful artifacts. Jasmine was drawn to works of art from the Southern Lands. She saw a statue of a woman that resembled herself.

"She looks like you, Jasmine," Freeya said.

"Freeya, this is how my mother appears in my dreams." Jasmine responded.

A third door stood behind them. Behind the door they heard the bustling of activity, as the sorcerer's servants completed their tasks. Suddenly, the third door swung open revealing the Great Hall of Gaul. Queen Dora saw a long table covered with many exotic dishes. The centerpiece was a large boar complete with its head clutching an apple in its maw. At the head of the table, she saw a man of small stature wearing a blue robe of unknown origin. He wore a pointed hat and clutched a crooked staff. She witnessed his ancient body. Dora was drawn to his lavender eyes which revealed his vast intelligence.

Suddenly, the sorcerer doubled his size, "Illusion can be a powerful tool," spoke the Sorcerer Gaul. "Welcome my friends. Your Majesty, your beauty overwhelms this old man's heart."

"Thank you, Great Sorcerer," Dora responded gracefully.

"We have many things to discuss," spoke the Sorcerer Gaul. "First you must feast and drink from the bounty of my table."

Dora and her family sat on one side of the table facing the princesses and their escorts. Dora asked to change places with her captain, as she did not care to partake of the boar while its eyes seemed to stare at her. They consumed the Boar from silver platters and drank mead from golden goblets. Freeya's favorite part of the meal was the freshly baked bread.

"Sorcerer, please join us in the feast," Shraonn said.

"Thank you, child, but I have no need for nourishment."

The sorcerer's eyes met Dora's. "Queen Dora, Captain, I have a request."

"Yes, Sorcerer." Queen Dora responded.

"I wish for you to care for a young boy. His name is Tyree. His father was slain at the battle of Lund, his mother by the Kreigg when she tried to flee from Nevau.

The young boy entered the hall. He shook from the fear of his ordeal. Sharonn ran to the boy without hesitation. "Tyree my name is Sharonn, you can sit by me."

A tiny smile crossed the boy child's face.

"He shall be our son," Dora said.

When the feasting had ended the servants cleared the table. Dora brought her daughter and new son to a small room adjacent to the great hall. When she returned, the Sorcerer Gaul began to speak.

"Our common enemy continues to expand his power, while my powers are waning. His Kreigg army will soon regain its full strength, and he is making an alliance with the Troblins—a demonic race that dwells within the dark places of the earth. I fear if my brother Raggnor cannot be stopped, he will soon conquer all the lands of this world."

"Sorcerer, you called Raggnor your brother. How can this be?" Captain Eric asked.

"Captain, Raggnor and I are both the spawn of the God Odin. My Earth Mother was a kind woman who brought forth the wisdom and goodness that I inherited from my father. Raggnor's Mother was ambitious. She nurtured evil and hate, and brought forth the war-like qualities from our father's lineage. We must destroy Raggnor now before it is too late! Raggnor lies within the chamber of lights. He will remain there for ten days while his body rejuvenates. Jasmine, may I touch your hands?"

Jasmine presented her hands to the sorcerer. Gaul ran his hands across her palms and strong fingers. The sorcerer smiled, "Jasmine, I have an important task for you and Manchu."

"Yes, Sorcerer," Jasmine and Manchu responded in unison.

"If you succeed, we will proceed to the next phase of my plan," spoke the sorcerer. "If you should fail, all will be lost."

The Sorcerer Gaul removed a necklace of precious stones from around his neck and placed it into Jasmine's hand. She followed the sorcerer's instructions. "Jasmine, squeeze the turquoise gem—push it up then down." The pendant fell into the palm of Jasmine's hand. "Now squeeze the gem once more and place it near the necklace by the clasp from whence it came. Push it down than up." Jasmine watched the jewel realign its self with the silver clasp. "Jasmine you must replace Raggnor's turquoise pendant with mine and deliver his to me."

"Yes, Sorcerer. I will not fail," Jasmine promised.

"My pendant will cloak you and Manchu; the Kreigg guards will be unaware of your presence. Once you have exchanged the pendants, you will become visible."

"Manchu!" the sorcerer commanded. "You will go to the cells to free the prisoners who are forced to toil in Raggnor's mine. You must release them and create a diversion to cover Jasmine's escape."

"Sorcerer Raggnor's fortress is a great distance; it will take many days for our horses to reach it," Manchu said.

The sorcerer gave a shrill signal and within moments two beautiful unicorn stallions trotted into the hall. The white one nuzzled against Jasmine's shoulder, while the tawny-colored one stood beside Manchu.

"These are my children; I have raised them from tiny foals," the sorcerer said. "They are faster than the wind and can leap great distances. They do not require saddles or reins. Whisper into their ears and they will take you any place you ask."

"What are their names?" Jasmine asked

"Odin has chosen you to be his rider," the sorcerer replied. "Thor has chosen Manchu."

Gaul knew he was taking a great risk. Without his own turquoise pendant attached to his necklace, he could not control the power of the Black Dragon. His advantage lay in the knowledge of his lack of control over the beast, while his evil brother remained unaware of his loss of power.

The Sorcerer Gaul spoke to Jasmine's sister. "Freeya, when I have Raggnor's turquoise pendant within in my possession, you will continue your quest. The dragon you seek is encased within my glacier, and only you are able to awaken him. I do not know how; I only know you must bring him back to life. Remember many things are possible within my realm."

"I understand, Sorcerer," Freeya acknowledged.

"Freeya, if you are successful, I will show you how to ride the dragon."

Gaul turned his attention to Khrom. "Go with Freeya, give her protection and comfort on her perilous quest."

"Yes, Sorcerer," Khrom replied.

"Captain, you are to form an army from those that take refuge in my land," the sorcerer commanded. "Within three days you should receive reinforcements to retake the Kingdom of Vall and return it to Queen Dora and Prince Khrom."

"Sorcerer, I promise to retake our Kingdom," Captain Eric said.

"Will we slay all the Kreigg after we have taken Vall?" Jasmine asked.

"Jasmine, I know of your desire for revenge," Gaul said. "Raggnor has used the Kreigg to do his evil bidding against you and the people of Nevau. The Kreigg are a race of simple beings who were once hunters and gatherers that lived in peace with their neighbors. As you know, their race has no males or females. Long ago Raggnor entered their valley and used his power of illusion to frighten them, and forced them to worship him as their God."

"I understand them, yet I will fight the Kreigg when I must," Jasmine replied.

"Each phase of our plan depends upon the success of the one before," the sorcerer said. "Return to your cottages, my friends, and rest."

When they mounted their horses they were met by a cool evening mist. The mist dissipated leaving a full moon to illuminate their path. Thor and Odin led the procession. Jasmine saw the lunar rays reflecting from their horns of ivory. She could not control herself.

"Odin, come to me, precious." The unicorn trotted beside Jasmine's mount within a twinkling she stood on her horse and leaped on to Odin's back.

"Manchu, join me!" Jasmine shouted.

Manchu called to Thor and joined Jasmine.

"To Queen Dora's cottage, Odin," Jasmine whispered into the magnificent creature's ear. She felt a rush as Odin leaped over the trees. His hoofs barely kissed the earth, when once more they where airborne. At first she clung to his neck, but she became more confident, knowing the stallion would not let her fall. After the third leap Odin cantered then walked to the front of Queen Dora's cottage. Jasmine dismounted, hugged her special new friend and kissed his horn. Odin heard the approach of Thor and Manchu.

Manchu dismounted and looked into Jasmine's eyes.

"I saw you kiss the unicorn. Do you have a kiss for me?"

"Odin is very special," Jasmine responded.

"Am I not special?" Manchu asked.

Jasmine touched the Asian Warrior's lips with her fingers. "Manchu, you are very special to me. Come join with me in the cottage."

On the trail Freeya led her sister's horse behind her, while Khrom led his brother's.

"I envy them, Khrom," Freeya said, "they are not afraid to lead life to the fullest."

"Freeya, tomorrow they go on a mission they may not return from," Khrom said.

"As shall we Khrom," Freeya responded.

Queen Dora held Sharonn, while Captain Eric held his new son. After a two hour journey they came to Queen Dora's cottage. Jasmine heard the arrival of the procession.

"Manchu, go outside, greet your brother and tell him I am sleeping."

Khrom saw the unicorns frolicking in a nearby meadow. Manchu stepped from the cottage that once belonged to him and his brother.

"Manchu, did you enjoy your ride?" Khrom asked.

Manchu hesitated for a moment waiting for his thoughts to clear. "Yes, Khrom. Thor is magnificent. We came here in three bounds."

"Where is Jasmine?" Khrom inquired.

"The Princess sleeps," Manchu answered.

"I need your help, brother," Khrom said. "We must take the mounts to the stable and ready them for the night."

"Yes, Khrom—and I hope we can find clean straw for our bed."

Queen Dora carried her daughter, while Captain Eric carried Tyree to the interior of the cottage. For this night the children would share the same room.

"Tomorrow we prepare a room for Tyree," Dora said.

"Yes, My Beautiful Queen."

"Join me in my chamber, my dear Captain."

Freeya entered her new cottage. "Jasmine, I know you are not sleeping."

Jasmine laughed softly in the near darkness. Freeya touched the wick of a candle to a hot ember in the fireplace. Jasmine rose from her bed.

"Freeya, join me in the hot spring. I wish to remove Manchu from me!"

"Jasmine!"

The young women ran through the frigid air, and with a loud

splash plunged into the warm pool beneath the spring. Queen Dora heard the merriment coming from the spring. "Oh, to be young once more," she mused.

Once the horses had been made ready for the night, Khrom and Manchu lay on their beds of straw. Manchu didn't mind the smells of the horses, for to him they were kin. His thoughts turned to Jasmine and their dangerous mission. He feared not for himself, but for the beautiful woman who had fulfilled all of his desires.

Though Khrom liked horses, he did not share the same feelings towards them as his brother. He detested their odor and the constant thumping sound coming from their stalls. He closed his eyes and pictured Freeya as the Queen of Vall.

Dark clouds shrouded the moon. Thunderclaps announced the arrival of a fierce storm. Both princesses ran through the torrents of cold rain to the shelter of the cottage. They used dry straw and kindling to return the fire to life. Within moments the flames brought heat and light into their new home. They fell asleep knowing they were safe from the raging elements.

Nogard

Chapter 19   Lair of Evil

Jasmine fell asleep into a deep slumber. Her mind entered the realm of dreams. She saw a beautiful ebony queen wearing a long white gown, and felt the woman touch her lips.

"Do not be afraid my daughter," spoke the woman. "I am always with you."

"I love you, Mother," Jasmine whispered in the darkness.

The world of the night passed swiftly, replaced by the full light of a midday sun. Jasmine arose to the sound of Odin prancing in front of the cottage.

"I am coming, my beautiful unicorn."

Jasmine put on her tunic, then her chain-mail armor and her new riding boots. She ran a stone over her broadsword to give it a killing edge. Placing it into its scabbard, she fastened the weapon to her waist.

Freeya awoke to join her sister. "Is it time?"

"Yes, it is time," Jasmine replied. "Freeya, I dreamed of my mother."

"I know, I heard you speak to her."

"I wish you were going with me, Freeya."

The two sisters embraced one another. Together they had faced many dangers and hardships. Now Jasmine would embark on a dangerous mission without her.

Thor entered the stable. The unicorn walked past the horses that he considered to be a breed apart from himself. Manchu awoke with a start from the sound of Thor's approaching hoof beats. Khrom awoke to join his brother.

"Take my armor, Manchu," Khrom pleaded.

"No, Khrom! My armor will be my skill."

Manchu dressed quickly. He inspected his Mongol sword before inserting it into its scabbard, then placed the scabbard beneath a sash secured to his waist. Thor started to pace nervously in place.

"It is time, my brother," Manchu said.

Khrom embraced his brother. Manchu leaped to the back of the unicorn.

"Do not fail us!" Khrom shouted.

"We will succeed, Khrom! The Sorcerer Gaul will have Raggnor's pendant."

Khrom ran behind his brother. He watched Manchu join Jasmine in the sunlight. He saw Freeya weeping in front of her cottage. He joined her to comfort her.

"They will succeed, Freeya."

"How can I know this?"

"My brother promised me. He said, 'We will return with Raggnor's pendant.'"

Freeya placed her hand into Khrom's. She feared for her sister, but it was good to have someone to talk to. She spoke to Khrom. "There was a boy once not so long ago—his name was Vass. We shared a kiss. He was not a prince or even a knight, and I liked him very much. He died for me in the battle of Lund. I do not wish for my sister to meet his fate." Khrom held the Princess of Nevau and kissed her forehead.

Jasmine felt the power of the creature beneath her. She felt her body joining with the unicorn and her soul merged with the rhythm of the steed. The trees of the vast forest became a blur as Odin raced past. He slowed his pace when he ascended the hill overlooking Gaul's castle and halted at the summit. Thor joined his brother. Their eyes met and without warning both unicorns bounded over the precipice. Jasmine's heart nearly stopped when she saw the castle rushing towards her.

Odin's hooves gently touched the earth. He trotted forward then slowed to a walk, as he came to the sorcerer. Jasmine saw the Sorcerer Gaul standing atop a stone platform in front of his castle. Odin halted beside the platform.

The sorcerer placed a gold locket attached to a silver chain around Jasmine's neck. "Within this locket lies the future of our world," he said resolutely.

"I understand, Sorcerer."

"I thank you, Princess Jasmine. Watch over her, Manchu. Remember you will be cloaked from the eyes of the Kreigg until the pendants are exchanged. Once the exchange has taken place, both of you will be visible to them. The time has come; you must leave now."

"To Raggnor's Lair," Jasmine whispered into Odin's ear. The unicorns turned to the west and raced over the forested hills. Odin took the lead while Thor followed in close tandem. They felt a tingling sensation when they passed through the barrier guarding Gaul's Realm. Jasmine saw a fleeting glimpse of the ruins of Nevau, as Odin raced past. The unicorns bounded over the three rivers leading to Lund. At the third river the unicorns paused to drink from the cold spring water. Jasmine heard the sounds of many horses coming toward them. She recognized the leader of the herd as the horse her father once rode into battle. Jasmine pondered, could her father still be alive? Once more the unicorns raced toward the frontier. Odin slowed his pace when they crossed into Raggnor's Realm.

Jasmine detected the foul odor of death hanging in the firmament. She saw hundreds of Kreigg Soldiers huddling around large fires. As Odin proceeded, she saw a massive fortress looming before her. The *lair of evil* merged into a dark mountain.

They crossed a stone bridge spanning a moat of swirling acid. The unicorns moved cautiously between the Kreigg Guards. When they began their approach, Jasmine could see three entrances to the fortress. High above the entrance in the middle she made out a huge platform. This is the place from where the dragons arise, she thought. Her unicorn trod slowly forward. Jasmine could see a ramp from the left descending into the bowels of the earth. A huge iron door sealed the middle. The entrance to her right led to the dragons' rookery. She removed her necklace and took the stone from the locket. Somehow she knew the pendant would guide her to Raggnor's necklace of power. The pendant pulled her toward the ascending path.

The pendant guided Jasmine past the dragons and their Kreigg Handlers. Though she was invisible to the Kreigg, she felt the eyes of the dragons watching her every movement. Odin trod softly over the stone surface. Jasmine saw a small passage at the far end of the dragons' loft. When she pointed the pendant toward the cave it began to glow. "We are close, my friend," she whispered to the jewel.

Jal had survived with many of his men. They were held in two cells adjacent to the mine they were forced to toil in. Raggnor needed the men to mine for amber. He planned to use the precious material to buy the services of the Troblin. While many of his men had become despondent, Jal clung to a ray of hope. He lived to be reunited with his daughter.

Thor began his descent into the tunnel leading to the amber mine. Manchu sensed the tunnel contracting. He dismounted at a side passage. At the rear of the passage he saw two large cells crammed with men. Between himself and the men stood three Kreigg Guards and a hideous creature clutching a chunk of the precious amber. The guards were groggy from the dim light and lack of air while the creature was preoccupied with the stone.

Jal heard the head of the creature from the underworld thump, when it struck the floor of the passage. In rapid succession the Mongol Sword decapitated the Kreigg Guards. Jal woke the man beside him, who in turn woke the man next to him. Jal watched in amazement, as a ring of keys were taken from a Kreigg Guard, and moved towards the iron door of his cell. A key entered the door to his cell and sprung it open. The key moved to the second cell. Jal heard a voice, but could not see its source.

"I have been sent by the Sorcerer Gaul to free you. My name is Manchu. I must speak with your leader."

"I am General Jal. These men are under my command."

"General, I need you and your men to create a diversion to enable Princess Jasmine to complete her mission."

"Jasmine lives!" Jal cried.

"We must hurry. Jasmine's cloak of invisibility is short lived. Follow me to the dragons' stable. Once the Princess has escaped, bring your men to the Realm of Gaul."

Manchu mounted Thor. When they began their ascent, he used the guard's keys to unlock the armory, which held Jal's and his men's weapons. Jal's army obeyed the invisible voice. Manchu halted their advance halfway to the top of the ramp to the dragons' stable. He did not wish to alert the Kreigg of their presence until Jasmine had exchanged the pendants.

Sensing it was too narrow for him to pass, Odin halted by the entrance. Jasmine dismounted and entered the tunnel. She saw a light reflecting off the walls. Her pendant grew ever brighter, directing her to a loose stone. When she removed the stone, she was dazzled by the beauty of Raggnor's necklace of power. Jasmine remembered the Sorcerer Gaul's instructions. She squeezed the turquoise pendant and felt a tingling sensation, then pushed the pendant up, then in a downward motion. The powerful stone broke free and floated in midair. When Jasmine opened her palm it joined her hand. She placed the pendant into the golden locket around her neck. She followed Gaul's instructions with his pendant, and the jewel aligned itself within Raggnor's necklace. Upon exiting the passage Jasmine saw many Kreigg guards advancing toward the now visible Odin. Leaping onto the unicorn's back she drew her sword.

Jal and his men were surprised by Manchu's sudden appearance. Before them was an Asian Warrior mounted on a unicorn. Manchu saw over thirty Kreigg advancing toward Jasmine.

"Slay the Kreigg! Save the Princess!" Manchu shouted.

Within moments Jal's army clashed with the Kreigg. Manchu charged through the Kreigg's line to be with Jasmine.

"Follow me, Princess! Thor and I will breach their ranks."

While most of the Kreigg fought with Jal's army, several blocked Jasmine's escape. Manchu's Mongol sword slew two Kreigg, while Thor rammed through their lines. Jasmine and Odin escaped through the breach before the Kreigg could close ranks.

In the midst of the battle, a Kreigg thrust his spear into Thor's left shoulder. The unicorn winced from the pain and continued his forward movement. Both unicorns leaped from the precipice. Odin landed gently. Thor faltered, nearly landing in the moat of acid. He was unable to maintain Odin's pace.

Jasmine slowed Odin. She turned to see the broken shaft of the spear imbedded in Thor. When they came to the first of the three rivers of Lund, Thor was unable to leap across. Manchu dismounted and led Thor to the opposite side of the cold shallow stream. Jasmine waited.

"Manchu, I will not leave you."

"Jasmine, complete your mission, I will stay with Thor."

Though she desperately wished to remain with Manchu, Jasmine knew the importance of her mission. She wiped the tears from her eyes and urged Odin forward. Odin shared her feelings, as he did not wish to leave his wounded brother.

Manchu pulled the spear from Thor's side. He did not know how to cure a unicorn, but he did know how to treat horses. He packed green mud into the wound and covered it with moss that grew beside the stream. Manchu led Thor into the wood to hide from the Kreigg and their dragons. In the distance he heard the sounds of battle between Jal's army and the Kreigg.

Jasmine raced to Gaul's Realm with the precious turquoise pendant. She saw the sorcerer's castle. The joy she felt at completing her mission was tempered by the thoughts of the dangers facing Manchu and the wounded unicorn.

Gaul had monitored Jasmine's dangerous mission. He witnessed the battle and felt the pain when the spear struck his unicorn. He made a special potion to mend Thor. Jasmine met the sorcerer in front of his castle. She removed the necklace with the prized pendant encased in its locket and returned it to him.

"Thank you, Princess Jasmine. I am in your debt!"

"I must return to Manchu. Thor has been wounded."

"Wait, Jasmine, I have medicine for Thor. Odin, will take you home first then deliver my potion to Manchu. He will know what to do. Manchu will return, riding Odin. Thor will follow."

He fastened a small container containing the potion to a large necklace and placed it around his unicorn's neck. Odin took Jasmine to her cottage then raced to be with his brother.

Manchu saw the blackened firmament being parted by the first glimmers of sunlight. He felt a sudden rush of wind hovering directly over him. He could only hope the dragon rider did not detect his presence, or the wounded unicorn's. He watched the dragon continuing her flight toward the border of Gaul's Realm. Two Kreigg soldiers forded the stream and nearly stepped on Thor as they rushed past. Manchu stood behind a large tree clutching his sword. Moments later he heard a large force crossing the river. He thought it could be Jal's Army, but he could not take the risk of revealing their presence.

Odin had taken Jasmine to her cottage and began the journey to save his brother. When he entered a large meadow, he felt a large shadow covering him. He pivoted with his nimble feet to change direction and bound to the safety of the wood.

Odin continued his dangerous mission. When he came to the stream where he had last seen his brother, he could not find him. He feared his brother had been captured or even worse. For a brief moment he emitted a high-pitched signal from his horn. He heard a weak response. Within moments he stood beside his brother.

Manchu, saw the message fastened to the container around Odin's neck. He read the instructions. *'Pour my potion into Thor's wound. Odin will know what to do.'* Manchu followed the instructions. He removed the moss and poured the potion into the wound. Manchu saw a glowing green light emitting from the standing unicorn's horn. Odin inserted his horn into the gaping wound. Thor's body shook violently for a brief moment. Odin stepped back; his horn exited the wound. Manchu witnessed the wound closing, leaving only a tiny scar. Thor rose to his feet to join his brother. Both unicorns drank from the cold spring-fed stream.

Manchu rode Odin while Thor followed at a steady pace.

They crossed the bridge over the second river of Lund without incident. When they crossed the last of the bridges, Manchu saw two Kreigg soldiers guarding the approach. He drew his Mongol sword and prepared to charge. The Kreigg had never seen a Mongol warrior, let alone one mounted on a unicorn. Fearing him to be a God, they fell to the ground to pay him homage. The unicorns increased their pace. Though he had not fully recovered, Thor traveled thrice as rapidly as any mortal steed.

Nogard

Chapter 20 Tears for a Dragon

Jasmine entered her cottage. Freeya embraced her sister.

"I feared for you, Jasmine."

Jasmine did not respond. A look of despair covered her face.

"Jasmine, what is wrong?"

"Thor lies wounded," Jasmine sobbed. "Manchu stayed behind to protect him."

"Did you make the exchange?"

"Yes. The Sorcerer Gaul has possession of Raggnor's pendant."

Sensing his unicorn was safe Gaul sent forth an image. "Princess Freeya, the time has come for you to continue your quest."

"Yes, Sorcerer," Freeya responded.

When the image waned, Freeya saw a beautiful black robe with a matching hood.

"Jasmine, I must go now. The time has come for me to continue the quest for the dragon. I hope you will soon be reunited with Manchu."

"I love you, Freeya," Jasmine said as she hugged her sister.

Khrom received a vision telling him the time had come for him to assist Freeya in her quest. He saddled two horses, before approaching the door to the cottage.

"Freeya, I heard Jasmine's voice. Where is my brother?"

"Thor lies wounded. Manchu stays with him," Jasmine responded.

Khrom felt an urgent need to help his brother, but he knew

the importance of his mission. He would not let Freeya face the unknown perils of her quest alone.

Freeya rode through the wood with Khrom. She saw a large herd of wild pigs rooting for nuts and mushrooms. As she ascended, Freeya saw the broad-leafed trees giving way to stately pines. She saw the height of the pines shrinking when they neared the Realm of Eternal Winter. When her horse trod on barren ground and stone, she dismounted.

"Khrom, stay with the horses. I must find the dragon alone."

Khrom dismounted in silence. He obeyed the princess's command, though he feared for her safety.

Freeya felt the hard surface of ice beneath her. She walked cautiously over the slick surface, where the morning sun had melted the glacier's mantle of snow. She searched in vain for the better part of the day. All signs of the Black Dragon eluded her. The rays of sunlight, which had given her a measure of warmth, began to wane. Freeya was nearly blinded by the glare of the setting sun, reflecting from the glacier. Exhaustion took control of her body. Unknowingly, Freeya fell beside the breathing hole of the Black Dragon. She fell into despair. "All is lost," she cried. "I have failed. The legend of the Black Dragon is false." She began to weep. Volumes of tears cascaded from her eyes.

While the majority of her tears merged with the glacier, a few entered the breathing hole of the Black Dragon. One tear fell a hundred feet and entered Kee's left eye. A second touched his right. The tears were the sign he had waited for these many seasons.

Sensing her despair, Khrom entered the glacier to comfort Freeya. He found her curled in a ball on the frozen surface.

"Freeya, I am here. Let us leave this place."

"Khrom, I have failed. My quest is doomed. I fear the stories of the dragon encased within the glacier are only fables."

Khrom lifted Freeya to her feet. He held her body against his own to give her warmth.

Far below many hearts began to beat. The first heart had been joined by a second, then a third. Soon all six of the Black Dragon's hearts began to pump life into his massive form. Heat from his body softened the ice. The massive dragon began his climb to the surface. The ice started to move. At first, fissures spread throughout the glacier, followed by growing chasms.

"The dragon lives, Khrom!" Freeya shouted. "I can feel his power."

"Run, Freeya! Run for your life!"

A massive head broke through the frozen mantel, blocking Freeya and Khrom's escape. They stood in awe, as the huge dragon emerged from its icy tomb. They watched its massive wings unfurling. Freeya felt the glacier shake when the starving dragon collapsed. She felt pangs of hunger coming from the creature. Freeya did not know how or why, she only knew she was able to communicate with the dragon.

"Come, Khrom! He is starving! We must bring him food."

She remembered the herd of wild pigs. They moved carefully past the dragon to their horses. Together they descended the trail to the hardwoods. Freeya removed her short bow and quiver from behind her saddle. She saw movement. The wild pigs were but a short distance from where they had been that morning. Khrom watched in amazement. Freeya urged her horse into a gallop then charged into the herd. Her first arrow struck a large boar her second arrow struck a smaller pig. Khrom rode behind a tree to protect himself from the panic stricken herd.

"Khrom, help me with the pigs!" Freeya commanded.

"Yes, Princess," Khrom replied.

Khrom grabbed the boar by its hind legs, while Freeya carried the front. He secured the boar to Freeya's mount then secured the smaller one to his. They rode once more to the glacier and unloaded the pigs. Cautiously they dragged the boar to the head of the dragon. Though Freeya felt compassion for the starving beast, Khrom feared the dragon would devour both of them without hesitation.

The dragon tasted the scent of the pig. He elongated his neck to grasp the boar in his jaws to sever it two and swallowed the first half with a single gulp. The dragon devoured the second half without hesitation. He watched the two humans returning with the second pig. He devoured it whole.

The Sorcerer Gaul sent forth his image to Freeya. "You have done well, Princess Freeya."

"Thank you, Sorcerer."

"The dragon awaits. He wishes for you to ride with him to a warmer place."

Freeya saw the dragon lowering his head. She approached the dragon cautiously and placed her left leg over his neck. She felt his cold wet skin against her buttocks. When the creature lifted his head, she felt herself sliding down his neck until her body met his shoulders.

Freeya, held tightly to the dragon, when he stood erect on his hind legs and began to move toward the precipice at the edge of the glacier. Fear and excitement dominated her being. She heard a loud snapping sound when the dragon's wings expanded to their maximum span. Suddenly Freeya felt the power of the dragon when his legs vaulted them from the edge of the cliff. She saw the ground racing towards her. She closed her eyes and prepared to die. She felt the rapid descent slowing. When she bravely opened her eyes she saw the dragon was gliding effortlessly toward a distant hilltop. Freeya felt the dragon's thoughts and sensed he read hers as well. She barely felt the ground when her new friend alighted gently onto a lush meadow. She dismounted from the dragon once he lowered his head.

Khrom had watched in horror and disbelief. He did not trust this giant creature, after witnessing how rapidly the dragon devoured the wild pigs. He wondered if the beast had taken his future queen to a distant place to eat her at its leisure. Khrom made the distant trek to the place where the dragon had landed. He rode to the hill leading Freeya's horse behind. Khrom dismounted and followed a game trail to the summit of the hill in the near darkness. He saw the huge shape of the dragon, but no sign of Freeya. He feared for the worst. Khrom drew his sword and prepared for battle.

"Freeya! Freeya!" Khrom screamed.

Freeya awoke with a start. She had fallen asleep beside the dragon's head.

"Khrom, I waited so long for you," Freeya said in an angry

tone. "Why did you not make haste to come to me?"

For a brief moment Khrom pondered who should he slay—the dragon or the princess.

The dragon sensed the anger in the young man's thoughts. He did not like the sight of the unsheathed sword. The dragon stood erect, his eyes stared menacingly at the small mortal.

Khrom stood his ground. "Run, Freeya! I will protect you!"

Freeya ran between Khrom and the dragon. "Kee, please do not harm him. He is a friend; he means no harm."

Kee read Freeya's thoughts and responded to her with his own. "Sheath your sword, Khrom. The dragon will not harm us."

Khrom placed his sword into its sheath, while the dragon reclined.

"Khrom, you were willing to die for me. The day will come when I speak of this to our children."

"Let us leave this place, Freeya."

They descended the hill to their tethered mounts. As they rode Khrom asked. "Freeya, I heard you call the Dragon Kee. How could you know his name?"

"He told me; we know one another's thoughts."

Khrom did not speak. After this day he felt anything was possible.

Freeya rode to her cottage. When she entered the bedroom, she was surprised to see Manchu sleeping beside her sister. Freeya carefully left the cottage and closed the door behind her. She saw Khrom taking the horses to the stable.

"Khrom, I cannot stay here this night. My sister is with your brother."

Khrom felt a sense of relief his brother had returned. He turned his attention to Freeya. "You can spend the night in the stable. The straw is not as comfortable as your bed, but you may like the company."

"Alright, if I can sleep with my horse," Freeya replied hesitantly.

Jasmine awoke to the early morning sun. "I fear for my sister, Manchu. She has not yet returned."

"She came in last night. Perhaps she is with Khrom in the stable."

Nogard

Chapter 21　　One with the Dragon

"Why did you not awaken me?" Jasmine asked in an angry tone.

"I did not wish to disturb you," Manchu responded.

"Never mind, come with me to to the stable."

Upon entering the stable she saw Khrom saddling two horses.

"Where is my sister?" Jasmine demanded.

"Jasmine! I found him. The Black Dragon lives!" Freeya shouted from the loft above.

"Manchu has returned. He and Thor are safe," Jasmine announced.

"I know this. I saw him last night."

"Freeya, tell me of the Black Dragon." Jasmine asked.

"He is magnificent. His size dwarfs all other creatures. When I am with him I feel his power and I know Kee will protect me."

Jasmine did not ask her sister how she knew the dragon's name. By this time she had accepted the magic that encompassed the Realm of Gaul.

Freeya and Khrom rode to Kee's hill. They dismounted and climbed to the summit on foot. Freeya came to the place where she last saw the dragon. She saw the blades of grass and small saplings springing upright in the depression left by the dragon. Kee was gone. She felt betrayed. Perhaps she thought, Kee no longer wished to be her ally against Raggnor. Khrom held Freeya and tried to comfort her.

Suddenly an unearthly roar bellowed from the sky. A massive shadow covered the hilltop. "Run to the wood, Freeya!" Khrom screamed. They heard the thud of the carcass of a large bullock striking the earth. Freeya heard the sound of the dragon's wings capturing the wind. Kee landed gently beside his prey. Khrom watched the dragon singe the bullock with a blast of flames.

Khrom held Freeya's head against his chest. "Do not watch, Princess." Freeya shuddered when she heard the dragon's talons tear into flesh, and the sound of the bullock's bones being crushed by his massive jaws. Kee sensed Freeya's presence. His thoughts entered her mind.

"The dragon asks for us to leave," Freeya whispered. "He wishes for us to return when the sun is high and he has finished eating."

Khrom and Freeya descended the hill to their nervous mounts, and rode to a nearby valley. Their horses drank from a spring fed stream and dined on lush grasses. For a brief time Freeya and Khrom strolled through the beautiful valley. Freeya saw a Mother Unicorn and her foal frolicking in the meadow. She looked at the young man beside her.

"Khrom, I wish to be your queen and bear your children," Freeya announced.

"Freeya, I love you more than all things."

They held one another beneath the canopy of a giant elm. The sun was high when Freeya turned toward the dragon's hilltop. She saw vultures making a spiraling descent.

"It is time, Khrom. We must return to the dragon."

"Freeya, I fear for you. I do not wish for you to ride the beast. I forbid it!" Khrom demanded.

"You forbid me!" Freeya screamed angrily. "I must ride Kee! All will be lost, if I do not ride him into battle."

"Then I will ride the dragon," Khrom stated.

"No, only I can ride Kee. It is my destiny."

Freeya's will prevailed. She rode to the hill of the dragon followed by Khrom. Once more they climbed to the summit. Kee had finished his meal, only a few scraps of the bullock remained for the squabbling vultures. Freeya heard moans of pleasure coming from her new friend, absorbing rays of the midday sun into his black skin.

Freeya approached Kee's head. She had little fear of the

dragon, which could devour her with a single gulp. Her right hand caressed the base of Kee's lower jaw. "I wish to ride with you, my friend." Freeya said as her thoughts entered the dragon's mind.

Kee began to rise. He lowered his head and extended his neck. Freeya mounted Kee and gently slid downward to his shoulders. He stood erect on his hind legs and walked to the bluff of the hill. Freeya closed her eyes and clung to Kee's neck. Kee began to beat his wings slowly at first, than increased to a rapid cadence.

Khrom felt the wind being generated from the dragon. He was forced to retreat to the wood to escape the swirling clouds of dust.

Kee adjusted for the weight of the young woman balanced on his shoulders. When he sensed a rising thermal, his legs sprang his body skyward.

Freeya's fears began to subside. She opened her eyes slowly, during Kee's ascent. She saw distant mountains and broad plains. In the distance she made out the ruins of Nevau and far to the west, the sea which seemed to touch the sky. When Kee circled the Realm of Gaul, Freeya saw the spires of the castle of Vall. She felt Kee's reassuring thoughts. She felt at ease and released her hold on his neck and for a time dared to stand on his back. Her fear had been replaced by exhilaration. Kee continued his ascent. Freeya peered once more at the castles and villages below, which appeared to be merely tiny clusters of stones. When a thunderstorm approached Kee flew over it. Freeya outstretched her arms, and felt the dew contained within a cloud.

As they flew, both formed a pact to defeat Raggnor and his forces of evil. Kee needed Freeya to free his sisters. Freeya needed Kee to free her people. Together they formed a plan. Kee would fly close to his sisters and Freeya would slay the dragon rider with her bow. Kee impressed on Freeya her need for complete accuracy. She must slay the Kreigg without harming the female dragons. In turn Kee would lead Princess Freeya's army against Raggnor.

Kee returned to the hilltop. Khrom emerged from the wood after the dragon landed. Freeya shouted to Khrom from atop the dragon. "Khrom, I need to have my short bow and quiver of arrows!"

Khrom was beginning to have second thoughts of having Freeya as his queen. They had yet to wed and she was already giving him commands. He descended the hill and returned with Freeya's bow and quiver of iron tipped arrows.

"Khrom, make targets and place them around the hilltop!" Freeya shouted.

"Yes, Princess," Khrom responded.

Kee lifted once more into the sky. Khrom drew circles with a stick at intervals around the hill, and placed a stick upright in the center of the circle.

Kee made a slow pass over the hill. Freeya took aim at the first target. She was able to hit targets from horseback, but she never dreamed of striking targets from atop a dragon. Freeya released her bow string. The feathered missile took flight. Kee sighed, while Khrom screamed and ran for his life when the arrow nearly struck him. On the dragon's second pass Freeya struck the target, and on the third her arrow severed the stick in the center. Kee increased his speed, while Freeya's arrows continued to strike their mark. Both Khrom and Kee were impressed by Freeya's skill. Kee landed and lowered his massive head. Freeya dismounted to join Khrom.

"I am impressed, Freeya. You are truly a Master Archer."

Freeya gently pressed her lips against Khrom's. "Thank you for your support, Khrom. Kee thinks I am nearly ready; he wishes to continue training with me."

"You have practiced enough for today, Freeya."

Nogard

Chapter 22   Army of Nevau

Jal's army had taken the Kreigg by surprise. He wished to join Jasmine as quickly as possible. The general felt the cold water of the first river of Lund against his legs. When Jal and his men completed fording the stream, they heard the sound of horses coming from the wood. Jal's black stallion trotted to his former master.

"Mount the horses. We ride to Nevau for our saddles and lances!" Jal shouted.

The knights helped one another climb on to their mounts. The Peasant Soldiers marched behind the knights. Jal observed his army of free men, who where no longer slaves in Raggnor's mine. Jal's force crossed the remaining two rivers without incident. The army approached Nevau under the cover of darkness. Jal sent forth two scouts. He met with his scouts on their return.

"How many Kreigg guard the drawbridge and the stable?" Jal asked of the first scout.

"I saw five guarding the bridge and no Kreigg at the stable, General," the first scout responded.

"Where are the remaining Kreigg?"

"Their main force stays behind the inner wall, General," the second scout answered.

Jal turned to one of his lieutenants, a tall, gaunt man with long gray locks.

"Luce, once we have taken the bridge and stable, take twenty men and secure the inner wall," Jal commanded. "Keep the Kreigg trapped inside."

Jal's army moved with stealth in the blackness and quickly slew the Kreigg guarding the bridge, before they could sound an alarm. Luce and his men secured the inner wall. The Kreigg Commander heard Luce's approach. He ordered his army to repel the invaders. The fighting became furious, and several Kreigg where slain when they tried to force their way through the narrow exit into the main courtyard. Fearing he was facing a much larger force, the Kreigg commander ordered his soldiers to barricade themselves within the inner court-yard.

Jal's men removed all the saddles and lances before the light of the new day revealed their presence. Once the horses where saddled, the army of Nevau advanced at a steady pace. Jal planned to reach the Realm of Gaul in two days.

Nogard

Chapter 23   Incursion

For untold centuries the Sorcerer Gaul maintained an invisible barrier on the borders of his realm. Only the sorcerer allowed who could enter or depart his realm. As his powers waned, breaches formed within the barrier. Sensing his brother's weakness, Raggnor sent forth scouts to find the ruptures and probe the realm's defenses.

After a full day of practice with Kee, Freeya and Khrom descended the dragon's hill. Freeya detected a foul odor. "Khrom, draw your sword. Kreigg are nearby." Freeya whispered. Khrom stood guard while Freeya mounted her horse. Freeya placed the notch of her arrow into the bow string while Khrom mounted his steed. When he guided his horse onto the road, Khrom was nearly blinded by the light of the setting sun. Freeya saw four Kreigg soldiers who had slipped through a fold in the sorcerer's barrier.

"Khrom, we must slay these intruders, before they can tell their master of the breach in Gaul's barrier."

Freeya guided her mount into the swamp, which ran beside the road. Khrom followed catching a glimpse of the huge Kreigg, as they slipped past. Freeya wished to attack the Kreigg from the west and use the sun as her ally.

Unaware of Freeya and Khrom's presence, the Kreigg continued their trek. They held one hand over their eyes to block the rays of the blinding sun. The scouts wore no armor and were armed with iron headed axes.

The horses climbed the bank to the solid footing of the road. Freeya's horse pranced nervously waiting for the command to attack. Freeya knew the Kreigg's battle tactics—when under attack from mounted forces, they would form two lines to repel the knights.

"I will take two with my bow." Freeya said with assurance. "Take the one to my right when I break through."

"Yes, Princess," Khrom acknowledged.

Khrom did not have Freeya's confidence. He had been in combat with other men, but he had yet to be tested against the Kreigg. They were so huge and there were four of them to their two. He feared if he went for help, Freeya would think of him as a coward. Khrom aligned his mount with Freeya's. Freeya looked at him and smiled.

"Are you ready, Princess?" Khrom asked nervously.

"Yes!"

"Charge!" Khrom screamed.

The Kreigg were caught by complete surprise. They heard the thunder of the closing steeds and formed two battle lines. The rays of the western sun glinted off the metal of their drawn axes.

When the Kreigg came into her range, Freeya pulled her bow to its maximum draw. She aimed instinctively from the galloping horse. Her arrow took flight and struck the Kreigg with a resounding thud. The iron arrowhead pierced his chest and severed his heart. The mortally wounded beast-man fell backwards to the hardened earth. Freeya's fingers grasped a second arrow from its quiver. She was nearly on top of the second Kreigg when her arrow struck his throat. The third scout stepped aside to wield his axe into Freeya as she passed.

Khrom's horse crashed into the startled beast-man. The collision threw both Khrom and the Kreigg to the earth. Khrom's horse faltered from the impact. Khrom stood and faced the dazed Kreigg. He wielded his sword and struck a fatal blow to his foe's neck.

Freeya slowed her horse and returned to Khrom.

"Freeya, my horse is injured I will not be able to ride him. Did we slay all of them?"

"No. One still lives," Freeya responded. "I must find him and kill him."

Freeya began to track the beast-man. She knew the Kreigg where quite capable of ambushing their pursuers. She saw broken branches and mashed down grass springing back to its upright position. He is near, she thought. Freeya caught a glimpse of the Kreigg standing in the pines. She made out the large stone he held above his head. She notched an arrow to her bow string.

Freeya heard the sound of many hoof beats coming from the opposite direction. The Kreigg heard the approaching horses as well. He panicked and bolted past her running into the swamp. Freeya did not follow. She watched as he ran into a bog and started to sink. Within a few minutes, all that was visible of the Kreigg where large bubbles breaching the surface of the swamp.

The riders approached Freeya. She saw the captain leading Khrom's band of brigands.

"Freeya, where is my son?" Captain Eric asked.

"Follow me, Captain," Freeya replied. "I will lead you to him."

The captain saw Khrom standing beside his mount. He was surprised to see the bodies of the three Kreiggs.

"The two of you killed three Kreiggs. Did any escape?" the captain asked.

"One tried, but he was taken by the swamp," Freeya answered.

"Why did you not go for help? Both of you could have been slain."

"We had to slay them before they could tell Raggnor of the breach in the barrier." Freeya responded. She did not tell the captain of her desire for revenge.

"Why are you here, Captain?" Khrom asked.

"We have been sent by the sorcerer, to find the breach and place a sentry to guard it."

Khrom rode behind Freeya on her horse. Captain Eric led the procession. They followed the inside of the nearly invisible barrier and found a clear hole, large enough for a horse and rider to pass through.

The young knight from Vall took a special interest in the location of the breach. A plan to obtain wealth and favor with King Copen began to form within his mind. He would tell King Copen of

Khrom's planned rebellion, and take Khrom's sister Sharonn as a hostage.

The captain directed the band to build a large pile of brush atop the hill overlooking the rupture. Pitch was poured over the brush and a burning torch was placed a short distance from the pile.

"Two of you will be assigned to watch over the breach," Captain Eric commanded. "When you see intruders set the brush ablaze and ride for help."

"Yes, Captain," responded Khrom's men.

The captain gave assigned watches to his men. The young knight from Vall was given the morning watch, with an older man.

"Khrom, Freeya, the sorcerer wishes to speak with you this night. He will be in the village near his castle."

"Yes, Captain," Freeya and Khrom responded.

"Khrom, Freeya, cleanse the Kreigg blood from your bodies. I must return, and train our soldiers in the ways of war."

Freeya took Khrom to the place where he left his mount. His horse trotted to him. Khrom touched the horse's shoulder, at the place where it struck the Kreigg.

"I think I can ride him now," Khrom said.

"Do not force him to run, Khrom," Freeya said.

"Oh no, he is still shaken from crashing into the Kreigg," Khrom said. "I will ask my brother to care for him, he knows horses well."

They reached the cottages by the light of the stars. Manchu saw Khrom's horse limping, when he rode it into the stable.

"Khrom, what happened to your horse?" Manchu asked. "Did you run him into a tree?"

"No!" Khrom responded. "He collided with a Kreigg."

"A Kreigg—there are no Kreigg in the Realm of Gaul!"

"A breach has formed in the barrier; four Kreigg broke through," Khrom explained. "Please see to my mount. Freeya and I must go now to cleanse the Kreigg blood from our bodies."

Freeya and Khrom bathed together in the pool beneath the hot spring. Khrom lay in the magical waters with his eyes closed. He felt the blood of his enemy lifting from his body. His moment of tranquility was broken by a pleasant surprise. For a brief moment he felt Freeya's lips touching his.

"Thank you for risking your life for me, Prince Khrom," Freeya said softly. "The captain was right. We should have ridden for help."

"I know," Khrom responded. "I wanted to ride for help."

"Why didn't you?"

"I did not want you to think me to be a coward."

"I love you so very much, Khrom. We cannot tarry; the sorcerer awaits."

"Please, Freeya, can we stay a little longer?" Khrom pleaded.

When they returned to the stable, Manchu spoke to Khrom of his horse. "I can find nothing broken; he should be fine after a few days rest."

"Manchu, let me ride your steed. We are to meet with the Sorcerer Gaul this night," Khrom asked.

"Khrom, you know my horse will only allow me to ride him!" Manchu responded. "Take the queen's horse, he is not very swift, but nothing can stop him in battle."

Khrom looked fondly at the large horse his mother rode when he was an infant in her arms. He ran his hands over the steed's shoulders, to his amazement the old horse was sound.

"Freeya, this is the horse my mother rode when she escaped from Vall. I will ride him to victory, when I retake my kingdom."

They journeyed to the village near the sorcerer's castle. Freeya saw two foxes dancing in the moonlight.

"Why do they dance, Khrom?" Freeya asked.

"The captain tells me it is a mating ritual."

"Oh!"

When they entered the village, they were met by an old man clutching a crooked staff.

"Welcome, Your Majesties. The sorcerer awaits. I have been sent to escort you."

Freeya saw a hundred or more thatched huts in the torch light of the village. She followed the old one whose crooked staff thumped over the cobble stones of the main road. The Elder led them to the only stone structure within the hamlet. Upon entering the structure Khrom and Freeya saw the transformation of the old one into the Sorcerer Gaul. He was thrice the size of the old man and wore a blue robe. His lavender eyes entered Freeya's.

"Freeya, does all go well with Kee?"

"Yes, Sorcerer. We have become close friends."

"Do you still require Khrom's assistance?" the sorcerer inquired. "I have need of him."

"I can ride and train with the dragon alone, Sorcerer," Freeya replied.

"Khrom, I need you to prepare to lead your army."

"Yes, Sorcerer," Khrom replied.

"As you have witnessed, my powers have begun to weaken. We must take back your kingdom within three days or all will be lost."

"I understand, Sorcerer," Khrom said.

The sorcerer turned his attention to Freeya. "Tomorrow you must return to the dragon and continue to train with him. I am assured with his assistance, victory can be ours."

"Yes, Sorcerer Gaul," Freeya replied.

The sorcerer smiled for a brief moment and looked at the young prince.

"Khrom, take princess Freeya to the feast being held in your honor. Enjoy this night. You will not be with one another until the time of battle."

Khrom was surprised. He had no idea a feast was being held in his honor.

"Thank you, Sorcerer," spoke both Khrom and Freeya as they departed.

Freeya overheard the cook speaking to the village herdsman.

"Where is the bullock you promised for the feast?"

"He was taken by a dragon," responded the herdsman. "I saw the beast with my own eyes. A huge Black Dragon came out of the sky and swooped down on the bullock and carried him away."

"You have been drinking too much mead my friend. What did you bring?"

"Two rams and a goat," the herdsman replied.

"Alright, the rams will be fine. Take that goat away from here."

Khrom heard Freeya's muffled laughter. "Freeya, my kingdom faces many dangers—Raggnor, The Kreigg, and now your new friend's appetite."

"Freeya, come join us!" Jasmine shouted.

Freeya did not respond. Her mind journeyed to another time—another feast. She remembered the young peasant youth from the Village of Lund. He was gone now, slain by the Kreigg, as he fought to defend her and her kingdom. Freeya walked to her sister and touched her hand.

"I am sorry, Jasmine. My thoughts were of Vass."

Tears formed in Princess Jasmine's brown eyes, sliding gently over her cheeks.

"Freeya, I think of Joran every day. Our life is here now. We must go on."

Manchu approached his brother with two goblets of mead. "Drink and be merry, My Future King."

Captain Eric approached his two sons. "Where is my mother?" Khrom asked.

"She will not be with us this night. Tonight is a feast for warriors and she thought it best to stay with her children."

"Does my army prepare for war, Captain?" Khrom asked.

"Only a few, save your band, know how to use a sword or spear. Their spirits are high. They will fight for you and the Kingdom of Vall."

"Do we have enough weapons?"

"Yes, our forge has made many spears and all of our swords have been sharpened to a killing edge," Captain Eric replied.

The captain approached Jasmine. "Princess, the sorcerer has informed me your father and his army will arrive tomorrow."

"Thank you, Captain."

"Are you and my son Manchu ready for your demonstration?"

"Yes! Oh yes!" Jasmine responded.

Two rows of twenty staggered poles had been erected in a large meadow, each pole placed a little over the length of a horse from the other. Atop each pole a torch was fastened to the height of a warrior on horseback. The forty torches where ignited.

Jasmine took her position at one end of the flaming poles, while Manchu the other. She felt her mount prancing beneath her. Captain Eric stood near the center of the poles and waved a torch to signal the riders. Jasmine drew her sword, as did Manchu. Their horses galloped rapidly toward the flaming poles and each other. Jasmine swung her sword the blade severed the handle of the first torch hurling its flames to the ground.

The New Army of Vall cheered as each torch was severed and held their breath when the riders approached each other, on their alternating course. Manchu felt Jasmine's leg brush against his, as they passed one another in the center.

They continued the demonstration until all the torches had been severed. Khrom's band showed their quickness and agility by jumping through rings of fire. The captain and members of the sorcerer's guards gave a demonstration on the use of the sword and spear in combat.

The aroma of the rams cooking in the spit saturated the night air. A portly cook approached Khrom. "The rams are ready, Your Highness."

"Thank you. What is your name, cook?"

"I am called Klaus. I will be a good soldier, for I am to fat to run from battle."

"I admire your courage, Klaus," Khrom said. "You will be in charge of my kitchen when we retake Vall. Now I need you to feed my army and give them strength."

"Thank you, Your Majesty."

Khrom took Freeya by the hand, together they stepped on to a platform facing all who had taken refuge from Raggnor and Copen. Khrom spoke to his army of villagers and peasants.

"My friends, tomorrow we train for our just war against Copen and his assassins. The following day we will march to retake our beloved Kingdom of Vall."

A loud cheer resounded from half of the villagers and peasants, while the other half remained silent. "What of us who have come from Nevau?" a peasant shouted.

Khrom turned to Freeya she touched his hand and replied. "When we have taken Vall, I will marry Prince Khrom. Our kingdoms will become one." Freeya embraced Khrom. A loud cheer from all that heard Princess Freeya echoed throughout the village.

"My head cook Klaus tells me the rams are ready. Enjoy the feast my friends," Khrom announced.

When Freeya steped from the platform, Jasmine held her in an excited embrace.

"I am so happy for you, Freeya."

"Thank you, Jasmine. You and Manchu were magnificent."

"Thank you, Your Highness, Queen of Vall, "Jasmine said while she made a courtesy. "Please, Freeya, I wish to be part of your wedding."

"Yes, of course. You will be my maid of honor. We will plan the wedding after we defeat Raggnor."

Everyone dined on the rams and fresh bread and drank golden mead. The musicians played their instruments till the first rays of the new dawn appeared. The young knight from Vall had departed to rest before he committed his foul deed.

𝕹𝖔𝖌𝖆𝖗𝖉

𝕮𝖍𝖆𝖕𝖙𝖊𝖗 24   𝕬𝖇𝖉𝖚𝖈𝖙𝖎𝖔𝖓

The sun arose from its cradle to begin a new day, while Freeya slept in her Prince's arms. Manchu felt Jasmine's warm body pressed against his own. The captain approached the young couples.

"Arise, my sons and daughters we must prepare for war."

"Can we not let the war wait a little longer?" Manchu replied.

"You heard the captain. We have to train for war!" Jasmine commanded.

"Yes, Princess Jasmine," Manchu responded.

"Freeya, I have spoken to the sorcerer," the captain said. "Tell Kee he will not be part of the assault on Vall. You must go now. The dragon awaits your presence."

The sleepy village turned into a military encampment. Khrom took command of half of the men, and Manchu, the remaining half. Jasmine formed a band of young women who wished to fight for their kingdom.

Freeya rode directly to the dragon's hilltop. She thought of Khrom on her journey and hoped she would be a worthy queen. Kee nervously awaited his friend. He felt his morning pangs of hunger and had witnessed several flocks of geese flying over the hilltop. Freeya had barely mounted the dragon, when they were suddenly in pursuit of a large flock of snow geese. Kee closed with the large white birds. When he came into his range the dragon sent forth a small measured ball of flame to ignite a single goose. Kee dove beneath the burning bird opened his large jaws and inhaled his breakfast. Freeya held her breath, as the dragon dove toward the forest below, nearly colliding with its canopy.

Freeya relayed the sorcerer's message to Kee, that he would not be part of the initial assault on Vall. She explained to him they must wait for the sorcerer's command. Kee read her thoughts.

While Queen Dora rested in her cottage, Sharonn and Tyree played in the morning sun. Each held a wooden sword given to them by the captain.

"I will be a *mighty soldier* like my father," Tyree stated proudly.

"I will be a *warrior princess* like Jasmine," Sharonn responded.

The sounds of the toy weapons clashing echoed throughout the wood.

The young knight from Vall and his partner relieved the two men guarding the breach in the barrier. When the sounds of the departing guards grew silent, Orin spoke to his partner. "Lon, you look weary, I will take the first watch." When the older man closed his eyes, Orin struck quickly with his sword. Lon's limp body slumped forward without uttering a sound. The assassin rode swiftly toward Queen Dora's cottage.

The treacherous knight watched the children from the cover of the pines. Sharonn was unaware of the eyes of evil watching her. Tyree heard the sound of a horse snapping the pine boughs. He sensed the impending danger.

"Sharonn, run! I will protect you!" Tyree shouted.

Sharonn screamed and ran across the meadow toward her mother's cottage. Tyree clutched his wooden sword with both of his hands and stood between his sister and the charging knight. He heard the thunder of the horse's hoofs. Tyree stepped aside to avoid being trampled and thrust the point of his toy weapon into the horse's side. He heard the wooden blade snap an instant before he was struck by the knight's boot. The boy was hurled to the ground. His body was nearly trampled by the galloping steed.

Orin urged his wounded mount forward. He leaned to his right and felt the squirming body of his prize within his grasp. "Do not struggle against me, child, or I will slay you and feed your body to the wild pigs."

Queen Dora heard her daughter's screams. She ran to protect

her, armed only with a broom. Dora watched in horror, as the evil knight carried her daughter from the meadow and raced toward the breach in the barrier. She saw Tyree lying before her in the meadow. She heard a moaning sound coming from the boy. She knelt beside the one who had given so much in his attempt to save her daughter.

Tyree's face was bruised and his nose was broken. He spoke softly in the arms of his queen. "He won't travel far, Mother. His horse bleeds from my sword." Tyree closed his eyes his body became limp.

Queen Dora carried the boy into her cottage and placed him onto her bed. She desperately needed help—immediately. Her daughter had been taken, and with every breath the evil knight took her closer to Vall. Orin knew of the plans of her son's rebellion and would soon warn King Copen. On her bed lay a child that would soon perish if he did not receive help. She knew the only horse in the stable was Khrom's lame one. Dora led the steed from the stable. She took a torch and set the structure ablaze to signal the captain. The fire soon tasted wood and straw, sending flames and plumes of smoke skyward.

A sentry in the village saw the spiraling smoke.

"Captain, I see a fire by your cottage."

"Khrom, Manchu, continue the training!" the captain commanded. "Jasmine, come with me. I fear my queen could be in danger."

"Yes, Captain," Jasmine responded.

While Captain Eric and Jasmine rushed to the cottage, the sorcerer sensed Dora and Tyree's plight. He concocted a special potion to cure the child. He summoned his unicorn Odin.

Orin had raced through the breach; he felt confident his plan would succeed. He was oblivious to his horse's wound and continued to push his mount forward. The point of the wooden sword began to take its toll. When the wooden point fell from the horses flesh, it no longer restrained the blood in its severed artery. The trickle became a torrent. The horse collapsed from lack of blood. Orin and Sharonn tumbled to the earth.

From a rise in the plain a single pair of yellow eyes watched the movements below. He tasted the scent of the horse's blood. The creature watched the knight dragging a child behind him toward the road that led to Vall. The wolf lifted his head and sent forth an unearthly howl to his brethren. Soon the tall grass became alive with large silver coated creatures.

Sharonn broke free. She ran toward the wood to escape her captor. Orin pursued her with his drawn sword. Sharonn tripped on an exposed root and fell to the ground. She turned to face her captor who was about to bash her into unconsciousness.

Orin stopped his forward movement. He heard a low growl coming from behind. When he turned to face the threat a large black wolf leaped between himself and the child. Sharonn scrambled to her feet and hurried deeper into the wood.

The nimble wolves dodged the swinging sword of the evil knight. When Orin faced exhaustion the predators struck. Orin felt a fierce pain from canine teeth biting into his hand. His sword fell from his grasp as four of the snarling creatures hurled him backwards. The last thing he witnessed in this world was the maw of a great black male, an instant before it ripped out his throat.

While most of the pack stripped the flesh and bone from the horse's remains, the black male followed Shraonn's trail. In a short time he stood beside the child. Somehow Sharonn did not fear the wolf. She followed the alpha male deep into the wood. They passed many bogs and heard the chatter of squirrels, as they passed. The large wolf led her into a small cave. Her eyes adjusted to the dim light of the den. Sharonn heard the sounds made by many cubs crying for their mother's milk. She saw six little wolves playing on the dirt floor. She noticed one cub was smaller than the others. Sharonn held the smallest cub next to her chest. She placed the cub on to the floor of the cave. The black male pushed the little creature to Sharonn. She accepted the leader's present.

Sensing Tyree's fate, the sorcerer rode his unicorn Odin to be with the boy. He stepped inside the cottage.

"Sorcerer, please save this child," Dora pleaded.

"Yes, Queen Dora. His courage must be rewarded. I have brought a special potion."

The sorcerer held the vessel containing the potion near Odin. The unicorn placed his horn inside the vessel. When the unicorn retracted the potion began to glow. The sorcerer opened the boy's mouth and poured the magic liquid into his very soul. The youth levitated from the bed. His body changed many colors before he fell peacefully on to his back. Before her eyes, Dora saw Tyree's bruised and bleeding body transforming into rapid remission.

"He will be fine after a day's rest," the sorcerer said. "Did he say he wounded the knight's horse?"

"Yes," Queen Dora responded. "He told me 'he won't go far, Mother. My sword bleeds his mount.'"

The sorcerer looked into the ball of his staff. He saw Sharonn walking with a large pack of wolves toward his barrier. "Fear not for the safety of your daughter, Queen Dora. Your daughter approaches my realm and she is with friends."

The captain and Jasmine rode swiftly toward the beacon of the burning stable. When they neared the queen's cottage Jasmine saw Odin prancing near its entrance. "The sorcerer is inside, Captain."

Captain Eric dismounted and hurried to be with his queen.

"Eric!" Dora cried. "The knight from Vall took Sharonn and hurt Tyree when he tried to protect her."

"Jasmine, we must ride to save my daughter!" the captain shouted. "Orin has taken her."

"Captain, wait! Your daughter is safe now," the sorcerer said reassuringly. "She is at the barrier where the meadow meets the wood. Go to her; return her to her home."

"Yes, Sorcerer. I must leave to bring home my daughter."

"Jasmine, your father and his army near my realm. You may escort him to the village."

"Thank you, Sorcerer."

Captain Eric crossed the meadow and felt the tingling of the barrier as he left Gaul's Realm. He witnessed many wolves vanishing into the wood at his approach. Suddenly, he felt his heart leap. Standing before him stood his daughter holding a tiny furry creature in her arms. When he dismounted tears cascaded from his eyes. Sharonn held onto her new pet, as her father lifted her onto his mount.

"He is mine, Father," Sharonn said. "The leader of the wolves gave him to me."

"You and your brother must take care of him together."

"Tyree! Will Tyree be alright?" Sharonn asked.

"Yes, Sharonn," her father responded. "The sorcerer gave him a special medicine. What happened to the one who took you?"

"When he tried to hurt me the wolves killed him," Sharonn said. "They saved me, Father; they are my friends."

The captain did not speak for a moment. He had seen promise in the young knight.

"Orin was slain by his greed, child."

When they arrived at the cottage the captain dismounted and lifted his daughter from his mount. He held the small cub, while Sharonn ran to be with her mother.

"Mother, I was so frightened," cried Sharonn. "I thought I would never be with you again."

Queen Dora embraced her daughter.

"Sharonn, my love, Tyree nearly gave his life for you."

"Tyree, Tyree, we have a pet." Sharonn said. "The leader of the wolves gave him to us! Father said we can keep him."

Dora looked directly at the captain holding the tiny wolf.

"Did he? And without asking me?"

"Can we, My Queen?"

"Yes, Eric, of course," Dora replied.

Eric placed the baby wolf in the bed with Tyree. Tyree smiled when the small creature licked his ear.

Nogard

Chapter 25   Spirits of Nevau

Jasmine hurried to be with her father. She rode to the plain of tall grass and from atop a small hill she scanned the surrounding terrain for signs of the Army of Nevau. To the south she detected a rising dust cloud. She rode cautiously toward the cloud knowing it could be a patrol from Vall or even worse—Kreiggs. She proceeded, keeping a vigil for dragon riders. From atop a knoll she made out the form of her father leading a dust-covered column of men on horseback. The thick gray dust made the men appear as apparitions. For a brief moment her mind saw Joran, King Rugar, Vass and all who had been slain by the Kreigg marching with her father. "The Spirits of Nevau march with us," she mused to herself.

"Father! Father!" Jasmine shouted.

"Jasmine!" shouted Jal.

Jasmine rode to her father. She bent over and placed her moist lips against his parched ones. A tear fell from the general's eye, carving a tiny river into the covering of dust on his face.

"Father, I have been sent by the Sorcerer Gaul to escort you and your men to his realm."

"Jasmine, we are in desperate need of provisions and water!"

"All will be provided for you and your men. You can cleanse yourselves and your horses in our pools."

Jal felt a tingling sensation when he passed through the barrier of light. Jasmine and her father led the procession into the village. The people cheered as they passed and children threw flowers in front of their path.

The Village Elder approached Jal. "We welcome your army, General. My people have made new tunics for all who ride with you. Please cleanse yourselves and your horses. We will clean your armor and place an edge on your weapons."

"Thank you for your services. My men are truly grateful." Jal and his men stripped off their armor and tunics. Many of the women of the village joined the soldiers as they bathed in the clean cool water. The horses entered the pools beneath the men. A woman shrieked for joy when she recognized her husband, as the dust lifted from his body. A cart filled with new tunics was brought to the pools where the men bathed. The knights armor was shaken and cleaned free of the gray dust. Sparks danced in the armory, as weapons where made ready for battle.

Jal detected the aroma of goats being roasted in the village spits. When he had cleansed himself, he dressed in his new tunic and joined his daughter.

"Jasmine, where is Freeya?"

"Ride with me, Father. I have a surprise for you."

Jal followed his daughter through the mystical Realm of Gaul.

"We must dismount and climb this hill, Father."

Jal followed his daughter to the summit of the hill. He detected a strange odor and saw a large area of flattened grass and saplings.

"Why do you bring me here, Jasmine?"

Jasmine did not respond. She had never seen the dragon, let alone Freeya riding it. Yet she trusted her sister, and Freeya said she would be coming to this place on the back of the dragon.

"Father, look to the sun!" Jasmine shouted.

Jal saw the sun being blocked out by a huge black object. As it closed, the object took the form of a massive Black Dragon.

"Flee, Jasmine!" Jal shouted as he drew his sword.

"No, Father! Look—Freeya rides the dragon."

Freeya circled over Jal and her sister. Jasmine took her astonished father into the wood to give a clear landing zone. Jal tried to speak. His words tumbled from his mouth.

"How can this be?"

"Speak of this to no one father. The dragon is part of the

Sorcerer Gaul's plan to defeat Raggnor."

Jal watched the dragon circle the hilltop once more. He felt the rush of wind generated from the dragon's wings when it slowed its descent. He witnessed the creature landing softly upon the hilltop and lowering its head to allow Freeya to dismount. Jasmine ran toward her sister, while Jal walked cautiously to his adopted daughter.

"Freeya, your dragon is magnificent! I have brought our father."

"Freeya, I missed you," Jal said as he sheathed his sword.

Jal embraced Freeya in front of the watchful eyes of the dragon.

"Jasmine! I wish for you to meet my friend Kee."

Jasmine touched Kee's snout. Kee responded with a whimper of pleasure. Jal maintained his distance. He did not trust the dragon's intentions. For his part Kee remained wary of Jal, as he did not trust strangers armed with swords.

"Freeya! Jasmine and I cannot tarry. We must return to the village. I must council with the Captain of Vall."

"Thank you for coming, Father."

"Remember, Freeya, I love you as I love Jasmine."

Jal and Jasmine descended the hill and began their ride to the village.

Jal saw Khrom's army of peasants being trained for battle. For a moment he was reminded of the defenders of Lund and their sacrifice. He saw a handsome young man approaching his daughter.

"Jasmine, please introduce me to your father," Khrom said.

"Father I wish to present Prince Khrom, the rightful ruler of the Kingdom of Vall and..." Jasmine hesitated. She took a deep breath and regained her composure, "and the future husband of Princess Freeya of Nevau."

Jal nearly fell from his horse. He wondered how long it had been since he was with his daughters.

"I place my sword at your service, Prince Khrom."

"Prince Khrom, may I present my father, General Jal, leader of the Army of Nevau and the rightful ruler of the Kingdom of Nubia," Jasmine announced.

Before Khrom could continue speaking, Manchu rode beside Jasmine.

"Manchu, I believe you have met my father."

"Yes. We first met in Raggnor's mine, but I was invisible at the time."

"My men and I are in your debt," Jal said. "We thank you for our freedom."

"Khrom, the Sorcerer Gaul wishes for us to council with him," Jasmine said.

"You must join us General. We have need of your experience."

"Yes, Khrom, of course."

As they rode toward the sorcerer's castle, Jal turned to Manchu. "Manchu, what are your intentions toward my daughter?"

Manchu felt awkward, as he did not know how to respond.

"We are just friends, Father." Jasmine responded.

"We are very good friends, General," Manchu replied.

Once they had entered the castle's grounds, Khrom spoke to Jal of the Sorcerer Gaul's plan to defeat Raggnor. Khrom saw the sorcerer speaking with Captain Eric in the hall.

"Welcome my friends. I hope you enjoy goat's meat. I fear my realm's livestock has been decimated by our new ally."

"Goat's meat will be fine, Sorcerer," Khrom said. "Sorcerer, I wish to introduce General Jal."

"Thank you, Khrom. Welcome, General. Both of your daughters' courage has given us renewed hope."

"Thank you, Sorcerer," Jal responded proudly.

The sorcerer rose from his seat. His body doubled in size as he spoke. "The first phase of our plan has succeeded. We must press forward or all could still be lost. Vall must be taken tomorrow!" The sorcerer looked across his hall and saw the determination in Captain Eric's eyes. He spoke to him. "Captain, please share with us your knowledge of Vall's defenses."

Captain Eric stood while the sorcerer returned to his normal size. He began to speak. "Copen will send his knights to crush our foot soldiers. If they do not succeed, his knights will retreat across the drawbridge into the castle. His archers will target our knights from Vall's walls. If he senses defeat he will signal Raggnor for help."

Jal listened intently to the captain, a strategy formed within his mind.

"Captain, how loyal are Copen's men?" Jal asked.

"Most would not be willing to die for their King."

"What of the land that surrounds Vall. Are there any passes near the castle?"

The captain drew a crude map with a quill pen. "General, the main road traverses both wood and grassland. Two hills overlook the castle of Vall. The road passes through the narrow pass between the hills."

"Captain, can your men hold the pass against Copen's Knights?"

"Yes, General!"

"Prince Khrom, your band's mission will be to take the drawbridge!"

"I will lead them, General."

"You are very courageous, Prince Khrom," General Jal said. "Do you think it wise to place yourself in such danger?"

"Perhaps it is unwise, General. I will not ask any of my men to bear a risk that I would not."

"You will truly be a noble ruler, Prince Khrom. Jasmine, you will serve as my aide."

"Yes, Father."

Jal grabbed the side of the table. He nearly fell from exhaustion and lack of food. The sorcerer stood and faced the faltering general. "Jal, let us finalize your plan of battle later."

The aroma of the goat did not match that of a wild boar. Jasmine and Manchu took small mouthfuls of its rancid tasting flesh and washed it down with bread and mead. Jal ate ravenously, as he hadn't eaten a meal of substance in a very long time.

Nogard

Chapter 26 Vall

At the first signs of the new dawn Khrom and Manchu awakened to be with their men. Khrom dressed for battle then mounted the old warhorse. Manchu grabbed a last kiss from Jasmine before joining his brother. Jal and his daughter mounted their horses to lead the army of Nevau. As per his plan, Jal and his mounted force prepared to depart Gaul's realm on a trail leading through the wood. The first rays of the morning sun glinted off the polished armor of the Knights of Nevau as they passed through the barrier of light.

Jasmine led the procession over the narrow trail that forced the army into a single file formation. She felt the branches of the elms brushing against her face, as she proceeded. Jasmine stopped the advance near a clearing in the wood. She heard the beating sound of huge wings and knew a dragon was overhead. From his perch the dragon rider saw only the canopy of the wood, which appeared as a massive green tapestry.

Jal watched the dragon depart he could only hope the first part of his plan would be successful. He knew Copen would have twice his number of knights. His plan depended upon the element of surprise and the lack of will of Vall's Knights.

Khrom's small force marched in the open over the main road leading to Vall. He felt the shadow of a dragon and watched as it winged toward the Castle of Vall. Khrom halted his army when several villagers armed with pitchforks and picks blocked his path. A young man approached him.

"We will not allow you to sack our village!" the youth stated.

Khrom looked into the eyes of the villager. "Fear not. We mean you no harm. I have no quarrel with you. I am Prince Khrom, son of King Handamar, rightful ruler of Vall. I have come to free you from Copen's tyranny."

The young man bowed before his prince.

"My name is Brian, Sire. I wish to join with you."

"Brian, go forth to all the people of Vall. Ask them to join with me!" Khrom commanded. "Tell them we march against Copen on this day!"

The dragon rider flew to the tower of Vall. He spoke to the Kreigg Envoy of the approaching army. The Envoy walked into Copen's chamber.

"Your Highness, I regret to inform you one of my dragon riders has seen an army crossing your frontier."

"Did he say how large a force? Where they mounted?"

"He said there were a hundred or more men. Most of the soldiers where on foot."

King Copen feared an insurrection. He knew the people of Vall despised him. He sent for General Vicker, one of the assassins who slew King Handamar.

"General Vicker, I fear a rebellion has begun in my Kingdom. The Kreigg Envoy has informed me one of the dragon riders has seen an army marching on the road to Vall."

King Copen looked into his general's eyes as he continued speaking. "At present they are a small force. Most of them are on foot. Smash them now, General, before this rabble can create an uprising!"

"Yes, Your Majesty! My knights will destroy them!"

"General, slay only their leaders. The rest of the insurgents will serve as slaves in Raggnor's mines."

"A wise decision, Your Majesty."

Within a short time the large courtyard of Vall filled with knights and their nervous horses. A trumpet blared as the huge drawbridge fell across the deep moat. The wooden planks of the heavy bridge echoed the ironclad hooves of two hundred warhorses. The Knights of Vall dressed in full armor, armed with lances and swords crossed the moat and entered the road confident of victory.

Khrom witnessed his force growing in strength and numbers. He was pleased many of his new allies were former members of Copen's army. Khrom halted the procession midway through a narrow pass.

"Captain, make this place ready for battle!" Khrom ordered.

"Yes, Prince Khrom! Men of Vall, I need a wide trench. Dig it across the narrowest place in the pass." Twenty of the peasants followed the captain's instructions. They dug a wide shallow trench and filled it with hay then covered the hay with a thick coating of pitch. Behind the trench, the captain instructed more of the peasants to build a barricade of pointed poles designed to stop charging knights.

Khrom planned to make his first stand behind the barricade. He knew he would need to win many battles to retake his kingdom and Copen would need but one to destroy him. He continued to ride toward Vall with his brother, four knights and a small contingent of foot soldiers. When the road ascended a steep hill, he saw the spires of Vall. Khrom heard the single hoof beats of a single horse rapidly approaching the base of the hill.

"They come, Prince Khrom!" his scout shouted. "The Knights of Vall will soon be upon us!"

From atop the hill Khrom saw the rapidly approaching column.

"Manchu, when they reach the bottom of the hill signal our foot soldiers to retreat to the pass! We will engage the first of their knights, when they climb the hill."

"It is a daring plan, Khrom."

The first of the Knights of Vall reached the base of the hill. General Vicker saw Khrom's small army. When he saw the foot soldiers retreat he ordered his knights to charge. Khrom waited at the top of the hill. He struck while the Knights of Vall were caught off balance by the loose gravel on the steep incline. Khrom's small force clashed with General Vicker's Knights struggling to reach the summit. Many of their horses fell backwards, throwing their riders into the path of the charging knights behind them. Khrom ordered a retreat when he felt his foot soldiers had reached the pass.

Vickers' knights paused briefly to regroup at the summit, before pursuing Khrom's force. The foot soldiers rushed into the pass to join their comrades behind the barricade. Khrom's knights raced toward the pass. Manchu slowed his horse's pace to match his brother's old warhorse. Khrom heard the sounds of hostile hoof beats closing behind him. He rode into the pass and saw the trench and barricade before him. His brother's horse bounded over the trench, while his old steed plodded through the ooze—Khrom rode through a breach in the barrier.

"Torch the trench!" Captain Eric shouted.

Two of Vicker's knights where caught in the inferno. They were trapped between the rising flames in the trench and the pointed poles of the barrier. Captain Eric felt compassion towards the two men and their horses.

"A knight should not die this way, Khrom."

"Let these two pass," Khrom shouted.

Both men were brought before Khrom.

"Thank you for saving us," spoke the first knight.

"Why did you not slay us?" replied the second.

"I have come to reclaim my kingdom. I have need of your sword."

General Vicker saw the wall of flames in front of his army. Within the confines of the narrow pass his knights were unable to maneuver. He heard the sounds of heavy stones raining down on his knights from both sides of the passage.

Jal's force waited in the wood near the pass. The battle hardened veterans of Nevau prepared to strike, as coiled serpents. Jal pointed his sword forward. The Knights of Nevau burst from the wood, charging across the pass. The hooves of the warhorses made the sound of charging thunderclaps, as they left the soft grass and entered the hardened surface of the road. The polished surface of their armor glinted in the sunlight. Within in moments Jal's force sealed the pass.

The Knights of Vall where caught by complete surprise. Too late, General Vicker realized his arrogance had lured him into a trap. "Turn around! Fight your way through!" General Vicker shouted. "This battle is not lost!" His knights hesitated. He heard many of their weapons striking the earth. "Do not surrender. Raggnor will destroy this army and you with his dragons."

Khrom climbed to the top of the barricade with the two knights from Vall. "I am Prince Khrom the rightful ruler of the Kingdom of Vall. I have come to retake my kingdom and bring justice to the assassins who slew my father, King Handamar. I ask you to join me in my quest for justice and freedom. I ask you to turn over General Vicker for trial."

The first of the two knights spoke. "Prince Khrom spared me. He will be a fair and Nobel Sovereign, as was his father. I would rather die in his service than continue with Raggnor and his servant King Copen."

The second knight led a resounding cheer. "Hail Prince Khrom! Free Vall!"

General Vicker attempted to make a desperate escape. He drew his sword and urged his mount forward. His horse broke from the pass. Jal signaled to one of the young knights. The knight lowered his lance to a killing angle and braced for the collision. General Vicker felt the head of the lance piercing his chest.

Khrom and Captain Eric watched from atop the barricade. They knew the assassin was dead before his body struck the earth.

"He died a soldier's death, Khrom."

"Yes, Captain."

Khrom spoke to the Knights of Vall, who by now were in a state of disarray. "Knights of Vall, if you do not wish to join me, leave your weapons; you will not be harmed. This I promise you. Leave now!" A hush fell over the pass. None of the men departed. "For all who remain, I ask you to pledge your life and your sword to the people of Vall and myself. Our quest is the pursuit of freedom and justice." Khrom, was pleased when he heard his words being repeated from the lips of two hundred of his new knights.

"Dragon!" shouted a sentry. The dragon rider had seen the merging of the two armies and heard the chanting of the knights. He urged his mount to wing to Vall, to report once more to the Kreigg Envoy.

Once more Raggnor's Envoy entered King Copen's chamber. "I have grave news, Your Highness. General Vicker has been defeated and his knights have joined the insurrection against you."

"Does the dragon rider know who leads them?"

"He is called Prince Khrom, Sire."

King Copen thought for a moment. He remembered his cousin King Handamar had an infant son at the time of the coup. Yes the boy's name was Khrom, he thought. A rush of fear filled his being.

"He has come for vengeance!" King Copen shouted. He ordered his servant to bring the captain of his guard to his chamber. He spoke to the Kreigg Envoy, "How long will it take for Raggnor's army to reach Vall?"

"Four days Sire. One day to prepare the army and Raggnor's fortress is a three day march from Vall."

The Kreigg Envoy did not care for King Copen, or his master Raggnor. He reluctantly did his master's bidding out of fear for himself and his race. He departed King Copen's chamber and climbed the tower to witness Khrom's approaching army. He felt a soft breeze kissing his face. *Perhaps it is time for a change,* he thought.

King Copen knew he could only trust the captain of his guard and his henchmen who, like himself, would be held accountable to Prince Khrom.

"You sent for me, Your Highness?" Copen's captain asked.

"Did you slay all of Handamar's family?" The captain did not respond to his king; his silence spoke for him.

"His son marches against us," King Copen said in an urgent tone. "We must hold Vall until Raggnor's army arrives or face the wrath of Prince Khrom. How many of your men can we trust?"

"About thirty of my guards, Sire."

"Bring your men to the towers. We will make our stand there until Raggnor's army arrives. Tell my archers they will be rewarded handsomely if they fight for me, or they will be slain by Raggnor if they join with Khrom."

Copen's captain prepared the defenses around the perimeter

of the towers, behind the inner wall of Vall. He spoke to the leader of the archers, who promised the loyalty of his men to King Copen. Ten of the captain's most trusted men were assigned to guard the drawbridge.

Khrom's army grew ever larger and more powerful as it neared the castle. "We must take Vall this night, General," Khrom said.

"Is your band ready, Khrom?"

"Yes!"

Khrom ordered his army to halt near the moat, which surrounded Vall. He gathered his band of brigands to take the massive drawbridge.

When darkness enveloped the Kingdom of Vall, a hundred peasants started to beat their drums. The loud drumbeats soon dominated the sounds of the night. Khrom used the sound to mask the noise of three small boats provided to him by the people of Vall. His band wore no armor. Each carried lengths of rope to scale the wall near the drawbridge. As the small boats began the crossing, Khrom felt their vulnerability. He knew if they were detected Copen's archers would cut them down. Khrom felt his craft bump the opposite bank of the moat. The band hugged the castle's wall, as they worked toward the drawbridge. Two of Khrom's men heaved their grappling hooks. The first took hold. The second pulled a stone free and crashed against the side of the wall. Two fire arrows struck the earth in front of the band. Khrom was exposed and his men were trapped. They huddled against the wall to avoid the flaming arrows. Three of Khrom's men were wounded by the first volley.

"What is your command, Khrom?" Manchu shouted.

Before he could respond, Khrom saw a hole in the wall open before him. He saw a torch and heard the voice of a woman.

"If you wish to live, follow me."

"Follow me! Everyone follow me!" Khrom yelled.

The band ran quickly to the shelter of the hidden passage. Khrom saw the face of a young woman holding a torch.

"I thank you for saving us."

"Are you in the service of Prince Khrom?" the woman asked.

"Yes!" Khrom replied not wishing to identify himself.

"I am called Mlia. I know these passages well. Most of our people hate King Copen, but we fear Raggnor's dragons. Now we wish to join Prince Khrom in his just cause."

"Where does this passage lead, Mlia?"

"The castle's kitchen."

The passage descended then ran flat for a considerable distance. Khrom and his band had entered the bowels of Vall. Their feet trod through small pools of stagnant water. They heard the sounds of rodents scurrying before them. Only the flickering light of Mlia's torch parted the blackness. Khrom felt an ancient stone staircase, as he began to ascend. Mlia leaned against a stone door. The door opened into the kitchen of Vall. Khrom saw a group of poorly armed servants and an archer.

The archer spoke to Khrom. "I am certain our archers will join with your prince, once you take the bridge."

Khrom led his band through the kitchen and hall of Vall. His plan was to cross the courtyard swiftly and silently. He left his wounded in the care of Mlia and the servants. His band moved silently over the cobblestones of the courtyard. They nearly reached the chains holding the bridge, when one of Copen's guards saw their approaching shadows.

"Invaders in the courtyard!" screamed the guard.

"Slay the invaders with fire arrows!" the master archer commanded.

The archer who followed Khrom to the courtyard took aim. He saw the outline of his commander in the torchlight on the wall. His arrow took flight in the blackness. The master archer clutched his chest and fell to the cobblestones below.

Copen's guards held their ground and defended the bridge. Manchu fought his way to the lever that would release the chains holding the bridge.

Mlia heard the fighting. She led the servants in a desperate charge. They attacked the guards with skillets, wooden paddles and their bare hands. The fighting became intense. A cook was impaled by one of the guard's spears. A servant girl screamed when the blade of a sword pierced her shoulder.

Mlia bashed the head of a guard fighting Manchu with her iron skillet. Manchu pushed the lever forward. Suddenly the bridge was in freefall. After a loud crash the structure spanned the deep moat.

"Forward!" Jal commanded.

Three hundred knights, followed by a hundred foot soldiers and hundreds of the peasants of Vall stormed across the bridge.

Sensing Copen's defeat, the Kreigg Envoy departed the tower. When Copen's guards attempted to stop him, he used his greater strength to push them aside. He descended the spiral stairs to the wall. He walked past the bewildered archers who were still unsure of their loyalties. The Kreigg Ambassador addressed the army below.

"I wish to speak with Prince Khrom. I wish to join him in his cause."

A hush fell across the courtyard. Like the rest of his army Khrom was startled by the ambassador's words.

"I will meet with you in my hall, when we have taken the rest of my castle," Khrom said before turning to his army. "Give this Kreigg safe passage."

"You did not tell me you are the Great Prince Khrom," Mlia said.

"I am sorry, Mlia. Would you care to join my army?"

"Yes. I do not wish to remain a servant girl."

He heard the voice of a spokesman from the archers on the wall. "We pledge our service to Prince Khrom. We pledge our bows to his cause."

Khrom's victory lie within his grasp, yet he knew Copen and his assassins would fight to the death. He met with General Jal, Captain Eric and Lon the archer who had helped him take the bridge within the hall of Vall.

"Lon, from this time forward you are my Master Archer."

"Captain, are your soldiers able to storm the tower?"

"Yes, I will lead them."

"No, Captain, I need you here!"

"Khrom, I must. Please do not deny me this."

"Yes, you may lead the final assault, Captain." The Prince of

Vall embraced the only father he had known.

"Lon, your archers must provide cover for our soldiers!"

"Yes, My Prince."

All of Khrom's army where exhausted from the fighting. Within a short time the sounds of slumber echoed throughout the vast hall of Vall. Jasmine slept in Manchu's arms, beneath a large oak table. They were unaware of the dangers lurking in the darkness.

𝔑ogard

𝔠hapter 27   𝔄ssassins

King Copen met with his captain. "Captain, we must act quickly or all will be lost. Prince Khrom and his officers must not be allowed to live through this night. How many men do we still command?"

"Only twenty, Sire."

"Send half of them to the hall through the hidden passages. Tell them to strike swiftly while Khrom and his force sleep."

"Our assassins will not fail, Majesty."

The captain assembled his force. Soon eight swordsmen and two archers crept down the hidden passages which honeycombed the thick walls of the castle. They came to a hidden door that opened into the Hall of Vall.

Unlike the rest, Mlia did not slumber. Her strong eyes penetrated the near blackness of the large hall. She saw Khrom's guards at the entrance, and though they gave her a sense of security, she felt the presence of evil lurking nearby.

The hidden door opened silently. The two archers were the first to enter. Their stocking covered feet muffled the sounds of their movements. The swordsmen followed the archers into the hall. They moved silently across the room toward Khrom. She grabbed a torch and began to scream, as she ran to warn Khrom.

"Assassins! Assassins!" Mlia screamed in the blackness.

Copen's archers took aim at the screaming maid. Two arrows struck Mlia in her chest. She fell beside Khrom. Khrom awoke suddenly to see the silhouette of a killer hovering over him with a dagger aimed at his throat. He acted instinctively to avoid the blade. Khrom leaped to his feet and grasped his sword. With a single blow he severed the assassin's head from his body. "Rise, soldiers of Vall!" Khrom shouted. "Slay Copen's assassins!"

Jasmine and Manchu found themselves behind the killers. Manchu beheaded one of the archers, while Jasmine slew the other. Khrom's guards rushed to join the battle. In a matter of moments seven of the assassins where slain. The remaining three dropped their weapons to surrender.

Jasmine held Mlia's hand. The servant girl spoke softly, hesitantly.

"Do you know the young knight called Skoll?"

"Yes, he died fighting the Kreigg."

"I go now to join him."

Mlia closed her eyes. Jasmine felt the spirit departing from the young woman.

"What do you wish to do with these prisoners, Khrom?"

"Bind them, my brother! We hang them tomorrow with the other assassins!"

Jasmine fell once more into her lover's arms.

"Jasmine, you are crying," Manchu said.

"I weep for Mlia, Manchu. I pray Odin will take her to Valhalla to be with Skoll."

The night turned cold. On the distant plain a wolf howled for his mate.

Nogard

Chapter 28   The Deadly Tower

Captain Eric awakened thirty of his soldiers to make preparations for the final assault. His men put on full battle armor with reinforced breastplates. Each carried a heavy shield. He knew this would be a battle of brute force.

"Lon, are your archers ready?"

"Yes, Captain!"

The foot soldiers marched across the wall past the archers. They saw the first rays of sunlight reflecting from the spires above the tower. A heavy wooden door blocked the entrance to the stairwell.

"Use the ram!" Captain Eric shouted.

"Yes, Captain!" his soldiers responded.

The defenders of the tower rained stones and arrows on the soldiers below.

"Archers, ready!" Lon shouted. A hundred bowmen took aim. Lon dropped his arm. A volley of arrows arched skyward wounding a number of Copen's Henchmen. The survivors retreated from the wall.

The battering ram smashed through the door. The Soldiers of Vall stormed up the spiral stair case. Eric heard the clash of steel and the sounds of men in combat. He waited for the sounds of battle to abate.

"We have taken the stairway, Captain," shouted a soldier.

Captain Eric did not respond. He stepped into a fresh pool of blood as he ascended the stairs. He passed the bodies of two of his men and four of Copen's Assassins. Eric came to a large oak door near the top of the tower. He knew this door guarded the entrance to King Copen's last place of refuge.

King Copen, his son Prince Luffin, his captain and a handful of his men huddled within the chamber. Copen heard the pounding of the ram splintering the door. His men stood before him forming a human barrier.

The ram smashed through the door. Eric and his men burst into the chamber. Copen's men fought like cornered beasts. One by one they fell from the onslaught. Eric faced the assassin who slew his king so many years before in this very chamber. The assassin lunged forward to slay him with his sword. Eric stepped aside to avoid the blade. With a single blow he severed Copen's captain's left arm at the shoulder.

"Slay me with your sword, Eric! I beg you, let me die a soldier's death!"

"No!" Eric responded angrily. "You will be hanged with your king and the remainder of his assassins for the murder of King Handamar! Bind this one's wounds. I do not want him to avoid the hangman's noose. Bind Copen and his son for trial."

Khrom heard the cheers of his army as King Copen and his son where led into the courtyard for trial. He formed a tribunal in the hall consisting of General Jal, Captain Eric, Jasmine and himself.

"Bring the accused before this body!" Khrom commanded.

"Yes, My Prince," his guards responded.

Copen, his son and the remaining assassins were prodded into the hall. All accepted their fate save Prince Luffin, who shook in fear. Khrom addressed the former king and his men. "You have been charged with the murder of my father King Handamar, and the beheading of Knight Joran. You have been charged with numerous crimes against the people of Vall and Nevau. How plead you?"

Copen spoke, "I have only obeyed the bidding of my master, the Sorcerer Raggnor. I ask only that you spare my son. He is only guilty of being my son."

The tribunal retired to a small chamber adjacent to the hall. Captain Eric was the first to speak. "Hang them all, Khrom. Luffin may return one day to avenge his father."

"I agree with the captain." Jal said.

"No!" Jasmine shouted. "The son should not be punished for the crimes of the father!"

Khrom thought for a moment. "Copen and his assassins are to be hanged from the castle's wall. Luffin will be stripped of his title and banished from Vall. This is my final decree."

Copen and his henchmen where stoned when they were dragged through the courtyard and forced up the stairs of the outer wall. A large crowd gathered outside the castle to watch the execution. Khrom removed Copen's crown and robe. Suddenly he realized this man who had wielded such power had been reduced to a fat man with a rope around his neck. Khrom shoved his father's murderer from atop the wall. He heard the snapping sound of Copen's neck being broken by the hangman's noose. Copen's captain did not fare as well as his king. Eric pushed the one who had slain his king from the wall. His body being off balance due to the loss of his arm, twitched and dangled for several minutes until the rope took his life. One by one the remainder of Copen's assassins met a similar fate.

Jasmine did not leave the hall. She did not witness the hangings. She thought of Joran, her beautiful knight. Her vengeance had been satisfied. Copen was dead. His lifeless body dangled from the wall of the castle he once ruled. The empty feeling in her began to dissipate.

Manchu entered the hall. "Jasmine, it is done!"

"Yes, I know, Manchu. Please hold me—hold me tight."

Luffin had watched the hanging from the hilltop. A great sadness overcame his being. He looked upon the body of his father and vowed to someday return.

Khrom called a council to prepare Vall for an assault by Raggnor. "Captain, ready the castle's defenses."

"Yes, Khrom!"

"General, continue training our men."

"Yes, My Prince!"

"Manchu, have the peasants bring provisions for many days, we may be forced to endure a siege."

"It shall be done, my brother!"

"Jasmine, take some men with you. Bring Queen Dora and her children to Vall."

Khrom was interrupted by an urgent cry. "Dragon! Dragon!" shouted a sentry from the tower. The dragon rider made a sweep toward the bodies hanging from the wall. The rider could not be sure, but he thought he recognized the body of the former king. He turned his dragon to make haste to his master's realm.

"They will be here in force in three to four days, Captain. I plan to be ready for them. Escort the Kreigg Ambassador to my chamber."

Within a short time the Ambassador entered the chamber adjacent to the hall.

"Prince Khrom."

"Ambassador, you wish to speak with me?"

"Yes, I wish to join you. The Kreigg despise Raggnor. We serve him only out of fear of his magic and his dragons. A few tried to resist, they were captured and fed to Raggnor's dragons. If you can somehow stop the dragons, I am confident most Kreigg will join with you."

"Then you will join in my cause, Ambassador."

"Yes!"

Nogard

Chapter 29   Ruler of Vall

Jasmine waited for the dragon to pass from view before she crossed the bridge with three of Khrom's men. It was dusk when she entered Gaul's Realm. In a short time she saw the cottages by the stream.

Queen Dora heard the sounds of the approaching horses. "Sharonn, Tyree, come with me quickly. I know not who rides toward us." Dora took the children into a root cellar behind the cottage. She closed the doors behind them and held her daughter and son, while their eyes adjusted to the darkness. She heard the horses stop in front of her home.

"Are they bad men, Mother?" Sharonn asked. "I am frightened, Mother."

"I will protect you," Tyree said.

"We must be quiet, children."

Dora heard a single horse approaching from the opposite direction. Her heart sank. She knew it was Freeya returning from the dragon and it was too late to give her warning. Dora's despair turned to instant joy when she heard Jasmine's voice.

"Freeya, Khrom has taken Vall!" Jasmine shouted. "I have come to escort Queen Dora and her children to their castle."

Dora and the children emerged from the cellar. "Jasmine, Freeya, you must spend the night in my cottage."

Jasmine turned to the escort. "Keep guard this night, two may sleep in the cottage, while the third keeps watch."

"As you command, Princess," responded the guards.

"Please, both of you enter my home. We have much to discuss."

As they entered the cottage, Jasmine felt a small furry creature brush against her leg. The small wolf became frightened and ran to the safety of Sharonn's arms.

"Jasmine, my sons and Captain Eric—are they unharmed?" Dora asked.

"They are fine. Khrom has established himself as the Ruler of Vall."

"What of our father?" Freeya asked.

"General Jal has become the commander of a great army. The knights and archers of Vall have sworn their allegiance to Khrom, and Jal is their general. Captain Eric and Manchu are charged with preparing the castle's defenses."

"Jasmine, were many of our people slain?" Queen Dora asked.

"Yes," Jasmine responded sadly. "I cried for a young woman who died in my arms. She gave her life protecting Khrom from Copen's assassins."

Freeya listened intently to Jasmine's words. A shudder ran through her when she heard the words, *'protecting Khrom from Copen's assassins.'*

"Freeya, are you and the dragon ready?" Dora asked.

Freeya hesitated for a moment. "Yes, the dragon grows impatient."

"We should help you pack your things, Dora," Jasmine said.

"I have a small problem. I am a queen without a carriage and horses."

"I am to blame. I failed to bring one from Vall," Jasmine said. "I will send one of my men in the morning to bring one."

The silence of the night was broken by the sounds of two large horses. The guard heard their approach. "Halt! Halt!" screamed the guard. Within moments Jasmine and her men bolted from the cottage with drawn swords. Freeya remained within the cottage, as the queen's last line of defense. The horses stopped in front of Jasmine. The light of the moon revealed two large gray steeds pulling a beautiful carriage with silver trim. Jasmine heard the voice of the driver.

"My name is Aronn," the Coachman said. "The Sorcerer Gaul sent me. I am to bring Queen Dora and her children to Vall. Many years ago I was her husband's coachman."

Dora recognized Aronn's voice. She stepped through the doorway into the night. She approached the large dapple gray horses. The queen touched the nearest one's muzzle. "I thank you, Great Sorcerer, for this wonderful gift."

The sorcerer spoke to Dora's thoughts. "You are welcome, Queen Dora. I wish you a safe journey."

Aronn wept when he saw his queen.

The night passed swiftly. At the time of first light, the beautiful carriage was packed with Queen Dora, her children and their belongings. Sharonn sat beside her mother, while her brother held the wolf cub on his lap on the opposite side. Freeya watched the carriage depart then rode to rejoin Kee.

The carriage left the safety of Gaul's Realm and entered a rut filled trail through the wood. Upon entering the plain, the trail became somewhat smoother. In the distance a male wolf howled. The small creature on Tyree's lap nearly leaped through the carriage's window. When Tyree reached for the cub it barred its fangs. The small beast calmed down, when a nearby female gave a reassuring howl.

Jasmine rode beside the carriage. "The main road to Vall lies ahead, Majesty. We must remain vigilant."

Dora saw the ravages of war once they began to travel over the small stones of the main road. She saw the remnants of a small village that had been sacked and torched by Copen's henchmen. The carriage moved through the pass where the first battle for Vall had taken place. The stench of burning pitch still permeated the foul air. She pondered how many of her people died to take this pass. Aronn brought the horses to a halt when they reached a hilltop overlooking the Castle of Vall.

Queen Dora's eyes drank in the beauty of the castle she had fled so many years before. Then she made out what appeared to be bodies hanging from the castle's wall. She surmised it to be Copen and his men. The mere thought disgusted her. It bothered her to know her son had given the order and her captain had sanctioned it.

"Jasmine, when we reach Vall, I want those bodies to be taken down! I did not raise my son to be a barbarian!" Queen Dora demanded.

"Your Majesty, this is part of the sorcerer's plan."

"Jasmine, those bodies are to come down! I have spoken!"

Jasmine saw a cloud of dust rising from the road before them. She was unable to identify the riders racing towards them. She had heard stories of highwaymen who preyed on unwary travelers on the road to Vall.

"Aronn!" Jasmine shouted. "Be ready if these riders try to stop us. We must break through to Vall."

"Yes, I understand!"

"What is happing?" Queen Dora asked.

"I fear a band of brigands is about to attack!" Jasmine replied.

Jasmine and her men formed a wedge, while Aronn drove the carriage behind them. Dora held her children on the floor, as the carriage raced down the steep hill towards the approaching band. Aronn braced for impact. Suddenly the riders in front of them forced their mounts off the road. Jasmine recognized their leader, as they raced past. She slowed her pace then signaled for the procession to halt.

"They are brigands, My Queen, but they are our brigands," Jasmine said. The leader of the band rode to the carriage. Dora rose to the window. She saw the face of a dust covered young man. "Welcome to Vall, Mother," Manchu said.

"Manchu, you nearly frightened me to death!" Jasmine said angrily.

"You nearly ran me down! I could have been killed!" Manchu responded.

"'You should have identified yourself! My duty is to protect Queen Dora."

"Stop bickering!" Queen Dora demanded. "Jasmine is right. I have spoken."

The peasants lined the road to see their queen. A young girl ran beside the carriage to give Dora flowers. Dora saw oxen pulling carts filled with grain moving into the castle. She heard the sounds of hammers repairing the drawbridge. She knew Vall was preparing for a siege. Soon the sounds of her large horse's hooves striking the planks of the bridge announced her arrival. Khrom met his mother at the gate to the courtyard. Queen Dora stepped from the carriage, while her son held her hand.

"Welcome home, Mother."

Queen Dora's eyes flashed with anger. "Khrom, how long do you plan to leave your father's cousin hanging from the outer wall?"

"I leave them hanging as a symbol of my power," Khrom responded.

"We must talk of this in private my son. Where is Captain Eric?"

"He awaits you in your chamber, Mother."

"Please escort me there. I need to speak to both of you."

Khrom escorted his mother to her new chamber. Eric met Dora in the hallway and held her in a tight embrace.

"I love both of you. I feared for your safety. Now I must speak as your queen. The people of Vall deserve better than to be ruled by fear and intimidation. They have suffered too long under Copen's oppression. I demand those bodies be taken down from the wall and buried."

Khrom told his mother part of the plan to defeat Raggnor was for the dragon rider to see Copen's body hanging from the wall.

"Has the dragon rider seen them?" Queen Dora asked.

"Yes," Khrom replied. "Well, I think he did."

"Khrom, leave them there until you are certain the dragon rider has seen them. Then take them down and have them buried."

"Yes, Your Highness."

"Khrom, what of Luffin's fate?"

"I did not execute him mother. I banished him from Vall."

"This was a wise decision, Khrom."

"Mother, have you seen Freeya?"

"Yes, she is well—she loves you very much."

Queen Dora turned her attention to Eric. "Captain, can we defend Vall against the Kreigg?"

"Yes! If Freeya is successful, we will defeat the Kreigg."

"Come Eric, I need your help with the children and your pet wolf."

"Yes, My Queen."

Jasmine joined her father in the courtyard. "I grow weary of war, Father."

"As do I, my daughter. Perhaps one day you will marry and raise children in peace and I will be an old grandfather."

"I love you General Jal, Prince of Nubia."

Once more the night fell upon the Kingdom of Vall. While the children slept in an adjoining room Captain Eric caressed his queen. Dora felt the first rays of sunlight penetrating the chamber. From the tower she heard the sentry's cry. "Dragon, Dragon!" When the dragon rider had departed, she heard her son's command. "Cut them down and bury them."

The Queen of Vall pressed her lips against those of her captain's.

𝕹ogard

Chapter 30　Rejuvenation

Raggnor's time within the cave of lights was completed. The 'Dark' Sorcerer's body had been rejuvenated. His youthful form had been transported to the portal, which opened to his realm. Once more he was shrouded within his dark robe. His fingers pulled the stone from the wall. He placed his necklace of power around his neck.

Raggnor felt the large flat stones against the soles of his feet, as he walked briskly past the stable of the dragons. He was confident with his new allies the Troblin he could conquer all the lands. His only concern was being able to supply the Troblin with enough amber from his mine to buy their allegiance. He saw his two generals approaching. Raggnor sensed all did not go well during his time within the cave of lights.

"Greetings, Master!" both of the generals said simultaneously.

"General Tog, have you found Princess Freeya?" Raggnor asked in a stern voice.

"She has escaped to the Realm of Gaul, Master."

A flush of anger raced through Raggnor. "You permitted Freeya to escape! What of her sister?"

"Princess Jasmine is with her sister, Great One."

"Master, the Troblin Ambassador awaits your presence. He has come to ask for his payment in amber."

"Thank you, General Hatin."

"Master, I must speak to you before you meet with the Troblin Ambassador."

"Speak to me, General Tog!"

"Production in your mine has ceased. The slaves from Nevau have escaped."

'What!" Raggnor screamed. "I leave my realm for a mere ten days and you allow the princesses to escape! Now you tell me the slaves that worked my mine are at large! If you and your inept army cannot find slaves to work my mine, I will force you and your soldiers to dig for amber!"

General Tog spoke no more. He dare not speak to his master of the incursion of the unicorns.

"Master, we have a larger problem."

"Yes, General Hatin."

"A young Prince called Khrom leads a rebellion against your Regent, King Copen. His army has surrounded the Castle of Vall. My dragon rider will be returning soon to tell what he has observed of the battle."

"General Hatin, report to me immediately upon his return."

Raggnor paced for a few moments before proceeding to his meeting. The Sorcerer Raggnor entered his chamber; in a darkened corner he observed movement. He heard a voice coming from the shadows.

"Forgive me, Sorcerer. I awaited your presence in the depths of your chamber, as I am not accustomed to sunlight."

"You are the Troblin ambassador, I assume," Raggnor stated.

"Yes."

Raggnor's eyes adjusted to the darkened room. He saw a horrific creature about half his size that possessed more bat-like features than that of a man. When the Troblin spoke, Raggnor cringed from the sight of his fangs.

"Does my appearance offend you, Sorcerer?"

"No! I mean—yes."

"Do not be concerned, for I am repulsed by yours," spoke the Troblin. "My emperor is very interested in your proposal. You wish assistance of his army to conquer all the surface lands, and in return my Sovereign will receive vast quantities of amber."

"Yes! How many soldiers will he provide?"

"I have brought five-hundred with me another ten-thousand will arrive in seven of your nights. He will send thousands more when he begins to receive shipments of amber." The Troblin Ambassador hesitated for a moment. "My emperor wishes control of the mine."

Raggnor thought for a moment. He knew once the Troblin took control of the mine, he would have little to bargain with. "No! I shall work the mine with my slaves. I will give you ten carts filled with amber for the first ten-thousand soldiers."

The Troblin Ambassador nodded his head in agreement. He felt this sorcerer did not realize the worth of amber. In his world, amber far exceeded the value of gold. He retreated to a tunnel near Raggnor's mine to join his five-hundred soldiers.

Raggnor heard a rapping against the door to his chamber.

"Master," General Hatin said. "My dragon rider has returned. He reports Prince Khrom has taken Vall. He has hung your Regent and his men from the wall of the castle."

"Prepare my dragons! Prepare my army! We march on Vall!" Raggnor paused for a moment. "Wait!! He hanged Copen from the wall. This prince is ruthless! I like that quality in a Regent; perhaps we can reach an arrangement."

"Yes, Master."

"I will send him a message, if he agrees to my terms I will not march on Vall."

Raggnor began to write his demands.

Prince Khrom:

You have deposed my regent and hung his body from the wall of Vall. You possess the qualities I seek in a regent. I can give you power and wealth beyond imagination. I will not march on the Kingdom of Vall if my demands are met in a timely fashion.

Find the Princess Freeya and have her brought to me.

Give me a hundred able men to work my mine.

Provide me with two thirds of your harvest.

You must agree to my demands, or my dragons and army will reduce your kingdom to cinders.

Your Lord and Master,

Raggnor

"General Hatin, have your rider deliver this message under a flag of truce and wait for Prince Khrom's reply."

"Yes, Master."

General Hatin watched the dragon lift from the top of Raggnor's fortress before disappearing in the direction of Vall.

As the dragon rider neared Vall, he unfurled a large flag of truce. "Dragon approaching!" screamed the sentry in the tower. Khrom and Captain Eric ran up the staircase to the summit of the tower.

"Khrom, look. The dragon rider appears to be displaying a flag of truce."

"Yes, I see it, Captain! Guard, bring the Kreigg ambassador to the tower."

"Captain, have ten archers watch the rider. If his intentions are not honorable, slay him."

Khrom heard a loud puffing sound coming from the stairwell. "You sent for me, Prince?" the Kreigg Ambassador said trying to catch his breath.

"Yes, a dragon rider approaches. I must know if his intentions are honorable."

"His flag of truce is genuine. I see he carries a pouch over his shoulder. I believe the Sorcerer Raggnor has a message for you."

"Thank you, Ambassador."

"Standby to take the pouch," Khrom commanded. The dragon hovered beside the tower. The Kreigg removed the pouch from his shoulder and placed its strap over the hook end of a large pole held by two of Khrom's men. Khrom felt the wind being generated from the dragon's wings. He felt the power of the huge creature hovering in place. He took the pouch and proceeded to his mother's chamber.

"Mother I wish to share this message from Raggnor with you; the fate of our kingdom rests with my reply."

Khrom removed the parchment and read the message from the evil sorcerer.

"What does it say, my son?"

"He offers to make me his regent—if I meet his demands."

Khrom's face flushed with anger. He spoke in an enraged tone. "He wants me to give him Freeya for his queen, and a hundred of my men to work his amber mine, plus two thirds of Vall's harvest. If his demands are not met soon he threatens to march on Vall with his dragons and army."

Queen Dora approached her son and embraced him.

"Khrom, I am with you. I would rather see our kingdom destroyed than bow to Raggnor. With the Black Dragon's help we will prevail."

Khrom poured himself a goblet of mead and began to draft his response.

> *Raggnor:*
>
> *I have no intentions of meeting your demands. Princess Freeya is to be my queen! I forbid you to take any of my people to work your mine. You will no longer receive any of my Kingdom's Harvest.*
>
> *My power increases daily and if you should dare approach my kingdom, my army will march against you and destroy your Realm of Evil!*
>
> *Prince Khrom*

The dragon rider flew in large circles over the castle waiting for Khrom's reply.

Khrom entered the tower.

"You have your reply, Prince Khrom?"

"Yes, Ambassador. I fear Raggnor will not take kindly to it."

The dragon rider descended. He placed the pouch over his shoulder and flew towards his master's fortress.

"Captain, we will be under siege in three days," Khrom said. "We must be ready for war."

"Yes, Khrom. We will win or we will die."

Raggnor waited for his dragon rider to return. He paced within the confines of his dark chamber. He desperately needed slaves to work his mine or the Troblin would not join their forces with his. Or even worse, they could try to take the mine for their own.

Raggnor heard a rapping sound against the door to his chamber. "I have Prince Khrom's reply, Master," General Hatin said.

"Bring it to me!" Raggnor demanded.

General Hatin entered the chamber with General Tog following close behind. General Hatin handed the pouch to his master. Raggnor removed the parchment and read Khrom's defiant response to himself. His face turned red, his neck swelled, his body shook with rage.

"Prepare my dragons! Prepare my army! We march on Vall at dawn! Take a hundred men for slaves. Kill the rest—men, women and children. Burn the Kingdom of Vall. Make it an example for all the kingdoms that dare to oppose me!"

"Yes, Master!" both generals responded in unison.

The Kreigg ate a hearty meal of grain then prepared their weapons for battle. The dragons would join the army at dawn, on the third day of their forced march. General Tog led fifteen hundred Kreigg soldiers across the frontier on the first day. They marched four abreast over the road leading to Vall. General Tog was pleased his army met no resistance at the pass of Lund.

The massive army appeared like a giant serpent to Khrom's scouts atop the pass. The scouts descended to their horses and rode through the night. The next day they arrived at the castle. Manchu escorted them into Khrom's headquarters within the Hall of Vall.

"The Kreigg come, Your Highness!" the first scout reported.

"How many did you see?" Khrom asked.

"All of them, Sire," the second scout responded. "They number in the thousands."

Khrom turned to his mother. "Perhaps you should return to Gaul's Realm."

"No, Khrom! I will not desert the people of Vall at this time."

"I love you, Mother."

"Yes, I know."

"Manchu!" screamed a peasant.

"What is so important?" Manchu asked.

"A bullock has fallen from the bridge into the moat."

Manchu directed his men to use a small boat to approach the animal and place a rope around its neck. With twenty men and two horses they were able to hoist the creature onto the bridge. Khrom walked onto the bridge to be with Manchu.

"We shall dine on this bullock this night, my brother," Khrom said.

"Yes, Khrom. It shall be done."

In the Realm of Gaul Freeya and Kee honed their skills on a herd of wild pigs. The swine ran an erratic pattern across an open meadow. Kee flew quickly in an effort to match the maneuvers of the fleeing prey. Freeya took aim and barely missed the first as it dove into a hole. Her arrow struck the second, sending it tumbling end over end. Kee's massive talons grasped his prey. The Black Dragon returned to his hilltop to dine at his pleasure.

Freeya was surprised to see the Image of the Sorcerer Gaul waiting for her on the summit of the hill. Once Kee landed she dismounted and approached him. He spoke with her while the dragon consumed the pig.

"The time is near, Princess Freeya. Are the two of you ready?"

"Yes, Sorcerer! When do we go into battle?"

The Sorcerer Gaul spoke in a serious tone to Freeya, "Raggnor's army and dragons will approach Vall at first light. You must slay the dragon riders or all will be lost!"

Freeya replied with confidence. "I understand, Sorcerer. We shall not fail."

The image of the sorcerer vanished before her eyes. Freeya slept beside Kee. A cold mist enveloped the hilltop followed by a bitter cold wind. Tiny ice crystals fell from the firmament. The crystals grew in size and intensity. She felt pain from their impact on her body. Suddenly, she no longer felt the stinging of the hail. In the near blackness she made out the shape of a massive wing protecting her body.

"I love you, Kee," she whispered.

Nogard

Chapter 31   Dragons

The pink light in the eastern sky served as a beacon for Raggnor's dragons. Three of the dragons labored from the weight of heavy stones. The largest and swiftest of the dragons carried Raggnor and General Hatin. Unlike her sisters, Raggnor's dragon enjoyed her status. She had bonded with the evil sorcerer and his dragon master. Raggnor felt the power under his command. He believed he had become a match for even the power of his father the God Odin. Soon he flew over his marching army. Raggnor saw the castle of Vall in the distance. He felt confident this would be his first victory in his quest to conquer all the surface lands.

Kee struggled to rise from the hilltop. Freeya had mounted his shoulders in the predawn. The dampness and cold from the previous night had taken its toll. Without warmth to dry his cold wet body, Kee could not lift from the ground. Freeya wept. She knew all would be lost if Kee were unable to fly. The Sorcerer Gaul sensed the situation. He waved his hand to send forth a warm rising thermal, and Kee became airborne. He rose to heights above the clouds to absorb the rays of the morning sun, then hovered above a large dark cloud to mask his presence.

Within Vall the defenders heard the sound of the closing Kreigg drums. Fear began to take its toll.

"Dragons!" screamed the sentry in the tower.

Khrom and Captain Eric rushed to the tower. "I see three, no four dragons, Captain."

"Where is Freeya, Khrom?"

"Do not fear; she will be here soon, Captain."

A cloud drifted over the castle, blocking the morning sun. A mighty roar bellowed from within the cloud. Khrom saw the mighty Black Dragon Kee emerge, with Freeya mounted on his shoulders. Kee dove toward the first dragon.

The startled dragon rider released the heavy load of stones sending them crashing into the moat below. Kee matched the Kreigg's desperate maneuvers. Freeya took aim a mere twenty feet from the dragon rider. Her arrow took flight. Within an Instant its iron head pierced the Kreigg's chest and heart. The mortally wounded rider slumped forward. Kee made a series of high pitched sounds. His sister reacted. She turned and dove toward the Kreigg Army. The body of her tormenter fell from her shoulders and crashed into the army below. The defenders cheered when Freeya struck the second rider and the green dragon dropped her heavy stones onto the Kreigg Army below.

Raggnor was in shock. He fumbled for his necklace of power and grasped his turquoise pendant. He pointed the jewel in the direction of Kee and began to chant.

"Drago be Doma! Drago be doma!"

The pendant glowed, but did not send a beam of lethal light into the Black Dragon. The Sorcerer Raggnor felt flames burning his hand. The turquoise pendant released itself from the clasp of the necklace and fell to the earth. Raggnor witnessed Freeya slaying the third of his dragon riders.

"General, return me to my fortress now!" screamed a panic stricken Raggnor.

"Yes, Master."

Raggnor's dragon flew an erratic pattern, which nearly clipped the treetops. Kee flew close behind trying desperately to match his sister's unpredictable movements. Kee knew he could bring her down with a blast of his flames, but he meant her no harm.

Freeya felt the rush of wind against her. She nearly fell when she released her hold on Kee's neck to notch an arrow to her bow string. She felt a rush, as she released her arrow. The green dragon banked to the left. The arrow flew harmlessly past her neck.

General Hatin commanded his dragon to climb into the morning sky then dive towards Raggnor's Realm. The green dragon's wings lifted Raggnor to the place of eternal night, then arced toward the earth.

Kee followed his sister's ascent. Freeya clung tightly to his neck, when he dove after the green dragon. Freeya heard her arrows rattling in her quiver moments before they were lost. Kee did not wish to harm his sister, but he knew he must use his flames to stop Raggnor. Once more they flew close to the trees. Freeya saw the tail of the dragon in front of her. With every beat of his wings, Kee closed with Raggnor.

Raggnor felt a surge of power within him when he entered the sky above his realm. He clutched his ruby stone.

"Give me cover, my jewel of illusion."

A thick fog masked Raggnor and his dragon. Kee was nearly blinded by the heavy mist. Suddenly, looming before him stood the blackened stone face of a cliff. Freeya clung tightly to Kee's neck when he climbed rapidly to avoid the collision.

General Hatin guided his dragon to his master's fortress. Raggnor dismounted and hurried to his chamber. He had yet to be defeated, but his losses where overwhelming. Three of his dragons of war and his powerful turquoise pendant where lost. His Kreigg army would be forced to fight Prince Khrom alone. He feared the Black Dragon could give Khrom the advantage. Raggnor knew if the Prince of Vall were to be victorious, he would march against him. The Sorcerer Raggnor began to form a plan. He still possessed one dragon and over a hundred loyal Kreigg guards. He sent for the Troblin Ambassador.

The fog dispersed when Kee departed Raggnor's Realm Both he and Freeya were exhausted from their pursuit. The Black Dragon flew slowly toward the scene of the impending battle for Vall.

𝔑ogard

𝔠hapter 32   𝔔ueen of t𝔥e 𝔎reigg

General Tog struggled to maintain control of his army. He no longer had the cover of the dragons and his master had fled the field of battle. Fear ran rampant throughout the Kreigg ranks. He paused for a moment. *I still have the advantage of numbers and brute strength,* he thought. General Tog ordered his soldiers to take up a defensive position near the castle of Vall. He planned a massive assault at midday, when his army had calmed.

Khrom watched the Kreigg from the tower of Vall.

"The time to strike is now, Khrom," Captain Eric said.

"What say you, General?"

"My knights are ready for battle. We would rather fight in the field of combat than behind walls of stone."

Khrom descended the tower to the outer wall to address his army. "Knights of Vall, mount your steeds take your lances and swords! Foot soldiers ready your spears! Archers clutch your bows! People of Vall, we shall take the battle to our enemy. I will lead you to victory!"

"Khrom! Khrom!" chanted the army of Vall.

"Is this wise, Khrom?" Jal asked, "If you are slain who will rule in your place?"

"Queen Dora, General."

Khrom mounted his old warhorse. He held his broadsword high and moved to the head of the column with General Jal by his side. Jasmine rode beside Captain Eric, followed closely by Manchu. The mighty drawbridge groaned as the clattering of chains lowered it into position. Khrom and Jal started the crossing. The planks of the span echoed the hooves of three hundred warhorses. A hundred foot soldiers, with as many archers, joined the procession. The peasants remained behind to serve as the castle's last line of defense.

Jal directed his force with his sword. The knights quickly formed a single broad line of battle facing the Kreigg. Captain Eric's foot soldiers formed behind the knights, while Lon's archers formed behind the soldiers.

The warhorses pranced nervously waiting for their commands. A mere two hundred meters separated the opposing armies. Khrom raised his sword. He stopped its downward motion, when he saw the Black Dragon approaching. "Wait!" Khrom shouted. "Let our dragon give them a taste of fire before we charge!"

Freeya looked below as Kee flew over the frightened Kreigg Army. Many of Tog's soldiers threw down their weapons and shook in fear at the sight of the dragon. Perhaps she thought, this battle could be avoided. Kee read her thoughts. He flew in a large arc over Khrom's force and faced the Kreigg Army, then turned and flew between the opposing forces. His neck extended as he pointed his head toward the earth. Freeya felt the heat generating from within the dragon. She released her hold on Kee's neck and turned her head away when the hot plasma erupted from his throat and deadly flames burst from his maw. Kee and Freeya were thrown backwards from the violent recoil. The field between the opposing armies erupted into an inferno.

General tog saw the fear in his soldier's eyes. He knew there was only one way to retain their obedience. When the flames subsided, he marched to the center of the field. He started to swing his axe and began shouting.

"What is he doing, Ambassador?" asked Khrom.

"He challenges you or your champion to a battle to the death. His army will follow the victor."

Jasmine heard the Kreigg Ambassador's words. She did not wish a great battle. She did not wish her father and her friends to be slain. Jasmine remembered the Sorcerer Gaul's words. "The Kreigg are a simple race, they only serve Raggnor because they fear his magic and his dragons."

"Jasmine!" Jal screamed when his daughter raced across the field.

"No!" Khrom shouted.

"Does she have a chance, Jal?" Manchu asked.

"Yes, Jasmine is the best champion among us," a worried Jal replied.

General Tog laughed when he saw his challenger was a mere woman. He heard members of his army cheering for him as the female warrior closed. General Tog stood motionless, holding his massive axe with both of his hands.

Jasmine clutched her lance. Her horse was on a collision course with the large Kreigg. She was unaware of the deadly iron tipped spear lying at the general's feet. She saw his eyes as he dropped his axe and bent forward to grasp his spear. Too late she realized the general's tactic.

The Kreigg General leaped aside to avoid the lance and thrust his spear into the horse's chest. He watched the horse tumble head first on to the charred field. He saw his challenger being thrown against a small tree. General Tog gave a savage war cry. He felt victory within his grasp. He had but to take the head of this human and his army would take Vall.

Jasmine's body racked with pain. She struggled to her feet. She felt her quickness and agility returning. Her anger surpassed her fear. She hated general Tog for killing her horse. She held her sword with her right hand and clutched a steel dagger with the other. Jasmine planted her feet and waited. The Kreigg General would have to come to her.

General Tog approached his victim. "It is a shame to slay this beautiful creature," he mused. He remembered his master's promise. *You can do with Princess Jasmine as you wish. She will be your victory prize.*

General Tog swung his axe. Jasmine dodged the blow and slashed his face. Tog made a second blow. The flat of his axe struck Jasmine's buttocks. She turned quickly. The blade of her sword severed two of Tog's fingers. The duel continued, while both armies watched the combat. Though they cheered for their general, most of the Kreigg wished to follow the brave princess.

Jasmine heard the Kreigg's axe strike the earth and felt his hand wrenching her weapon from her hand. She reacted quickly. Her left hand drove the steel blade of her dagger into the general's right eye.

General Tog had never experienced pain of this magnitude. He staggered forward groping for his axe. His weapon no longer lay on the ground. He knew it was in the hands of his advisory. He fell to his knees and hoped his end would be swift.

Jasmine grasped the handle of the heavy axe and swung it with both of her hands. She heard the snapping sound of the axe's blade severing the neck of the Kreigg General. Once she had struck the fatal blow her hands grabbed General Tog's severed head by its horns and held it high for all to see.

Khrom heard the Kreigg cheering and screaming, even louder than his own army. "What are they saying, Ambassador? Do they wish to join us?"

"They wish to follow the brave princess. The Kreigg want her to be their queen."

Manchu raced across the field. When he dismounted to place Jasmine on to his horse, she collapsed in his arms. Manchu brought Jasmine to her father. Jal held and caressed his daughter.

"I love you and I am very proud of you, even though you disobeyed me."

"I am sorry, Father."

Jasmine began to cry.

"Are you alright, child?"

"Yes, Father," Jasmine responded sadly. "Father, he killed my horse."

"Take her to Vall, Manchu. Our queen will tend to her wounds," Khrom said. "Manchu, wait."

"Yes, Khrom."

"Before you leave, the Ambassador must speak to Jasmine."

"Princess Jasmine, the Kreigg Army has spoken," the Ambassador said. "They wish to have you as their queen. They will follow you into battle against Raggnor."

"Why do they not choose you as their leader?"

"I am a diplomat. At this time they need to follow a warrior. Please at least for now serve as our queen."

Jasmine looked at her father. Jal nodded his approval.

"Yes, for now I will serve as your queen. However, Ambassador, you must remain at my side and when the time comes you will be the King of the Kreigg."

"Agreed. Thank you, Your Highness," the Ambassador said.

"Manchu, take me from here. My backside hurts," Jasmine pleaded.

"Yes, Your Majesty."

Jasmine had dreamed of having her own kingdom. She never imagined a multitude of strange looking creatures with horns on their heads would be her subjects.

Jasmine rode behind Manchu on his horse. She felt the pain deep within her. A growing bruise spread across her face. Manchu's strong arms lifted her from his mount. She fainted when he carried her up the stairs to his mother's chamber.

Queen Dora saw the growing bruise on the right side of Jasmine's face and surmised she had wounds beneath her armor.

"Manchu help me remove her armor."

"Yes, Mother"

Manchu saw the bruises covering Jasmine's body. He saw the exposed flesh, where Tog had struck her buttocks.

"The Sorcerer Gaul has given me a special potion to cure the wounds of battle. He told me to save it for the rulers of Vall. I trust he will forgive me. I must give it to this brave young woman."

Manchu placed Jasmine on to his mother's bed. He held her mouth open while Dora poured the magic potion into Jasmine. When the queen placed the empty vessel beside her bed it was replenished. "Thank you, Great Sorcerer," Queen Dora whispered.

Jasmine recovered rapidly. Before his eyes Manchu saw the bruises vanishing from her body. She opened her eyes slowly. The room was strange to her. She recognized Manchu's voice.

"Manchu, come close to me," Jasmine whispered.

When Manchu bent over her, Jasmine placed her hands behind the back of his head and pulled him down. He felt her lips pushing against his own.

"I see the Princess is recovering," Queen Dora said.

"Yes, Mother," replied Manchu.

"Oh, Manchu. Please bring me a tunic and my armor."

"Would you care to wear one of my gowns for your meeting with the Ambassador?" Queen Dora asked.

"Yes! Oh yes! Thank you, Dora."

"It is I who should thank you, for risking your life for Vall."

The Ambassador arrived with Khrom. "Mother, I do not see Jasmine. Is she...?" Khrom asked solemnly.

"Jasmine is fine. She prepares for her meeting with the Ambassador. Ambassador, would you care for some wine?"

"Thank you, Your Majesty," the Kreigg Ambassador responded.

Khrom heard Jasmine and his brother's laughter from behind a closed door. The door swung open revealing a beautiful Princess dressed in a glowing pink gown with matching slippers. The Ambassador bowed before his new Queen. He had never witnessed such radiance. She possesses wondrous powers, he thought. A short time before his new Queen had been locked in deadly combat, and now she walked as a regal beauty.

"Your Highness, your army needs food and a night's rest. They will follow you at dawn."

"Khrom, do we have enough grain to feed the Kreigg?" Jasmine asked.

"Yes. We have the stores Copen held for Raggnor."

"Prince Khrom, as Queen of the Kreigg I request grain to feed my army."

"I shall grant your request only if your army marches with mine against Raggnor."

"Agreed!"

"Should the grain be made into bread, Ambassador?"

"No, we Kreigg prefer to eat our grain whole."

Khrom provided enough of his kingdom's precious grain to feed the army he once detested. From his tower he saw the exhausted Kreigg Army sleeping at the foot of his castle. *War can be a strange game,* he thought. Khrom feared Raggnor had yet to be destroyed and the march to his realm of evil would be frought with danger. In the distance he saw a lone rider closing with Vall. He became elated when he saw her flowing white hair.

Freeya clutched the most valued prize in the known world. She had found the Sorcerer Gaul's turquoise pendant. She had remembered the place where it had escaped from Raggnor's hand. The gem had beckoned to her, as it knew she would return it to its rightful owner. She had come to Vall to see Khrom before returning the pendant. Khrom met her at the gate and escorted her to his chamber.

"Khrom, I have missed you so very much."

"I have missed you, Freeya. I love you."

"I love you, Khrom."

"Your sister has slain General Tog. The Kreigg have made her their Queen. Did Raggnor escape?"

"Yes, he has returned to his fortress."

"I feared as much. Where are Kee and his sisters?"

"Kee and his sisters are together on his hilltop."

"My army marches at dawn," Khrom said. "I will need all the dragons' support in three days, at the frontier with Raggnor's Realm."

"You shall have it, Prince Khrom!"

"Freeya, please spend the night with me," Khrom pleaded.

Freeya smiled then touched her lips to Khrom's cheek.

Nogard

Chapter 33   Sorceress

Freeya awoke to a steady rain pelting the castle. "Rise, Prince Khrom. It is time for you to lead your army."

"No. I wish to stay with my fair princess."

Khrom heard a loud knocking against the door to his chamber.

"Your army awaits, Prince Khrom," Captain Eric announced

"Yes, Captain. I will be with them shortly."

Khrom embraced his future queen then dressed in his tunic and armor.

"I will think of you often," Khrom said.

Freeya did not speak. She felt a tear in the left corner of her eye when Khrom stepped through the doorway.

Khrom saw no signs of the Kreigg Army when he approached the outer wall.

"Captain, where are the Kreigg."

"They march with their queen and your brother, to retake their land."

"My knights, foot soldiers and archers—are they ready?"

"Yes, Sire. Your army awaits your command.

Khrom mounted his warhorse. He pointed his sword forward. Trumpets blared when the Army of Vall began its perilous march to Raggnor's Realm of Evil.

Freeya and Queen Dora watched the procession from the tower. Freeya remembered the Army of Nevau marching to the Pass of Lund and how only half returned.

"Will you stay with us for a time?" Queen Dora asked.

"No, I must return something of great value to its rightful owner."

Freeya watched until the army had disappeared from view before she mounted her horse. She was unaware others had watched the departure of the Army of Vall. A brigand watched the lone rider on the road to Gaul's Realm. He signaled to his band concealed in the wood. Ten outlaws began their pursuit, while five more rushed ahead to a place of ambush.

Freeya had fastened the stone of power to a leather strap. The precious jewel dangled from her neck. She heard the approach of several horsemen behind her. She surmised they were hostile. "Brigands. They have come for the pendant," she said to herself. Freeya urged her mount to a full gallop.

While ten outlaws continued their pursuit on the winding road, the remainder of the band rode quickly over a straight path in the wood to intercept the rider. They took a position where the trail intercepted the road. One brigand clutched his bow, while the other four drew their swords. They heard the approaching rider nearing their trap.

Too late Freeya saw the outlaws. Within moments she was surrounded. She drew her sword. Freeya sensed the leader of the band was drawn to the jewel hanging from her neck.

"Lower your weapon!" the leader demanded. "Give me the stone and you may pass!"

The Sorcerer Gaul sent his power through the stone. Freeya sheathed her sword. She felt her hand being guided to the pendant. Her hand aimed the stone towards the brigands. A blue light penetrated their beings. A piercing ringing filled their minds. Their weapons burnt their flesh and fell from their hands. The outlaw's horses leaped uncontrollably, throwing their riders to the ground.

Thinking she was a sorceress, the brigands groveled before Freeya.

"Please forgive us, Sorceress," spoke the leader in a trembling voice.

"The Army of Vall marches against Raggnor. Join with Prince Khrom and I will not destroy you!" Freeya demanded.

"It shall be done, Sorceress."

Freeya watched the men racing to join the Army of Vall. She

touched the pendant once more. She enjoyed the power it gave her. For a brief moment she wished to be a Sorceress. Freeya overcame her desire for power and continued her journey to deliver the pendant to its rightful owner. She passed through the barrier of light and entered Gaul's Realm. The Sorcerer Gaul met her near Queen Dora's cottage.

"Welcome, Princess Freeya. I have been expecting you."

"I have come to return your pendant, Sorcerer."

"I thank you for this and the many things you have accomplished."

Freeya handed Gaul the jewel. The gem joined with his necklace of power. Now that he possessed both of the turquoise pendants, he sensed he had become stronger than his evil brother.

"I wish to return to Vall, Sorcerer."

"Yes, I understand, child."

Freeya turned her horse toward Vall, while the sorcerer returned to his castle.

Nogard

Chapter 34　March Against Evil

Jasmine and Manchu rode at the head of the Kreigg column. For the first time, the Kreigg marched as a free army who no longer feared Raggnor and his dragons. Though they met no resistance on the first day of their march, Jasmine felt uneasy. She felt the presence of hostile eyes watching her army's movements. At dusk she halted her force a short distance from Nevau. She prepared to face her first challenge.

"Ambassador, I must know the loyalty of the occupiers of Nevau," Jasmine said.

"I understand, My Queen. I shall send forth a representative."

The Ambassador sent forth one of his trusted lieutenants to serve as an emissary. While the lieutenant trod to the Kreigg fortress, Jasmine ordered her army to make camp. A Kreigg sentry ran to Jasmine and the Ambassador. Jasmine could not understand his language, but she did hear the words Vall and Khrom. She heard the sounds of horses and marching feet.

Manchu rode to greet his brother. Khrom ordered the procession to halt when he saw his brother approaching.

"Manchu, why did you not wait for us?"

"Queen Jasmine feels we should march against our enemy before they can regroup."

General Jal smiled when he heard Manchu's words.

"Captain, make camp beside our allies," Khrom commanded.

"Yes, Prince Khrom!"

Khrom and Jal rode into the Kreigg encampment with Manchu.

Jasmine met with Khrom and her father.

"Khrom, we are near Nevau," Jasmine said. "I have sent an emissary to ask for their surrender. He should be returning soon."

"What if they refuse?" Jal asked.

"My army will storm the fortress at dawn."

The emissary staggered into camp. He had been beaten and one of his eyes had been gouged. He spoke to Jasmine while the ambassador translated. "The occupiers are loyal to Raggnor. They will follow Raggnor's orders no matter what the consequences," the emissary gasped. "They have many human hostages in the courtyard and will slay them if we attack."

"Ambassador, ask the brave lieutenant if he saw the hostages. Ask him how many hostages there are."

"Yes, I saw many," he responded slowly.

The lieutenant fell to the ground in front of his queen. Jasmine kneeled to touch his face as he died.

Jasmine rose to face Khrom. "I can rescue the hostages. I know of a hidden passage that leads to the courtyard of Nevau. Freeya and I used it in our escape. I need a band of men who can walk silently and strike quickly to follow me."

"Jasmine, you must not lead this expedition," Jal said.

"I must, Father. I alone know the way."

Jal nodded his head. An agreement was reached. Jasmine and Manchu would lead the rescue. She would take a small force of swordsmen and two archers into the cave and through the maze of tunnels leading to the courtyard. She would place the ambassador in charge of the Kreigg Army until she returned.

A sentry in Khrom's camp heard the approach of riders. Within moments the riders were surrounded.

"Who are you?" Captain Eric asked. "What brings you to this place?"

"Once we were brigands, now we wish to serve Prince Khrom and join his army," spoke the leader of the band.

"Who sent you and how did you find us?"

"A sorceress with flowing white hair told us we must join Prince Khrom's Army. It is not difficult to follow an army of this size, sir!"

The captain pondered, a sorceress with flowing white hair. He surmised somehow this band had been in contact with Freeya.

Khrom and Jal returned to their encampment.

"Captain, who are these men?" Khrom asked.

"A band of brigands who wish to join with us. They claim they were sent by a sorceress with flowing white hair. I am not sure they are trustworthy, Khrom."

Khrom approached the leader. "By what name are you called?"

"I am Jon, Your Highness. These men are loyal to me."

"Tell me, Jon, of the sorceress who sent you."

"She is a woman of great beauty with flowing white hair. When we tried to take a jewel from her that hung from her neck she pointed it at us. A blue light came from the jewel that nearly killed us all. She said if we did not join Prince Khrom's Army she would destroy us."

Khrom knew the brigands had had an encounter with Freeya. He remembered she had found the Sorcerer Gaul's powerful turquoise pendant. Khrom looked at the gaunt faces of the band. He saw the poor condition of their horses. He remembered not so long ago he was an outlaw himself. Somehow he knew he could trust these men. He would send them on a perilous mission with Jasmine.

"Captain, feed these men and their horses!" Khrom ordered.

"Yes, Khrom!"

"Jon, I have need of your services. If you succeed in the mission I am about to assign you, I will grant you full amnesty and you and your men may join my army."

Jasmine and Manchu rode into Khrom's camp.

"Queen Jasmine, I wish to introduce you to Jon. His band will join you on your mission. They were sent to us by your sister," Khrom said.

Jasmine looked at the scurfy band feeding ravenously.

"Khrom, these men are not soldiers!"

"No, Jasmine, they are brigands. They are silent and quick and will follow their leader without question."

"Alright. Did you say Freeya sent them?"

"Yes. They believe she is a sorceress."

"Jon, if I select you and your band to join with me on this mission," Jasmine stated, "I will demand your complete loyalty and obedience to my every command!"

"You have my word, Your Majesty," Jon pledged. "My men and I shall obey all that you command. Please tell me the nature of this mission."

"Many of our people are being held by Raggnor's Kreigg in the courtyard of Nevau. Your mission will be to help me rescue them. I will tell you more when we have entered the cave. We leave in a short time, after you have completed your meal and cleansed yourself."

"Thank you, Your Highness."

Jon wondered why he was thanking the queen. She had asked him to join with her in a suicide mission against the Kreigg, and did she say 'cave'. Jon did not like caves and other dank places, yet he had given his word to a queen.

𝔑ogard

Chapter 35   Rescue

They began their journey by starlight. Jasmine and Manchu led the procession. Jon and his band with two of Lon's archers followed single file over the path leading to the cave. Upon entering the grotto, Jasmine ignited her torch.

"Jon, I escaped through here when the Kreigg overran Nevau," Jasmine said. "This cave leads to a tunnel, which leads to a passage to the courtyard where the hostages are being held. The Kreigg cannot see well in the darkness. Your band must overpower their guards quickly and silently while I free the hostages."

"Lead, and I shall follow, My Queen."

"Jon, on this mission you may address me as Jasmine."

"Thank you, Your Highness—I mean Jasmine."

"Archers, you must slay the Kreigg in the tower if we are seen!" Jasmine commanded.

The cave's long chamber was illuminated by Jasmine's torch and two more held by Jon's men. Jasmine guided her men through the labyrinth of the cavern. For the most part, the noisy bats had departed for the night to hunt for prey. Jon shuddered when he felt a dead bat brush against his leg in the knee deep water.

Jon felt the cave beginning to narrow. At the end of the chamber he made out the tunnel's entrance. When they entered the narrow tunnel, the footing on the clay bottom became slippery, but free of water. Jon heard the squeal of rodents and for a moment, thought he had entered the realm of the dead.

The thick musty air became ever harder to breathe. One torch died from lack of oxygen. Jasmine found the narrow passage.

"We are nearly there," she whispered. She crawled beneath the moat and the cover, which blocked the entrance to the courtyard.

"Manchu, Jon, remove the cover," Jasmine commanded.

Jon and Manchu lifted the heavy stone and slid it from the hole. A surge of refreshing cool air filled the passage. The two men slowly shoved the oxcart from the passage's entrance. Manchu was the first to emerge. He placed the cart where it would serve to shield their escape. Jasmine followed. Jon and his band climbed into the courtyard. The archers took a position near the cart to cover the escape route.

Jasmine's eyes adjusted to the near blackness. She saw the hostages tethered to several poles. She estimated fifteen poles with two hostages tied to each. Two groups of three Kreigg guards huddled beside small fires. On the outer wall's tower she made out two sentries.

Jon led his band silently across the courtyard. He felt the damp cool air against his face and the hard cobblestones beneath the soles of his feet. The band divided to attack the guards simultaneously. The Kreigg guards were caught by complete surprise. The band worked quickly as a team. While one jerked back the Kreigg's head, another slashed his throat. The struggle was over in a matter of moments.

Jasmine and Manchu rushed to the hostages. In his haste Manchu's foot struck a wooden bucket, sending it clattering noisily into the night. Both sentries on the wall heard the sound of the bucket and peered into the courtyard.

Lon's archers took aim. The first sentry fell from the wall. The second, though mortally wounded, sounded an alarm with his shell horn.

Jasmine and Manchu quickly severed the bonds of the hostages. Many were unable to walk and had to be carried by Jon's men. They began to lower the former hostages into the passage when Manchu saw many torches coming from the inner wall. He heard the clatter of Kreigg armor and the sounds of heavy marching feet.

The archers aimed near the closing torches. A Kreigg soldier screamed when he was struck.

"Jasmine, go into the passage now!" Manchu shouted.

"Come with me, Manchu."

Two of Jon's men carrying injured hostages were separated from the entrance. Jon heard their screams when the Kreigg severed them in half. He felt tears streaming from his eyes as he slid through the entrance into the passage. The archers slowed the Kreigg advance with their remaining arrows and followed Jon's men.

Jasmine led the procession through the passage into the tunnel. Behind her she heard the sounds of the Kreigg who were stuck in the narrow confines of the passage. She knew they must hurry before the Kreigg could dig through to the tunnel. She sighed when she entered the main chamber of the cavern. At the cave's mouth she saw many torches and from behind, she heard the sounds of loud footsteps and clattering armor.

"The Kreigg have broken through!" Jasmine shouted. "Move quickly to the cave's entrance!" She saw the torches at the front of the cave moving rapidly towards her. She could only hope they were not being held by her enemy.

"Your Highness!" shouted a friendly voice.

"Ambassador," Jasmine responded with a sense of relief.

"We await your command, My Queen."

"Slay these soldiers of Raggnor. Take no captives."

The battle was fought in near darkness. Jasmine heard the savage sounds of hand-to-hand combat. Large axes smashed through heavy armor, severing limbs and heads. Jasmine heard the hissing sounds of torches being snuffed out by the water on the floor of the cavern. The battle shifted to the interior of the cavern. Raggnor's Kreigg were being routed. At the end of the melee, twenty of Raggnor's and eleven of Jasmine's Kreigg had been slain.

"Thank you for coming to our aid, Ambassador. I am sorry for the loss of so many of our soldiers."

The ambassador was heartened by his new queen's words. *Raggnor would have not shown any compassion for his soldiers,* he thought. *He only demanded obedience and would have fed his dead to his dragons.*

Jon and his men placed the rescued citizens of Nevau upon their horses and led them on the trail to Khrom's camp. Jasmine rode to Jon's side and dismounted.

"You and your men fought bravely tonight. I am truly sorry for the loss of two of your men."

"Thank you, Jasmine—I mean Your Highness."

"I will speak to my father," Jasmine said. "If you and your men desire you will be trained in the ways of knights."

"Can we be trained together?"

"Yes!"

Jon watched Jasmine and Manchu ride together toward Khrom's encampment.

It had been a very long day, thought Jon. This morning he was the leader of a starving band of brigands. He remembered making a foolish mistake when he tried to steal a magic jewel from a sorceress. She had placed a spell upon him and his band, and forced them to join the Army of Vall. Now after rescuing hostages from Raggnor and losing two of his men in battle with the Kreigg, he and his men were to be made knights.

Khrom and Jal met Jasmine and Manchu.

"Jasmine, are you unharmed?" Jal asked. "The hostages are they...?"

"I am fine, Father. We lost two of the hostages and two of Jon's men. The rest are free and journey to this camp as we speak. Father, I have a request. I promised Jon he and his men would be trained as knights."

"I shall honor your promise, Jasmine—after we have defeated Raggnor."

"Jasmine, what are the Kreigg defenses at Nevau?" Khrom asked.

"They have been weakened. My army slew many of them this night," Jasmine replied. "I will march on Nevau at dawn. I am confident my army of free Kreigg will liberate Nevau in a short time."

"I will lead the Army of Vall to the pass of Lund. We will await you there." Khrom said.

"This is a good plan," Captain Eric said. "Manchu, if Jasmine needs our help to free Nevau, ride to us."

"Yes, Captain!"

"Jasmine, please try to rest," Jal said. "Tomorrow will be a difficult day."

"Yes, Father."

As Jasmine and Manchu departed for the camp of the Free Kreigg, Jon led the former hostages into Khrom's camp.

"Welcome, Citizens of Nevau. I am Prince Khrom of Vall."

𝕹ogard

Chapter 36   𝕱rontier

Manchu felt the warmth of Jasmine's skin pressing against him. He saw a great cloud passing between the earth and the stars. He witnessed bolts of lightning flashing above the pines and heard the crashing sounds of thunder. *Thor has come to join us,* he thought.

Jasmine slept peacefully through the brief storm. She dreamed of her first love Joran and of a life that could never be. She awakened to the sight of the morning sun refracting through the raindrops still clinging to the needles of the pines.

"Your army awaits your command, My Queen!" the Ambassador announced.

"Thank you, Ambassador. Please give me a little time."

Manchu had made tea from the root of a special tree. "Drink this, Jasmine. I have honey and bread I brought from Khrom's camp."

"Where is Khrom?" Jasmine asked, while splashing water onto her face.

"He marches to the pass of Lund."

Jasmine dressed quickly into her Tunic and armor.

"Ambassador, we march to free Nevau!"

Jasmine and Manchu led the column of free Kreigg to the former Castle of Nevau. The fortress of Nevau lay still like the carcass of a dead beast. The main gate lay open and the drawbridge spanned the moat.

"I sense a trap, Jasmine," Manchu said.

"As do I, Manchu, as do I!"

Jasmine pointed her sword toward the bridge. A hundred of her soldiers raced across the open field. She heard the clatter of their feet crossing the wooden bridge. Within in moments her army captured the former castle. Manchu rode across the bridge into the courtyard. When he felt it safe he signaled to Jasmine. She saw the bodies of several Kreigg, Jon's men and the slain hostages.

"They have fled, Princess!" Manchu shouted.

Jasmine thought for a moment. Suddenly she realized her enemy's plan.

"Manchu, ride quickly to warn my father and Khrom! A trap has been set for them at the pass of Lund. Tell Khrom not to enter the pass without my army."

"I will be with you at Lund, Princess!" Manchu shouted.

Manchu rode quickly across the drawbridge. He could only hope his steed would carry him to Khrom's army in time.

The Army of Vall moved steadily forward. Khrom's force crossed the first of the three bridges without incident. On the second bridge Khrom passed the bodies of two Kreigg soldiers.

"General, I feel we should take the pass as soon as possible. What say you?" Khrom asked.

"Our foot soldiers should secure the high ground first Khrom. I fear an ambush from above."

A scout rode to Khrom and Jal. "Prince Khrom, I have seen many Kreigg preparing defenses at the far end of the pass!"

"Did you see any on the top of the cliffs?"

"No, I did not look to the cliffs."

In his haste to battle Raggnor's Kreigg, Khrom ignored his general's advice.

"General, prepare your knights! Captain, ready your foot soldiers and archers! The time to take the pass is now!" Khrom commanded.

Many Kreigg lay hidden on the top of the precipice. They waited for the Army of Vall to march against their soldiers below. They planned to create an avalanche to slay most of the army and slay the rest with stones from above.

"A rider approaches from behind!" shouted a sentry.

"It could be Manchu!" Jal said.

"Halt the advance!" Khrom shouted.

Jal waited nervously for the rider to approach. He worried his daughter could be in jeopardy. The rider rode past the column to join his brother.

"Raggnor's soldiers have abandoned Nevau! Jasmine fears they have set a trap for you! She said you must wait for her before you enter the pass."

"General, Captain, have your men stand down! We will wait for Jasmine," Khrom commanded.

Jasmine's column arrived at dusk. She counseled with Khrom and her father.

"Khrom, my soldiers will take the high ground. I will need cover from your archers when they ascend the cliffs."

"Agreed. The Army of Vall will not advance until the high ground is secure. Jasmine, I give you my archers."

"Jal, Captain, prepare to take the pass!" Khrom commanded.

"Yes, Prince Khrom!"

Jasmine's Kreigg Soldiers prepared for the assault. They wore a bright red sash across their chest to distinguish themselves from their enemy. Raggnor's Soldiers hurled stones upon Jasmine's force as they began to climb the cliff face. The Archers of Vall responded with a volley of arrows. Five of Raggnor's Kreigg were slain in the first volley. A second volley drove them from the edge of the precipice. In a short time the ascent of the soldiers was complete. Jasmine's army became locked in bitter combat on both sides of the pass of Lund. She heard the screaming of the soldiers and saw bodies being hurled from the cliffs above.

The Ambassador stood beside his queen, tears streamed from his eyes. "It bothers me to see so many Kreigg slaying each other, Majesty."

"This will end soon, Ambassador," Jasmine said. "The Kreigg will soon have their own kingdom, were they can live in peace and freedom."

"Thank you, My Queen."

Khrom saw flags waving from both sides of the pass.

"The high ground is secure. General, advance your knights!" Khrom shouted.

The pass shook from the onslaught of three hundred warhorses. Raggnor's Army was quickly overrun. A Kreigg lieutenant threw down his weapons and surrendered to Manchu. Manchu brought him to the Ambassador for questioning.

"Ambassador, what has the prisoner told you?" Jasmine asked.

"I have grave news, Majesty. Raggnor has forged an alliance with the Troblin of the Underworld. Many of them have entered his realm and tomorrow night thousands more will come."

"We must take Raggnor's Realm before the main force of the Troblin Army can join with him!" Jasmine said to Khrom and her father.

"Our assault will begin at first light," Khrom said. "Tonight we make camp on the frontier."

Nogard

Chapter 37   An Unknown Ally

Raggnor had been informed of the death of his general at the hands of Princess Jasmine. He knew his main army had turned against him and made the princess their queen. For the first time he felt he could be defeated. *If I could hold Khrom's force at bay for just one more day,* he thought, *the Troblin Army could grant me victory.* The first part of his plan began in the middle of the night. A hundred Troblin archers slipped across the frontier in the blackness. Their eyes were accustomed to the darkness. The soldiers from the Underworld crept past the Kreigg encampment to the periphery of the Army of Vall. They moved within range of the sentries and slew two of them. The hideous creatures moved with stealth to surround Khrom's force.

Khrom awoke to the nervous sounds being made by his horses. "Captain, General, I fear we are about to be attacked! Sound the alarm!" Khrom yelled.

"Put out the fires! Grab your weapons!" screamed Captain Eric.

"Knights, to your mounts!" General Jal shouted.

The camp was in a state of chaos, trying to defend itself from an unseen enemy.

The Troblin prepared to send their first volley of arrows into the camp. They hoped to slay enough of Khrom's men to delay his assault on Raggnor's Fortress.

Troblins were not the only creatures prowling the night. An army of silver coated beasts ran silently over the shadowed forest trails. They scented the Troblin and closed for the kill. The pack caught the Troblin by surprise. They did not have time to aim at the attacking wolves. The soldiers of the night screamed in terror when the fangs of the predators tore into their flesh.

Khrom heard the screaming and savage growling in the blackness, followed by a chorus of howling.

"Captain, take your foot soldiers to assist our ally."

"Yes, Khrom!"

The captain tripped over the body of one of his fallen sentries. He saw the shapes of the surviving Troblins running toward him in the darkness.

"Draw your swords and slay them all!" shouted Captain Eric.

He beheaded a closing Troblin with a single blow of his sword. His soldiers slew nearly all the fleeing soldiers of the night. Eric heard the approach of hundreds of padded paws and saw yellow eyes glowing in the blackness.

"Lower your weapons!" Captain Eric demanded.

Eric remembered the wolves saving his daughter from the evil knight. He laid his weapon on the ground and walked toward the leader of the pack. The large black male approached. Eric dropped to his knees. "I thank you my friend for saving my daughter and now I thank you for saving my men." The alpha male brushed his muzzle against Eric's cheek then turned to join his pack. The wolves carried the Troblin into the wood to feed on them at their leisure.

Captain Eric returned to Khrom's camp.

"We are no longer threatened, Khrom. Only a few escaped."

"Did you see our ally?"

"Yes, their leader is the same wolf that saved your sister."

"They shall have their own realm and my protection."

Eric and Khrom both laughed. They knew the wolves where quite capable of defending themselves.

"Try to rest, Captain. Tomorrow will be the day of judgment."

Nogard

Chapter 38   Sons of Odin

Raggnor had made plans for his escape if he was defeated. He had his remaining dragon moved to a cave on the opposite side of his mountain, connected to his chamber by a hidden passage. In the middle of the night he walked to the frontier to create a massive image of a serpent bird. He held his pink stone and chanted in a tongue known only to the sorcerers and the gods. The image formed rapidly. He knew the Kreigg would believe the giant serpent with its fangs and wings to be real. He knew they would be too terrified to enter his realm. Without the Kreigg's help he felt the Troblins could hold Khrom's army until their reinforcements arrived.

The Sorcerer Gaul feared Raggnor's magic could cause harm to Khrom's army when they crossed the frontier. Until this time Gaul dared not to face his brother within the borders of his evil realm. Now with his necklace of power at its zenith and knowing his brother was weakened by the loss of his turquoise pendant, Gaul became confident he could defeat him in his own land. He mounted his unicorn, Thor, and rode through the night to join Khrom.

At first light Jasmine rallied her Kreigg Army. When she reached the frontier, her eyes beheld the image of a massive beast blocking her path. The Kreigg Army froze in terror, refusing to advance.

"Ambassador, speak to them. Tell them what they see is only is only an illusion," Jasmine said.

189

"Our eyes do not see the same as yours, My Queen. We believe the creature to be real."

"Manchu, ride through the creature!" Jasmine commanded.

To Manchu, the creature appeared to be little more than a cloud of mist, which vaguely resembled a giant snake with wings. Yet he saw the fear in the Kreigg and felt a bit hesitant. Manchu felt the droplets of mist against his face as he penetrated the creature. The Kreigg watched in horror. To their eyes the beast had swallowed the young knight.

Suddenly, Manchu faced a real threat. A Troblin arrow nearly struck his head and several Kreigg loyal to Raggnor advanced toward him. He turned his horse and rode back through the mist to rejoin Jasmine.

"Our enemy awaits us on the other side of the illusion," Manchu said.

Khrom and Jal rode to join Jasmine.

"Why does your army not cross the frontier?" Khrom asked.

Jasmine pointed to the faded image.

"The Kreigg believe the illusion to be real and fear they will be devoured if they try to pass."

Suddenly, with a wave of his staff the Sorcerer Gaul changed the image of the serpent bird to one of himself. He spoke to the Kreigg in their language. "Soldiers, the time has come to retake your land. Follow your queen to victory."

Manchu saw Gaul riding his unicorn, Thor. He was overjoyed at the sight of his fully recovered friend.

Jasmine pointed her sword forward. The Kreigg surged across the frontier. The Troblin fled to the fortress while Raggnor's Kreigg joined forces with their brothers. Khrom's army followed Jasmine's into the foul smelling realm. A group of Troblin archers tried to stop the advance from behind a wall of stone at a bend in the road. The archers of Vall took aim at the defenders, while their Kreigg allies charged. Jasmine heard the sounds of battle as large Kreigg axes hacked the helpless Troblin.

Freeya felt the power of Kee as she flew above the morning mist. She looked over her shoulder to see his three sisters flying in tandem behind them. When the mist cleared, her eyes beheld the armies of her sister and future husband. "The prophecy has come to pass," she whispered to Kee.

Raggnor continued to receive reports of one disaster after another. One of the guards from his mine barely escaped to tell him the Troblin had taken control of the amber for their own. Raggnor knew if the Troblin were victorious they would have little need of him and would destroy him. He knew as well Prince Khrom would grant him no mercy and would most likely have him hanged. His only chance for survival was to escape into exile. He trod quickly through the hidden passage, to the hiding place of his dragon and waited for the cover of combat to mask his escape.

The Troblin archers waited beneath an outcropping above the entrance to Raggnor's fortress. From this place they planned to hold off the Kreigg and the Army of Vall. The Troblin Envoy had failed to mention to Raggnor his Emperor's true intentions were more than mere amber. He wished to conquer all the surface lands and make them part of his empire.

Jasmine's Kreigg army approached the massive fortress. An arrow struck one. Then a volley felled several more.

"Take cover!" Jasmine screamed.

The archers of Vall responded with a volley. Their arrows struck the stone ledge protecting the Troblin. Jasmine remembered the stables of the dragons and the intercepting tunnel which connected the stables to the outcropping above the entrance. She signaled for Freeya to hover over her. Kee held Freeya in place, while Jasmine shouted her request.

"I need your dragons to lift my army to the stables above the Troblin!"

"We will assist you!" responded Freeya.

Kee spoke to his sisters.

The Kreigg created large carriers to take them to the plateau above the Troblin. Manchu joined the Kreigg soldiers in the first carrier. They lashed ropes to each corner of the carrier then merged the ropes together over the center.

A female dragon swooped over the carrier and snared the ropes with her talons. Manchu nearly fell to his knees when the dragon made contact. He felt the down draft of powerful wings when she ascended, with himself and the Kreigg in tow. He closed his eyes for a moment, knowing if the dragon released too soon, he would be dashed onto the stone surface below.

The Troblin commander recognized the threat and sent archers to the plateau. Freeya saw the Troblins emerge from the tunnel. Kee read her thoughts and unleashed a blast of flames. The Troblin archers screamed and perished in the inferno. Manchu waited until nearly two hundred Kreigg had been ferried into position. He led the charge into the dark tunnel. Jasmine saw him briefly as her army took control of the outcropping.

Raggnor's opportunity for escape had arrived. He mounted his remaining dragon with his loyal subject, General Hatin. The dragon lifted from the mountain.

The Sorcerer Gaul was aware of Raggnor's escape. In his right hand he held his powerful turquoise pendent and prepared to destroy Ragnor's dragon. Gaul hesitated for a moment. He did not wish to destroy his brother. *We share a common bond. We are both Sons of the God Odin. Perhaps exile and banishment from his kingdom is a just punishment,* he thought.

Raggnor's dragon flew due west beyond the forest and mountains. For the first time in his life, Raggnor wept. He knew he could never return to this land he had ruled for so many centuries. General Hatin guided the dragon over the froth of the waves of the Sea of Infinity. Their destination being a large island peopled by a race called the Britons. In the days to come Raggnor endeavored to change his ways and took the name Merlin.

Nogard

Chapter 39   The Troblin War

Jasmine watched the gates to the fortress swing open.

"The Troblin flee before us. Only a few remain in the tunnels below!" Manchu shouted.

"What of Raggnor?"

"Fear not, Queen Jasmine; he is in exile and banished from these lands for all time," the Sorcerer Gaul responded.

The surviving Troblin abandoned the mine and retreated through the labyrinth below to join with their Emperor's army. The Troblin Ambassador spoke to his general of their defeat. A decision was reached to tunnel through the surface within a massive cavern some distance from the fortress.

Jasmine and her father surveyed Raggnor's former chamber. Jal walked through the evil sorcerer's den of alchemy. He saw lizards, bats and serpents being held in many cages. Shelves filled with exotic ingredients to make potions of evil lined an entire wall. Jal sensed a presence behind him. He turned quickly.

"This room must be cleansed of its evil purpose!" said the Sorcerer Gaul in a stern voice. He waved his hand. The cages sprung open releasing all the creatures within. "Jal, take your daughter from this room!" When he felt they were safe he held his necklace of power. The turquoise pendant glowed. The room exploded with a force that rocked the mountain. Gaul emerged shaken and covered with dust from the rubble. He looked at Jasmine.

"I fear I have made a bit of a mess, Your Majesty. I must return to my realm to recover."

The dragons returned to the stables of their own free will. The Kreigg and the dragons had become friends and allies. Khrom watched the Black Dragon circle the fortress and land on the far end of the plateau. Freeya dismounted Kee and ran across the stone expanse. Khrom met her in the middle of the plateau. They embraced in front of the dragons.

"Freeya, it is over! We have won!"

"We are victorious, Khrom," spoke Freeya with a cautious tone. She felt confident of Raggnor's defeat, but the Troblin could be another matter. The dragons were exhausted. Kee closed his eyes and began to slumber.

"We should find a safe chamber, my love," Freeya said. "The dragons can be dangerous in their sleep."

Freeya spoke from experience. She knew Kee moved in his sleep and once released a small snippet of flames before awakening. Freeya held Khrom's hand. They descended into the bowels of the fortress to find a place of privacy. They discovered a beautiful room with a facing of amber. A shaft ascended to the surface allowing an abundance of clean moist air to ventilate the chamber. Within the center of the chamber resided a large round bed.

"This must be the place where Raggnor took women after he cast a spell upon them," Khrom said.

Freeya kissed Khrom then backed away. She was repulsed at the thought of the evil sorcerer taking her in this very room. Suddenly, Freeya felt the room casting an erotic power over her. She began to laugh. Her hands grasped Khrom's.

"Join with me, King of Vall," Freeya said in a beckoning tone.

The Kreigg and the soldiers of Vall celebrated their victory over Raggnor and the Troblin. Jal stood beside his daughter in the fading sunlight.

"You look worried, Father. Are you not pleased with our victory?"

Jal brushed his hand against Jasmine's cheek. "I fear the Troblin have not given up. We must remain vigilant. Where is your sister?"

"She was last seen with her future husband."

"Oh!"

Jal saw a look of sadness in his daughter's eyes.

"Father, I miss Joran," Jasmine said sadly. "He will always be part of me."

Jal held his daughter.

"Jasmine!" Manchu yelled, "I have found a clean pool! Come join me."

"Jasmine, join your young man," Jal said.

From deep within the recesses of the earth Troblin handlers brought forth a pair of Grubmaw—giant worm-like creatures with massive teeth used for grinding through solid stone. Under the direction of their handlers the beasts began to grind and tunnel their way to the base of the cavern above. The creatures worked as a team. When one became exhausted it would pull back and the other would take its place.

While Khrom slept, Freeya heard an eerie grinding sound.

"Khrom, awaken," whispered a frightened Freeya. "Do you hear the sounds?"

"I hear nothing, Freeya. Come close to me."

One Grubmaw pierced the surface. When it backed from the tunnel an avalanche of small stones rattled down the sides of the new passage. Khrom heard the sounds of thousands of feet climbing into the cavern. He fell from the round bed.

"Put on your armor, Khrom!" shouted Freeya. "The Troblin are breaking through." Within moments both Freeya and Khrom where dressed for battle and ascending to the surface.

"I must alert my army!" Khrom said.

"I go to warn my sister!" Freeya said.

"Jasmine, Jasmine!" Freeya screamed, as she ran into the blackness. Jasmine pushed Manchu's arm from her shoulder. She heard her sister screaming for her in the night. Freeya saw the form of her sister standing before her.

"Freeya, why do you cry out my name?"

"The Troblin are breaking through. Khrom and I heard them from below."

Jal had heard Freeya's cries. He rushed to be with her and his daughter.

"General, the Troblin are breaking through! Khrom and I heard them. Khrom needs your help!" Freeya said in an excitable tone.

The Kreigg Ambassador rushed to Freeya when he heard the words *'the Troblin are breaking through.'*

"Freeya, where are the Troblin?"

"I know not, Ambassador."

"Where were you and Khrom when you heard them?"

"We were in a chamber covered with amber."

"I know this chamber," the Ambassador said. "The sounds—were they from near or far?"

"They were some distance." Freeya thought for a moment. She placed herself in the room of amber. She pointed to the west. "From this room, the sounds came from this direction."

The Ambassador paused for a few moments, then turned to his guards and signaled for them to awaken the Kreigg army.

"Our enemy masses at the cavern of Sybradine. We will meet them on the plain where they are most vulnerable. Do you agree, General?"

"Yes, Ambassador," Jal responded. "I am glad we have become allies."

"Jasmine, I must join my knights," Jal said.

Jal was pleased when he saw the brightness of a full moon. *It is far easier to slay one's enemy when they are visible,* he thought. He saw the Kreigg soldiers being awakened by the Ambassador's guards.

"Jal, come quickly. We must sound an alarm to alert our men," Khrom said.

"No, Khrom. We must awaken our men without sounding an alarm. We do not want to warn our enemy. The Troblin think they can catch us sleeping. We will surprise them on the plain."

𝕹ogard

Chapter 40   𝕻eladine

Within a short time both Khrom and Jasmine's armies where roused. Khrom, with General Jal by his side, led the column. Khrom saw Jasmine and her Kreigg army marching to his left. Her column appeared as an army of giant shadows moving steadily forward over the moonlit terrain. He heard the muffled sounds of his knights' horses treading over the short tufts of grass. Turning, he saw the glint of lunar light reflecting from his soldier's armor.

"Can we defeat them, Jal?" Khrom asked.

"Of this I am not certain. I know we must try. If we slay enough of them perhaps the rest will flee."

From behind the column a chorus of howls drifted across the plain.

"Our ally follows us. General, I am confident of victory."

The Troblin quickly secured the cavern of Sybradine and the land around its mouth. Thousands of Troblin foot soldiers and archers formed their ranks. Though they were only half the size of men and less when facing the Kreigg, their strength lie in their vast numbers. Over nine thousand of the horrific creatures began their march across the plain to take the fortress. Seven thousand Troblin soldiers where armed with spears and swords, backed by two thousand archers. The vastness of their army resembled a horde of locust. The Troblin commanders planned a two pronged attack. While the main army would assault the fortress from the outside, a thousand additional soldiers would tunnel through the Kreigg barricade and attack from within.

Jasmine saw a line of ridges rising in the plain before her.

"This is a good place to fight, My Queen," the ambassador said.

"I agree, Ambassador. Signal Prince Khrom."

Jal saw a torch waving from atop the ridge to his left.

"Our allies wish to make a stand from this place, Khrom."

"Deploy our force, General."

The knights spread out to form a single line of three hundred horses and men behind the ridgeline. The archers and foot soldiers took their position atop the ridge. The Kreigg army formed two lines to the left of the Army of Vall. They waited in silence for the approach of the closing Troblin.

The Troblin moved forward at a steady pace. Their general did not care for the brightness of the moon, which exposed his army on the open plain. He saw the ridges before him that folded the flat plain. He made a decision to send forth a thousand of his soldiers to secure the high ground.

Jal and Khrom peered across the moonlit field. They saw a wave of horrid creatures rushing towards them.

"This Troblin general is no fool, Khrom," Jal said watching the advancing horde. "He seeks to take the high ground before committing his main force."

"We shall deny him and slay his vanguard," Khrom responded defiantly. "General, prepare our knights for battle."

At the top of the ridge Jal halted the advance by pointing his lance skyward. He saw the swarm of Troblin nearing the ridge. To his left he saw the Kreigg descending into battle. Jal lowered his lance. The Knights of Vall descended the ridge as a single force. He pointed his lance forward. The plain shook from the pounding hooves of the large warhorses. The Troblin where caught by surprise. They had never seen horses. Many thought the knights and their horses to be a single beast. Jal aimed his lance and sliced through two of his enemy. He dropped his lance and drew his sword.

Manchu led five hundred Kreigg into the fray with their large double edged axes. Every blow of a Kreigg axe severed a Troblin in two. Manchu's Mongol sword felt little resistance when it took Troblin heads. He watched his panic stricken enemy flee across the plain. A mere handful of the soldiers of the Underworld escaped to their main force. Manchu and Jal halted their armies and retreated to the ridges. For a moment they paused when they passed on the plain of Peladine.

"Manchu, your Kreigg fight well! Where is my daughter?" Jal asked.

"The Kreigg protect her on the ridge. She sends me to lead the battle!"

Jal smiled and led his knights to the high ground.

The Troblin general saw the defeat and rout of his first wave. He would not be surprised so easily again. He summoned his commanders to council in the cavern of Sybradine. He planned to take the ridge with a massive assault using both soldiers and archers. His soldiers would advance, then retreat when the knights charged. The Troblin archers would strike when the knights and Kreigg were lured into the open plain.

Jal surveyed his knights. His losses were light. Two of his knights had been slain and five of his horses could not continue. His enemy's bodies littered the ground before him, his nostrils filled with the odor of their dead.

Khrom heard the loud beating of drums and saw the Troblin advancing at a deliberate pace. He witnessed a huge cloud beginning to pass between the moon and the plain. He knew his Kreigg allies could not see well in the darkness.

Jal watched the Troblin advance. Many of the soldiers he observed where carrying shields and long spears. When he made out over a thousand archers, he knew the Troblin general's plan.

"They plan to draw us into the open and slay us with their archers!" Jal said.

"Do you have a counter plan, General?"

"Yes. I will need the Kreigg to stop their advance while my knights attack their archers. I must speak with my daughter."

Jal rode quickly across the ridge line to council with Jasmine and Manchu. He returned to lead his knights.

The Troblin continued their slow advance. Suddenly, several thousand of their soldiers surged toward the ridge.

The foot soldiers of Vall joined with the Kreigg to advance against the Troblin. The battle was joined at the base of the ridge. Though they were severely outnumbered, the Kreigg and foot soldiers of Vall held their ground. The Troblin commander waited for the knights to commit themselves.

Jal's knights rode two abreast to the right of the Troblin army in a flanking maneuver. Jal pointed his sword forward. Warhorses smashed into the shields and spears of the Troblin soldiers defending their archers. Chaos ran through the Troblin ranks. A handfull of their archers directed a volley at the charging knights. Their position began to crumble.

Jal saw a young knight beside him being struck by two arrows. A group of Troblin soldiers drove their spears into a horse and slew the knight when he fell. Jal felt his horse breaking through. His knights waded through the Troblin archers and slew them without hesitation. Once the threat of the archers had been eliminated Jal directed his knights to attack the Troblin at the ridge line.

Khrom and Captain Eric fought alongside Manchu. Their arms grew weary from the whaling of their swords. The Troblin panicked and bolted from the battle when they heard the sounds of horses behind them. Jal did not pursue his fleeing enemy. He rode once more to the top of the ridge to be with Prince Khrom.

The Troblin opened their second front. While the main force of Vall and the Kreigg fought on the plain less than a hundred guards remained to defend the fortress. A thousand Troblin followed a Grubmaw through a tunnel leading to the amber mine beneath the fortress.

The massive worm-like beast burrowed and chewed its way through the Kreigg barrier. When the beast's head broke through, three Kreigg guards tried to slay it. The huge creature opened its massive maw. Twenty tentacles thrust forward to seize its victims. The screaming guards were pulled into its mouth and grinding teeth.

Freeya heard screams of horror followed by the sounds of combat when the Troblin rushed through the breach. She knew the Kreigg could not hold the Troblin for long. She awakened Kee and his sisters. She knew the dragons where not accustomed to flying in the darkness. Kee spoke to his sisters in their language. Freeya's eyes would be his. She would direct his flight and his sisters would follow. The Kreigg handlers quickly placed a row of torches at the edge of the precipice. Freeya held tightly to Kee's neck. He lumbered forward toward the row of torches, his massive wings pushing against the night air. Freeya felt the rapid descent when Kee plummeted from the cliff face. She sighed when the descent slowed and Kee ascended through the clouds, into the realm of moonlight.

A massive cloud shielded the light of the moon from the plain. The Troblin regrouped from their disaster. The dark sky served their purpose well and the Troblin commander knew with their superb night vision they had the advantage over the Army of Vall and the Kreigg were nearly blind in the darkness. The Troblin moved their remaining archers within range of the ridges. The archers aimed their first volley at the Kreigg. A thousand arrows flew as deadly birds of prey in the blackened sky. They struck the Kreigg soldiers defending the ridge. A hundred were slain and more where wounded. A wave of Troblin assaulted the Kreigg position.

The Troblin archers turned to aim their second volley into the army of Vall. Sixteen horses and twelve knights where felled.

"Captain, hold the ridge as long as you can," Khrom shouted. "We cannot let our horses fall into our enemy's hands."

Khrom embraced the man who had been his father for the better part of his life. He retreated with General Jal and his knights to Jasmine's position.

Captain Eric surveyed his position. His force had been reduced to eighty-six soldiers and less than seventy archers. He saw thousands of charging Troblin. He made a decision to die fighting. There could be no retreat. His archers aimed at the dark forms of their enemy and released their arrows. For a brief moment a hole formed in the attackers' ranks. The gap closed quickly as the Troblin continued forward. Eric drew his sword. His archers sent forth a second volley. Eric watched the Troblin slowing when they climbed over the bodies of their dead.

Kee felt the warm rays of the early morning sun being absorbed into his dark skin. The clouds dissipated revealing the desperate battle below. He ignited his internal furnace.

Captain Eric was surprised to see the Troblin halt their advance turn and flee in panic. He felt the rays of the new sun on his back and saw the shadow of the dragon fall upon the plain.

Kee flew to the mouth of the cavern. He opened his maw and a massive blast of flames erupted from deep within. Freeya closed her eyes and turned her head. She held Kee's neck tightly when the recoil repelled the two of them to the far side of the plain. The flames feasted on the Troblin. Their horrid screams filled the dawn. Within moments the proud Army of the Underworld had been reduced to ashes.

Captain Eric and his men retreated to the opposite side of the ridge to avoid the fire storm on the plain. He heard the sounds of combat. The Kreigg's vision had returned with the light of the new day. They soon slew the remaining Troblin.

Kee hovered over Jasmine and Manchu.

"Jasmine, the Troblin are invading the fortress from within!" Freeya yelled.

The Troblin general peered from the mouth of the cavern of Sybradine. His army had been reduced to a shadow of its former self. He knew his army attacking the fortress from within could not go beyond its walls. He sent orders for his soldiers to retreat from the Kreigg fortress and hold the amber mine. The Troblin Ambassador returned to his Emperor for instructions.

While the army of Vall and the Kreigg regrouped, the Troblin general hurried through the labyrinth of tunnels to the fortress. He did not wish to lose any more of his soldiers in a war he felt could not be won.

Kee flew over the top of the fortress. Freeya saw the Trioblin retreating into the tunnels. When Jasmine approached the fortress she saw the Troblin General and two of his aides standing in front of the entrance. The general spoke in the tongue of the Underworld.

"What does he say, Ambassador?"

"He wishes a truce. His soldiers have withdrawn to the amber mine. His Ambassador speaks to their Emperor. He will return with a plan for peace."

Khrom joined Jasmine.

"The Troblin wish to stop fighting. They have retreated to the mine."

"Can they be trusted, Jasmine?"

"I believe they can. The Troblin fear our dragons. I am sending a hundred Kreigg to secure the fortress."

The Kreigg moved cautiously through the upper levels of the fortress and slowly descended into its bowels. They found the bodies of the courageous guards who died in defense of their home. The Troblin had taken their dead into the Underworld. They halted their advance near the entrance to the mine of amber.

Jasmine's army and the army of Vall entered the fortress. Kee circled the plateau. When he felt assured the Troblin were gone, his massive wings slowed his descent. Freeya dismounted to be with Khrom. She clasped his hand and led him to a secluded pool to cleanse the battle from his body.

Jasmine conferred with the Kreigg ambassador. "How important is the amber mine to the Kreigg?" she asked.

"We have no need of amber, Majesty. Our needs are simple. We desire food, shelter and the freedom you have given us."

"Do you agree to give the mine to the Troblin in return for peace?"

"Yes!"

Nogard

Chapter 41   Emperor of the Underworld

The truce held as the Kreigg cleansed their fortress. On the third day a loud beating of drums rose from the mine beneath the fortress. A Troblin envoy climbed the stairs to Jasmine's chamber escorted by two Kreigg and her ambassador. The envoy spoke to Jasmine. She did not understand his words, but she knew his message to be of great importance. She thought he said "Emperor." Jasmine turned to her ambassador.

"The Emperor of the Underworld is coming tomorrow evening. He wishes to make peace and see your dragons."

"Tell him I wish for peace and he may see my dragons."

The ambassador spoke with the Troblin envoy, and then turned to his queen.

"He thanks you, and will convey your message."

"Manchu, find my advisers!" Jasmine commanded, "I must council with them before I meet with the Emperor."

Manchu found Jal and Captain Eric and asked them to join Jasmine. He found his brother and Freeya on the plateau. He spoke to Khrom while Freeya stroked Kee's massive head. They all met in the hall of the Kreigg to discuss strategy. Jasmine looked into the eyes of her friends and allies.

"To be a queen is not an easy task. I have sent for you to ask for your advice in a crucial matter. Tomorrow I meet with the Troblin emperor to discuss peace terms. He wishes to see our dragons."

"I do not trust him. He was once an ally of Raggnor," Khrom said.

"I agree with Khrom," Manchu said. "He wants the dragons for his own!"

Freeya spoke in a calmer tone.

"This war must end. We cannot slay all the Troblin—there are too many of them. Let us give the emperor a show of strength."

"Freeya speaks with wisdom," Jasmine said. "The dragons must be moved to another mountain. Captain, General, I need your help to make our army appear even more powerful than it is. Ambassador, prepare the Kreigg army. The Emperor must think we are a formidable force. I thank you for your council. I release you now to perform your important task."

Khrom held Freeya's hand as they departed the chamber.

"You are not only beautiful, you are wise beyond your years."

"I know, and I have a handsome prince who loves me."

The Troblin emperor rose from his throne to begin his journey to the surface world. He was far greater in size than his subjects, more the size of a man than that of a Troblin. He wore a crown fitted with stones of amber to symbolize his wealth. His robe was made from a type of silk—from worms that thrived on fungi. His red eyes peered into a pool, which revealed his reflection. Though a human would be repulsed by his appearance, the females of his kind worshiped him and thought him to be quite handsome.

He climbed on to the back of his grubmaw beside its handler. The giant creature moved effortlessly through the labyrinth of tunnels and passages. He passed underground caverns being cultivated with mushrooms and other fungi by the Trolls. Nearing the surface he saw many soldiers bowing to him as he passed. His journey was long and tiresome. The grubmaw was forced to make many switchbacks in its ascent. The Emperor was devastated by the loss of so many of his soldiers. He dare not risk more of his army, who he needed to keep the Trolls and other beings of his world from revolting. He saw a flight of bats descending from a cave leading to the surface. The Emperor felt a kinship with the flying mammals and believed they shared a common ancestor.

Freeya directed Kee and his sisters to a nearby mountain. She would spend the night with the dragons.

The two armies worked together in preparation for their show of force. The knights cleansed their horses and polished their armor. The foot soldiers and Kreigg cleaned their weapons. As part of the ruse Manchu tied large branches behind two horses to create a massive cloud of dust. The Kreigg erected two large structures and covered them with mounds of hay and pitch. The parade route was established.

Jasmine awoke with the new dawn. She placed her armor over a clean tunic and placed her crown upon her head. Khrom and the Kreigg ambassador entered her chamber.

"Do you approve of my dress, Ambassador?"

"Yes, it is fitting to appear as a *warrior queen!*"

"Are we ready, Khrom?"

"Yes, Queen Jasmine!"

The emperor met with his general at the entrance to the amber mine. He needed to adjust his body to the thin air. The general ordered one of his soldiers to bring a sample of amber to his ruler. The Emperor touched the precious stone and admired its red translucent hue. It was midafternoon when a Kreigg guard entered Jasmine's chamber and spoke with her ambassador.

"The emperor has arrived," said the Ambassador. "He wishes for me to escort him at this time. With your permission, I shall bring him to your chamber?"

Jasmine smiled and nodded her head.

The ambassador descended the ramp leading to the mine. He faced many Troblin at its entrance. He bowed to the Troblin deity. Then he presented him with a special pair of glasses to help him see in sunlight. With his new envoy, the emperor followed the ambassador. They ascended the ramp, and climbed the stairs to Queen Jasmine's chamber. The emperor coughed when his lungs became clogged with pollen. The ambassador held the door open to Jasmine's chamber.

"Your Highness, I present to you the Emperor of the Underworld."

At first glance both the emperor and the queen were revolted by the other's appearance. Jasmine spoke to the emperor while her ambassador translated her words.

"Welcome to my kingdom, Great Emperor. I thank you for

coming. I thank you for your gesture of peace. I seek peace as well."

The envoy translated his emperor's words to the ambassador, who in turn spoke to Jasmine.

"The emperor thanks you, and wishes to know if you are ready to begin talks."

"Ask the emperor to join me on the plateau. I wish to show him my dragons and army before we speak of terms of peace."

Though the emperor did not wish to be exposed to sunlight, he had an overwhelming desire to witness the dragons. Jasmine led the emperor to a special viewing stand that partially blocked the afternoon sun. The Kreigg ambassador instructed the emperor on the use of the special glasses. The glasses where made from bone. Tiny slits cut into the bone allowed only a fraction of sunlight to enter the wearer's eyes. After a few moments the emperor's eyes adjusted enabling him to see the parade being held in his honor.

Jal led two hundred of his knights past the fortress. The sun reflected off their polished armor. A thousand Kreigg soldiers marched behind the knights. Suddenly, three female dragons dived from the sky to fly over the heads of the marching Kreigg. When the last of the Kreigg had passed, a giant shadow emerged. The emperor felt a sense of terror when the Black Dragon closed with one of the structures.

Kee opened his maw to release a massive ball of fire. The structure burst into flames, sending a blast of heat into the reviewing stand. The startled emperor turned to the wall and covered his face with his robe.

"Ambassador, tell the emperor I am sorry. I did not think the flames would be so intense."

While the confusion lasted on the reviewing stand, the knights realigned themselves to march once more over the parade route.

The Emperor recovered from his initial shock. He had heard of the awesome power of the Black Dragon, now he had experienced it for his own. He no longer desired to conquer the surface lands.

The emperor's envoy spoke to the ambassador. "My master accepts your queen's apology. He wishes only for peace between our realms."

The knights marched once more in front of the fortress. The ruse had been successful. Not only did the emperor fear the dragons, he believed Queen Jasmine's army was a formidable force. When Kee's shadow once more appeared the envoy spoke. "My emperor wishes to return to his realm. He asked me to complete the terms for peace."

Jasmine and the ambassador escorted the emperor to the mine. Jasmine was in awe of the huge worm like creature awaiting the emperor. She watched as the Ruler of the Underworld climbed on to his grubmaw to begin his descent into his subterranean realm.

The Kreigg ambassador spoke to the Troblin envoy once the emperor had departed.

"What happened to the ambassador of your realm?"

"My emperor had him killed and fed to his grubmaw when he told of the defeat of his army."

"Oh! What does your emperor want in return for peace?"

"He asks that you do not invade his realm and he wishes control of the amber mine. What are your queen's terms?"

"You may tell your emperor we give the mine to him as a gift. We will not invade his realm as long as he does not threaten ours."

"Agreed. We accept your terms."

A set of runes recorded in stone the agreements in the language of the Kreigg and the Troblin was placed on the border of the Underworld and the surface lands. The Troblin sealed the mine from the surface world. Though he thought they could never be allies, the ambassador was pleased. The Troblin war was no more.

Nogard

Chapter 42 　 Dilemma of the Dragons

Khrom's army returned to Vall. Some of the former villagers of Lund began the process of rebuilding their homes and making preparations for a spring planting. Jasmine had ordered a hundred Kreigg soldiers to assist in the reconstruction of Nevau. Freeya and Khrom stayed with Jasmine and her father for the better part of a month to help govern the Kreigg until the ambassador would become their king. They rode to Peladine. Khrom dismounted and pulled a tuft of grass free from the soil.

"Ambassador, I have been told of a type of wheat that could flourish in this place. With help from my farmers, I am sure the Kreigg could raise more than enough wheat to meet their needs."

"Yes, we shall farm this plain in the spring. I thank you for your council, Prince Khrom," said the ambassador, as he pictured a vast field of wheat.

A cold damp wind blew over the short grass of the plain of Peladine. "Let us leave this place," Jasmine said.

Upon their return to the fortress she spoke to the ambassador. "I wish to know the language of the Kreigg. Will you teach me?"

"With pleasure, My Queen."

The dragons returned to their stables above the fortress. Jasmine spoke to her sister of her dilemma.

"Freeya, I owe much to your dragon and his sisters, but we are unable to feed them and ourselves in the coming winter."

"I will travel to the Sorcerer Gaul and ask for his advice," Freeya said.

Freeya rode past the ruins of Nevau. She saw villagers who were once held hostage by the Kreigg working with their former adversaries to rebuild the castle of Nevau. She saw the blood stained waters of the streams being cleansed by bubbling springs. They had traveled but a short time when Kee's shadow crossed the road. Khrom looked into the sky to see the massive Black Dragon with a bullock in his grasp.

They made camp in a meadow halfway between Nevau and Vall. Wisp of snow hissed in the flames of their campfire.

"Winter will soon be upon us, Princess."

"Do we have enough food to feed our people?"

Khrom gave a blank stare. "I will ask my mother when we return."

Princess Freeya and her prince spent the night huddled together beneath a wool blanket, while the winter wind howled through the branches of the naked elms.

It was mid morning when they crossed into Gaul's Realm. They rode past the stream and cottages, which had been Khrom's home for the majority of his life. The wood and meadow still teemed with exotic creatures. For a time they were joined by the unicorns Thor and Odin. Freeya rode past the now abandoned village, which had served as a place of sanctuary for so many of her people. The sorcerer met them at the entrance to his castle.

"Welcome my friends. I am pleased of your victories over Raggnor and the Troblin." He saw a look of concern in Freeya's eyes. "I know the reason you have come. The dragons were your greatest allies and now that the wars are over you can no longer afford to take care of them."

"This is true, Sorcerer," spoke Freeya.

"On the day of the shortest time of the sun, the cave of lights will open to Nogard, the Realm of the Dragons. The three females will be able to pass into their realm."

"What of Kee, Sorcerer?"

"The Black Dragon must remain behind. I fear we will have need of him in the coming days."

"Where can they live at this time?" Freeya asked.

"Come into my castle, I shall show you a place on the map I have drawn."

Upon entering the passage to the castle Freeya saw the map fastened to the wall. The Sorcerer Gaul pointed to a valley to the south of his realm.

"This is the valley of the swine. Wild boars live here in great abundance. There are far too many of them. Their constant rooting has destroyed much of my forest. The dragons would be doing me a favor if they culled them for a couple of months."

Freeya surprised the sorcerer with a kiss.

"Thank you, Sorcerer! I will guide Kee and his sisters to this place. Khrom you will meet me here and bring my horse."

Khrom nodded his head in agreement. Once more he had become Freeya's servant and bowed to her whim. They spent the night in Gaul's castle. While Khrom slept, the sorcerer spoke to Freeya of his plans for the dragons.

Freeya awoke at dawn. She wished to return to Kee as soon as possible. As she rode she heard the sounds of recovery filling the morning air. Khrom heard hammers striking stones in the quarry to be used in the reconstruction of Nevau. They saw a crew of Kreigg filling holes and ruts, which littered the earthen road.

Jasmine awaited Freeya's return at the former frontier.

"Jasmine, I have spoken with the sorcerer."

"What did he say?"

"The dragons are to be relocated."

"Where will they go?"

"First they will go to the valley of the swine. There will be more than enough wild boar to feed them until the shortest day. On this day Kee's sisters will pass through the cave of lights to their realm."

"What of Kee?"

"The sorcerer said Kee must remain behind. He said we will have need of him in the future. I know not where he will stay when his sisters are gone."

Khrom rode behind the sisters to the fortress. Jasmine spoke to a Kreigg who took their horses to a newly constructed stable.

"Jasmine, you spoke to him in his tongue."

"Yes, the ambassador is a good instructor."

Nogard

Chapter 43   Valley of the Swine

Freeya mounted Kee in the time of the midmorning sun. Her thoughts revealed to the dragon his fate and that of his sisters. When they became air born she peered below to see Khrom riding his horse and leading hers on the distant journey to the southern mountains. Kee's wings beat a steady cadence. Freeya saw several flights of geese making their migratory passage to the southern realms. The wary birds gave a wide breadth to the flight of dragons. In the distance Freeya saw the jagged tips of the black mountains. It was late afternoon when they slowly closed with the giants. She saw steam enveloping the peaks from a source far below. When they passed through the heavy mist a lush green valley appeared.

Kee flew over a large plateau. He saw a deep cavern that had been carved into the cliff-face long ago. He felt the warmth of the rising thermals from the valley below. He saw a winding game trail descending to the valley. He circled to land. A herd of ibex fled to avoid the approaching dragons.

Freeya knew it would take several days for Khrom to arrive and even longer if he were to lose his way. She hoped his journey would be a safe one.

Kee spoke to his sisters and told them this would be their home until they would be returned to Nogard.

Freeya dismounted Kee and walked to the edge of the mountain's shelf. The scent of the flora mixing with the odor of the wild boars filled her nostrils. She peered over the edge to see what appeared to be a field of moving stones. She observed much of the valley to be barren, stripped of its vegetation by the rooting pigs.

While light still remained, Kee instructed his sisters in the ways of the hunt. Freeya remained behind, as the dragons spread their wings to descend into the valley. Kee spotted a large herd of swine feeding on a hillside. He lowered his talons and being the greatest raptor of all, swooped in to make his kill. The pig squealed once as the giant claws took his life. Kee flew above the plateau and dropped his meal to the surface, then returned to observe his sisters.

The first of the females nearly met disaster when she clipped her wings against a tree. The second dove over a pig and grasped a claw full of air. The third was a bit more successful than her sisters. She was able to grasp a large boar, but when she tried to lift the pig, it wiggled free. Kee swooped down to snare the wounded pig. He quickly ended the suffering of his prey and carried it to the plateau. *Tomorrow will be another day,* he thought. *I will teach them to hunt tomorrow.*

Freeya shared the swine with the dragons. She didn't care much for the burnt flavor after Kee had ignited the pig. She hoped her thoughts did not offend her friend. She spent the night on a bed of ferns.

Khrom's first day of travel had gone without incident. He felt the warmth of his campfire. His eyes closed, as his thoughts turned to his bride to be. Khrom awoke at first light; his fire had expired leaving only a few remaining embers. He fed the embers and in a short time was able to boil water for his tea. The second day of his journey to the southern mountains had begun. Khrom followed the map that the Sorcerer Gaul had sketched for him.

"The things a man will do for a woman," he spoke aloud. His horse trod over a game trail through a barren wood. Khrom emerged from the wood and started to ascend the foothills of the southern mountains. He paused when the sun was high to let the horses feed on the lush grasses, which touched their bellies. Khrom ran his fingers over the map. *I should soon see the black mountains,* he thought. Each hill appeared as the one before. He noticed the height of the grass had begun to diminish. At the summit of a steep hill he saw a herd of ibex. Beyond the ibex he made out what appeared to be black dragon's teeth rising into the sky. Khrom urged his horse and Freeya's forward.

Khrom was unaware of the danger he would soon face as he closed with the black mountains. The mountains loomed ever larger, as he ascended each hilltop. There was no sign of man during his trek. *Perhaps I am the first of my kind to be in this place,* he thought. At dusk he reached the base of the massive stone giants. A warm mist covered his face. Khrom knew the source of the mist would be in the Valley of the Swine. He made camp for the night hoping to be with Freeya on the next day.

A large carnivore watched the horses and tasted their scent. The beast felt droplets of saliva gliding over its saber teeth before falling onto its raspy tongue. The sabertoothed cat moved with stealth behind his prey. The beast which matched the size of Freeya's horse had never seen man.Within this place, all creatures feared his presence. The massive cat waited for the time of blackness to strike.

Khrom heard the nervous sounds of the horses. He grasped his sword with his right hand and thrust a large branch with his left into the fire to use as a torch. In the yellow light he saw the huge beast. Khrom screamed defiantly and charged. The cat snarled before fleeing into the night. Nothing had ever challenged it before.

Khrom inspected the horses. While his remained unscathed, Freeya's had several claw marks on its rump. He feared he had not seen the last of this killer beast. He spent the remainder of the night with his sword in his hand.

Dawn came late. The sun slowly penetrated the ever rising cloud of mist. Khrom untied his short lance from his warhorse. He prodded his mount cautiously forward. With his lance held high he followed the base of the mountain. He detected the aroma of exotic plants and saw an ever-widening breach separating the mountains. Upon entering the valley, a herd of wild pigs scattered before him. His search for Freeya had begun. In the center of the valley he saw massive hot springs, bubbling and expelling billows of steam skyward.

The sabertoothed cat waited for its prey's approach. The beast lay behind the cover of a large boulder downwind of Khrom's path. When the horses neared, the cat unleashed its retracted claws. Its muscles tensed as it prepared to spring.

Khrom heard movement an instant before the beast leaped. His horse surged forward to meet the descending sabertooth. In the collision, the cat was hurled backwards, while Khrom was thrown to the side. The old warhorse stood his ground, while Freeya's fled. The cat regained its footing and faced Khrom.

Khrom crawled to his lance and used it to stand. He planted the butt of the lance into the ground. Droplets of mist formed on the steel point of his weapon. His eyes of blue steel touched the yellow predatory eyes of the sabertoothed cat. Khrom stared into the elliptical pupils. He watched them expand into round dark pools. Neither he nor the cat wished to continue the confrontation. The sabertooth turned its head and began to stalk the pigs of the valley, its natural prey.

Khrom inspected his horse and kissed its muzzle. He spent the better part of the day searching for Freeya's horse. At the height of the sun he heard the beating of massive wings. He peered into sky and saw two green dragons carrying swine in their talons. *Freeya is near,* he thought. Khrom watched the dragons land on the side of a mountain. He knew even if Freeya were there he would be unable to scale the steep incline. He heard the approaching hoof beats of Freeya's horse.

Freeya saw Khrom and the horses far below. She was unable to descend to Khrom, and if Kee landed onto the valley floor he could not receive enough lift to fly back to the plateau. Her thoughts spoke to her friend. Kee lifted into the air and flew in a circle. Freeya stood on the edge of the precipice. She closed her eyes and felt Kee's talons close gently around her waist. Together they descended into the valley. Freeya opened her eyes when Kee began to hover. She felt the talons release and the hard surface of a large stone beneath her feet. A single tear fell from her eye, as her friend rose with the rising steam.

Khrom had witnessed Freeya being placed on to the boulder.

He rode swiftly to his future queen. His hands grasped her waist, as he helped her descend to the earth. They stared at one another for a moment before embracing.

"Khrom, did you lose your way? I expected you to come yesterday."

"It is a long journey, Princess."

Freeya saw the claw marks on her horse's rump.

"What happened to my horse?" Freeya spoke in an angry tone.

For a brief moment Khrom wished Freeya was still on the plateau.

Freeya looked at Khrom's face. She saw a bruise covering his right cheek and a cut on his brow from his encounter with the sabertooth.

"Oh Khrom, what has happened to you?"

"I will tell you on our journey. It is time to leave this place."

One of Kee's sisters flew low over their heads and dropped a freshly killed swine to provide them with food on their journey. Khrom and Freeya left the valley of the swine to begin their long trek to the Kingdom of Vall.

Nogard

Chapter 44   Preparations

Captain Eric rode to Sorcerer Gaul's Realm with a formal request from Queen Dora. As he approached, he could only hope his words would be understood. He knew his sword was his greatest attribute, not his speech. The war against Raggnor and the Troblin had taken its toll on the captain. At midday he saw the spires of the sorcerer's castle.

The sorcerer met the captain at the entrance.

"Dismount, Captain. Come join me in my hall."

"I have an important request from my queen."

Gaul detected nervousness in the captain's speech. "My dear captain, please come to my hall and drink some of my special mead. It will help the words flow from your tongue."

When they entered the hall, Gaul poured a goblet of golden mead for the captain. Eric placed his lips against the rim and felt the potent drink pass over his tongue. His words passed without hesitation.

"My queen wishes for you to perform the coronation of her son Prince Khrom and affirm him to be the rightful Ruler of the Kingdom of Vall. She also requests that you perform the wedding of her son to Princess Freeya."

"When would you like this coronation and wedding to take place? Do you have any further requests, Captain?"

"Six days from tomorrow. Yes, I have a request, Great Sorcerer."

Eric took a long drink of the mead and hesitated for a moment.

"I have loved Queen Dora for a very long time and she has grown to love me. I ask for you to marry us in a private ceremony."

The sorcerer did not speak for several moments. He closed his eyes and listened to his thoughts.

"Tell Queen Dora I shall honor her request only under these conditions. I shall marry Freeya and Khrom first. Then I will perform a joint coronation for both Princess Freeya and Prince Khrom. The Kingdoms of Nevau and Vall shall be as one. The new king and queen shall have equal power over this realm."

"Thank you, Sorcerer. I am confident my queen will honor your decision."

"Captain, I am honored you asked me to marry Dora and yourself."

"Thank you, Sorcerer."

When Eric tried to stand he faltered.

"Captain, I think you should sit awhile. Mead can be a powerful drink.

Eric spent the rest of the afternoon and night with his head lying on the table. He did not mount his horse until the next day.

Queen Dora worried about Eric. He had been gone far too long. She hoped he had conveyed her request in a proper manner. She hoped his words did not stumble from his mouth. Queen Dora would have spoken to the sorcerer herself, but protocol demanded a special envoy or friend deliver this request and she nearly always bowed to protocol. A guard knocked on her chamber's door.

"A lone rider approaches Majesty."

"Thank you, guard," the queen said.

Dora climbed to the tower. She made out the shape of a horse and rider. Her heart raced like a young girl when she recognized Eric. She hurried to her chamber to make herself more beautiful for her captain.

Eric rode swiftly to the castle. His steed slowed when it reached the bridge and halted on the cobblestones of the courtyard. He dismounted and handed the reins of his horse to a squire. His heart surged, as he rushed up the stone stairs to his queen's chamber.

Dora heard the rapping of Eric's knuckles against the oak door to her chamber.

"Who beats against my chamber door?"

"The captain of your guard, Your Majesty," responded Eric.

Queen Dora hesitated to respond and allow her captain entry. *Had it been so long ago that Captain Eric beat upon her door, to rescue her and her infant son,* she thought. She felt her hand unbolting the heavy door. Before the captain could speak she pressed her lips against his. Her lips parted, she smiled then spoke as a queen.

"Does the sorcerer agree to my request?"

"Yes, but only under his conditions."

"What conditions!"

"The sorcerer wishes to perform the wedding before the coronation. He wishes to coronate the new king and queen together. He said they should be given equal power over the Kingdoms of Vall and Nevau."

Queen Dora thought for a moment.

"The sorcerer is very wise. I agree to his decision."

Eric looked into his queen's eyes. "Dora, the sorcerer will marry us in a private ceremony."

"I love you, Captain Eric."

"I love you, My Beautiful Queen."

Eric noticed a strange silence surrounding him.

"Dora, where are the children?"

"They were playing in the courtyard with their pet. Did you not see them, when you arrived?"

"No, I did not see them there."

Sharonn and Tyree had outwitted their bodyguard and dashed across the drawbridge as he conversed with a maid. They entered the wood beyond the cleared land surrounding the castle. Sharonn breathed in the clean scent of the forest. Both she and Tyree did not like the confinement of stone which had become their new home. Tyree nearly stepped on a large hare. The rodent bolted with the wolf pup in rapid pursuit. Sharonn drew her wooden sword.

"I am Princess Jasmine and you are a Troblin."

"Yes, Sharonn, I will play the part of a Troblin."

"I am Princess Jasmine. Die, you Troblin scum!"

For a few minutes they clashed their wooden swords together. Tyree allowed Sharonn to place her sword next to his side. He closed his arms over it and fell backwards.

"You have slain me, Princess Jasmine."

"That was fun, can we do it again."

Tyree heard the wolf pup yelping as it ran towards them. He leaped to his feet and saw a huge brown beast crashing through the brush.

"Do not run Sharonn, stay perfectly still. The bear may pass us by. We cannot outrun it."

The children heard the beast roar when she stood upon her hind legs. The bear scented the air, in its search for the small wolf. Satisfied the pup was no longer a threat to her cubs, she dropped to all fours and retreated to the wood. Sharonn heard twigs snapping behind her. She turned to see her father.

"Come to me, my children. Your mother worries for you."

"Father, I was so frightened," cried Sharonn.

"You must never come here alone."

"Does this mean we can never leave the castle, Father?" asked Tyree.

"No, I am home now. I will bring you here and many other places.

Queen Dora waited in the clearing next to the wood. Sharonn ran to her mother with her toy sword still in her hand.

"Mother, Tyree and I saw a bear!"

Eric and Tyree approached Dora.

"Dora, shouldn't our daughter be taught the ways of a lady?"

"Yes, in due time. For now, let her learn the ways of a warrior. Our world is still a dangerous place."

Later that night Queen Dora began to draft invitations for the coronation and the wedding. To compound her task, Dora would serve as both the mother of the bride and the groom. She sent forth riders throughout her kingdom, and to Jasmine and her father.

With the new day the castle of Vall began a transformation from a bastion to a place of beauty. The grime and blood of war were cleansed from the stone surfaces. The tops of the spires were polished to once more reflect the light of the sun. Eric found two bullocks, which had somehow eluded the Black Dragon.

𝔑ogard

Chapter 45   Visions

In the fortress of the Kreigg, Jasmine peered from the plateau where once the dragons were stabled. She saw a lone rider coming from Vall. She sent a Kreigg guard to escort the rider to her chamber. Jasmine and her father met with the courier.

"What brings you to my kingdom?"

"I am to deliver a message from Queen Dora of Vall."

The courier handed Jasmine a rolled parchment bound by a leather string. Jasmine unbound the parchment and read its contents out loud.

> *"To Queen Jasmine, General Jal, and my son Manchu,*
> *   The three of you are cordially invited to the wedding*
> *of Princess Freeya to Prince Khrom. The coronation*
> *will follow the wedding. Please join me as soon as you*
> *are able. I need your help.*
>
> > *Thank You,*
> > *Queen Dora."*

"Father, we must leave now!"

"Jasmine, a queen must not leave her realm until it is secure. You should send for the ambassador."

Manchu met the courier in the stable.

"It is good to see a rider from Vall. What brings you to the land of the Kreigg?"

"I have delivered a message from my queen to yours."

"Have a safe journey on your return to Vall."

"Perhaps I will see you there in a few days."

Manchu pondered the courier's words. He hurried to Jasmine's chamber to read the message from Vall. He heard the ambassador and Jasmine conversing in the tongue of the Kreigg. The chamber door opened to allow the ambassador to leave. Jasmine saw Manchu standing in the hallway. She placed her arms around his waist and kissed him.

"We are going to Vall! Freeya is to marry your brother and they are to be made King and Queen over the Realms of Vall and Nevau."

"When do we leave?"

"Tomorrow. You can stay with me tonight."

A broad smile crossed Manchu's face.

The next morning Jasmine departed the fortress with her father and lover. They rode swiftly over the rebuilt road until they neared the emerging castle of Nevau. A sudden storm caused them to seek shelter.

"I see a cottage," Jal shouted.

In front of the cottage Jal saw a large wooden sign hanging from a pole, which read 'The Inn of Nevau.' The soaked trio made their way to the door of the structure. A thin man with a lantern met them.

"Welcome to my Inn. I will stable your horses. My wife will tend to your needs."

Jasmine and Manchu entered the log building while Jal and the innkeeper tended to the horses. A stout woman placed kindling into the hearth. A roaring fire quickly brought light and warmth to the structure.

"You and your wife should take off your wet clothes. I have a large blanket you can share," said the woman.

Jasmine's eyes twinkled while Manchu tried to keep from laughing. Jal entered to see his daughter's clothes hanging near the fire next to Manchu's.

"I have a blanket for you, sir," said the woman.

Manchu fell into a deep trance. His thoughts turned to his family in a distant eastern land. His thoughts became a vision. He saw his father being severed in half and his mother and sisters in chains. His mother's voice pleaded for him.

"Manchu, free us from this evil warlord! Please free us!"

He saw a crest on a shield and knew it to be the sign of Vin Po, the Southern Warlord.

The next day they rode at a steady pace, stopping only briefly to rest their horses. At dusk, Jal signaled to make camp. He planned to reach Vall on the next day.

Jasmine spoke to Manchu, "You cried in your sleep last night."

Manchu shook for a moment, "I had a vision. My father has been slain by Vin Po, the Southern Warlord. My birth mother and sisters have been taken away in chains. My mother pleaded for me to save them."

"What are you going to do? Do you wish my help?"

Tomorrow I ride to the east to find my family. Please tell Queen Dora why I cannot attend the wedding and coronation."

Manchu held Jasmine tightly. Cascades of tears flowed from their eyes.

"I must travel alone, Princess!"

That night Jasmine slept in the arms of her Mongol Warrior. In her heart she knew it would probably be the last night she would spend with him.

Freeya and Khrom huddled together by their fire. They had camped where the trail they had been traveling met with the main road to Vall.

"Add more wood to the fire, Khrom! I am cold."

"Yes, Princess!"

Khrom did not care to rise from Freeya's warmth.

"I am to be the King of Vall and my woman treats me like a servant," he mumbled.

"I heard that, Khrom," Freeya said angrily. "I am not your woman!"

"I am sorry, Freeya. I didn't mean to ...."

Khrom added kindling and a dry log to feed the flames.

"Thank you, King of Vall," Freeya said in a gentle tone. "You may join me if you wish."

At the first sign of light Khrom heard the hoof beats of a single horse on the hardened surface of the road.

"Freeya, awaken! A rider approaches!"

Khrom leaped to his feet with his sword in his hand. He did not have time to mount his horse. Suddenly he recognized the closing rider.

"Manchu!"

"Khrom!"

"Manchu, have your morning meal with us. We have much to speak of."

"Where are Jasmine and General Jal?" Freeya asked.

Freeya made tea and cooked flesh from one of the pigs the dragons had killed.

"Why do you travel alone, my brother?"

Manchu told Khrom of his vision.

"I will ride with you!" Khrom said.

"No, Khrom. I must ride alone. I am sorry I cannot attend your wedding and coronation. You and Freeya will be a just king and queen. Thank you once more. I must leave now."

Khrom held his future queen's hand and watched his brother ride to a trail leading to the distant eastern lands.

Manchu would cross many streams and ascend the Urals before reaching the broad grassy plains. He would see the Nomadic Tribesmen and their herds of wild ponies. In time, he would journey to the city of the Southern Warlord, Vin Po. Within the city he would face many dangers and find exotic things and began the search for his mother and sisters.

Freeya saw two riders approaching. She knew it had to be her sister and Jal. The riders closed rapidly.

"Freeya!"

"Jasmine!"

Jasmine rode to be with her sister. Freeya saw the tears in her eyes.

"He is gone, Freeya, and he may never return."

"I know. We spoke with him this morning."

"Freeya, I do not love him, but he has been a special friend."

"He must follow his quest, Jasmine."

"I know this, Freeya. I know this."

The four continued to Vall. As they neared the castle, villagers cheered.

"Long live King Khrom! Long live Queen Freeya!"

Captain Eric met them at the entrance to the drawbridge.

"Khrom, where is your brother?"

"He had a vision and must go on a special quest!"

"You must tell me more of this quest later."

"I will, Captain."

"Freeya, Jasmine. My queen requests the both of you stay with her. Khrom, you and the general are to stay with me until the preparations are completed."

Nogard

Chapter 46   Babadu

Queen Dora met the princesses at the summit of the stone stairs.

"Freeya, my child, I hope you do not mind I have begun making arrangements for your coronation and wedding to my son."

Freeya wished she had been consulted beforehand. Yet she knew Dora had little choice for she had been gone for a very long time. Freeya and Jasmine entered the queen's chamber.

"Your Highness, could you tell me when my wedding is to take place."

"In two days, Freeya, the Sorcerer Gaul will perform the wedding first, followed by the coronation."

"Jasmine, I wish to have you as my maid of honor. Sharonn, I wish for you to be my maid of flowers." Freeya held Dora's hands and looked deeply into her eyes. "Dora, I shall be a good wife to your son. I love him more than all things."

"I love you as a daughter, Freeya."

Dora saw the sadness in Jasmine's face.

"What is wrong, Jasmine?"

"Manchu rides to the east on a quest. He had a vision from his birth mother and sisters. He asks me to give his regrets for not attending the wedding."

The queen lowered her head for a moment. "I feared one day he would leave to return to the place of his birth. I loved him as I loved Khrom. May Odin watch over him and protect him. I wish him well on his perilous quest."

"I will be honored to be your maid, Freeya," Jasmine said.

"Can I wear a pretty dress?" Sharonn asked.

"Thank you, Jasmine. Yes, you will wear a beautiful dress, Sharonn."

"Where is Tyree?" Jasmine asked.

"He will be with our men this night."

Tyree felt special. He admired Khrom and Captain Eric, his adopted father, and to be with the great general was a special privilege.

Eric began to speak. "Khrom, your mother has taken charge of your wedding and coronation. I have arranged for a feast and entertainment. The Sorcerer Gaul will perform your wedding first, to be followed by your coronation. Tomorrow we ride to bathe in the hot springs near our former cottage."

"Queen Dora would have made a fine general," Jal said. "What part do I have, Captain?"

"Yes, she would, Jal." The captain and the general shared a hearty laugh. "General, you are to be the father of the bride."

Jal thought for a moment. He recalled Freeya as a little white haired girl playing with his daughter Jasmine.

"I thank both Queen Dora and you for this honor," Jal said humbly.

"Tonight we shall feast, drink mead and enjoy the entertainment in Vall's hall," announced Eric.

"Did the queen make these plans?"

"Oh no, I think you will enjoy the dancers, General."

Eric and Jal entered the hall together. Khrom followed holding Tyree's hand. They sat at a long table behind goblets filled to rim with mead. Khrom asked one of the servant maids to bring a cup of weak wine for Tyree.

The boy saw a man dressed in the headdress of stag. Another approached from the far end of the hall. They clashed their antlers in a mock battle. He watched a third man dressed as a hunter armed with a bow. The hunter stalked the stags and pretended to slay one. A trumpet blew to end the scene.

"I liked that play, Khrom!" Tyree's excitement ended abruptly when he saw the meal being served to him. "Eat this stag's liver, young prince. It will make you a man," spoke a woman with large bosoms. Tyree cut into the liver with his knife and with a gulp of wine placed the meat into his mouth. To his delight, it was delicious.

"Once we have eaten, I have arranged a special pleasure for your entertainment," Captain Eric said.

"I saw a wagon in the courtyard. Does it have anything to do with the entertainment?" asked Jal.

"Perhaps, General, perhaps," Eric said.

Jal had recognized symbols on the side of the wagon, which appeared to be of Nubian origin. He heard the beating of a drum. Suddenly, before him in the center of the hall two young dark women not much older than his daughter began to perform. In the background he saw a man of his age and ancestry beating a drum.

The girls walked on their hands and performed many acrobatic tricks. The man began to play a flute, as the young women began an exotic dance. Soon both women were bare to the waist. Tyree covered his eyes, only to peek through his fingers.

One of the dancers approached Jal. She recognized him as one of her countrymen. She spoke to him in the tongue of the Nubians. "You may join me if you desire, General." Jal smiled. The women paraded around the hall, clad only in their loincloths.

Khrom saw the sweat forming on the shapely beauties. He wanted to touch them, but he dare not especially in front of Jal and the captain.

The music stopped, as it had begun. The young women ran to the far side of the hall to be covered with long robes by the older man. The three performers returned to the center of the hall to take a bow. Captain Eric handed the man a small pouch of gold coins and a larger pouch filled with silver.

"They were wonderful, Captain! Where did you find them?" Jal asked.

"Actually, they found me. On my way to Gaul's Realm I saw a wagon covered with strange symbols. The driver was a dark skinned man traveling with his two daughters. He asked for directions to Vall. He told me they where entertainers from a distant land and they had been commissioned to perform for King Copen. When the man told me of the entertainment they provided, I hired them."

"Of course you did. I thank you for this special night, Captain."

Jal walked to the wagon while his companions returned to Khrom's quarters. He remembered the man vaguely. Of course they were much younger then. *The man's wife was a harlot and he was a thief. When the man tried to steal his mother's jewels his father banished him from the Kingdom of Nubia.*

The man greeted Jal in his native tongue. "Welcome Prince Jal, we shall speak after my daughters provide you with pleasure."

The young women removed Jal's armor and tunic. He looked into their beckoning eyes. For a moment he saw his wife's image and felt a twinge of guilt. His guilt dissipated with their touch. After the encounter the women bathed Jal in a wooden tub. They dried his body with a large cloth and helped him dress. Jal walked to the front of the wagon.

"What is the price for your daughter's services?"

"I ask not for gold or silver," said the man. "One day you shall return to Nubia, I wish to go with you. I wish to help you retake your Kingdom."

"Yes, it is true," Jal said. "I am in as much exile as you, my friend. I will return one day. I thank you for your offer."

"I hear things are very bad in our homeland, My Prince."

"Are you still a thief, Babadu?"

"You have a good memory, Prince. I have not practiced this craft in many years, but yes I still have the skills and I have taught my daughters the trade."

"Good, I may have need for your skills in the future." Jal hesitated for a moment before asking, "Babadu, do you have trouble with your daughters chosen occupation?"

"Not at all, their mother taught them well. She believed the art of pleasure to be an honorable profession. I loved her very deeply. She died from the plague in Constantinople. My daughters are very selective. You should be honored."

Jal nodded his head.

"Where will your travels lead you?"

"We return to our base camp near the city of Constantinople. You can find us there when you need us."

"Thank you my friend, and tell your daughters I thank them as well."

Jal passed two gold coins across Babadu's palm then walked briskly to Khrom's chamber.

Nogard

Chapter 47   A Merging of Realms

At dawn Queen Dora awakened her daughter and the two princesses. She heard the sound of large horse's hooves striking the cobblestones in the courtyard.

"Ladies, our carriage has arrived."

"Where are we going?" Freeya asked.

"We travel to the hot springs in the sorcerer's realm to cleanse ourselves. We must complete our task before the men arrive."

Freeya was the last to board. She heard the crack of a whip and felt the forward motion. The journey passed quickly as the women talked and laughed. The coach halted in front of Dora's former cottage.

While the two younger women and her daughter ran across the partially frozen ground to the hot steaming pools, Queen Dora strolled past the cottage. The cold air added a blush to her cheeks.

Freeya and Jasmine disrobed and entered the warm water beneath the spring. Sharonn followed her hero Jasmine into the inviting water. The warm water dissolved the sweat and filth from their bodies. Jasmine grasped Sharonn by her waist and held her in the air, then dropped her into the water. Sharonn popped to the surface.

"Did you enjoy that, little sister?"

"Yes, can we do it again?"

Dora stood by the spring. She disrobed revealing her mature body.

"Mother, Jasmine called me her little sister!" Sharonn yelled.

"Is that alright, Dora?" Jasmine asked.

Queen Dora smiled, then spoke. "Yes, we are all one family."

While Jasmine and her daughter played, Dora spoke to Freeya. "I thank you for coming into our lives. You will be a fine queen and wife to my son."

"Thank you, Dora."

The morning passed swiftly. The women dressed to depart Gaul's Realm. Sharonn squealed with delight when she saw the gowns the sorcerer had delivered to the coach while they bathed. Freeya read his note aloud, which had been placed on her white wedding gown.

> *Many things are possible in the Realm of Gaul. I shall be with you tomorrow.*
>
> *Sorcerer Gaul*

The coachman drove the coach toward Vall. He saw several men.

"Riders approaching, Your Highness," said the coachman.

"Close the curtains!" demanded the queen.

Freeya peeked through a corner to see Khrom riding past, with Tyree clinging to his waist. Jal and Eric rode behind.

The women remained mute until their men had passed.

"Who were the riders?" Sharonn asked.

"Your brothers, your father and Jasmine's father," Freeya said.

"I want to go with them. I want to play with Tyree in the water."

"Not this day, Sharonn," Dora said. "You are to be the maid of flowers."

Sharonn smiled. Like the rest of the women she could hardly wait to wear the gown that the sorcerer had given her.

The men soon entered the cleansing pools.

"Did you enjoy the Nubian's company, Jal?" Eric asked.

Jal smiled revealing a gold tooth in the center of his mouth. "They gave to me a pleasurable experience. I remembered the man; he was a thief. My father banned him from Nubia."

"Oh!"

The men did not stay in the water long. They wished to return to Vall before nightfall.

The women tried on their new gowns. Each took her turn looking into a large polished mirror in the queen's chamber. All of the gowns expect Freeya's sparked in many colors. Freeya twirled in her white shimmering gown.

"You are a beautiful bride, Freeya."

"Thank you Jasmine."

"Sharonn began to cry."

"Sharonn what is wrong?" her mother asked.

"I am to be maid of flowers and I have no flowers."

Queen Dora smiled and shouted to the guard on the opposite side of the door to her chamber. "Guard, find the coachman tell him to bring the flowers he picked while we were bathing."

Khrom and his party returned to Vall. The men returned to his chamber. A guard knocked on the door.

"I have a message for Captain Eric from my queen!"

"Enter and give me the message!"

Eric read the note aloud.

"Arrangements have been made for a wedding rehearsal and coronation rehearsal. Bring the men to the hall in one hour."

Eric flipped over an hour glass and watched the grains of sand recording the period of time.

"We have little time to prepare, my friends."

Only a quarter of the sand remained on the top half of the glass, when the men departed for the hall. Tyree was overcome by the aroma of baking bread and the slow roasting bullocks in the cooking pits. Khrom watched workmen hanging a massive tapestry featuring Freeya riding the Black Dragon. Below the dragon, he saw an image of himself leading his army into battle.

"Captain, I wish to have the Black Dragon to be our coat of arms."

"This shall be done, Prince Khrom."

Queen Dora entered the hall.

"Captain, I am pleased you arrived on time."

"Yes, My Queen."

Queen Dora announced her plans. "The wedding will take place in the hall in front of our honored guests. The coronation will be in the courtyard so all our people may witness the crowning of their new king and queen."

Khrom watched the women approaching. He became fixated on Freeya. Captain Eric stood in for the Sorcerer Gaul. Freeya walked beside Jal, followed by Jasmine.

While the captain preformed the mock wedding, the party heard the beating of hammers as workmen constructed a platform in the center of the courtyard.

"Once the wedding is over, Khrom, you and your bride will walk up a ramp to the platform for your coronation," Queen Dora instructed.

At the end of the rehearsal, Queen Dora clapped her hands. Servants brought wine and bread to the tables. Two minstrels entered the hall, one with a lute, the other with a flute. When the music began Dora and Eric started to dance and give the rest of the party instructions. Soon everyone joined in the dance. Sharonn and Tyree thoroughly enjoyed themselves.

"I want to marry Tyree," Sharonn said.

"Perhaps one day. Not now, my child," spoke her mother.

The party lasted well into the night. Sharonn and Tyree both fell asleep with their heads resting on a large wooden table.

"It is time to retire for the night. We have a long day tomorrow," Queen Dora said.

Freeya's lips touched Khrom's. "I will think often of you this night," Khrom said.

"Dora, when are you to wed Captain Eric?" Freeya asked after she entered the queen's chamber.

"After your coronation, when I have given my crown to you, I will no longer be bound to tradition, which only permits me to marry royalty. I will be free to marry the man I choose and I choose Sharonn's father."

Shortly after dawn, the sentry in the tower saw the Sorcerer Gaul approaching on his unicorn. The sorcerer heard the sounds of trumpets announcing his arrival as he crossed the bridge. Khrom heard the trumpets he leaped to his feet and began to splash water onto his face.

"Tyree, awaken your father. The sorcerer has arrived," Khrom said.

"Captain it is time to wake up. The sorcerer has arrived!"

The captain did not stir. The boy pulled at his adopted father to no avail. Tyree grabbed a pitcher, which he thought was filled with water. In desperation he poured the contents onto Captain Eric's face. Eric leaped to his feet then fell to the floor. He opened his eyes to see the room spinning around him. His head throbbed for a moment before it began to clear. He bellowed a loud laugh when he saw the empty pitcher lying beside him.

"What a waste of good ale. Tell me what is so important you awaken me in such a manner?"

"The Sorcerer Gaul has arrived. We must make ready to greet him," Khrom said. "I told Tyree to awaken you. Do not be angry with him."

Captain Eric held out his hands to the youth. "You did the right thing, Tyree."

While the men cleansed themselves and dressed in their uniforms, the sorcerer rode slowly around the courtyard. The peasants were amazed. Most had never seen a unicorn and even fewer had seen a sorcerer. Jasmine heard the commotion, dressed quickly and hurried to the courtyard below.

"Odin, Odin!" She ran to the unicorn and kissed his horn. Gaul placed his hand onto her head. She turned to face him.

"Welcome, Sorcerer Gaul. Forgive me. I should have addressed you first."

"It is alright, child. I know of the love you have for my unicorn."

"Thank you for coming, Great Sorcerer," spoke the voice of a beautiful woman descending the stairway. "We thank you for giving us the beautiful gowns."

"The pleasure is mine, Your Highness. I see the platform is complete."

"Yes everything is ready."

"You have done well, Dora."

"Thank you, Sorcerer."

"I must go now to meet with the future king and his party."

From the tower the sentry could see people arriving from all corners of the combined kingdoms. They came to witness the most joyous occasion of their lives. A warm sun began to dissipate the chill in the air.

The Sorcerer Gaul approached Khrom's chamber and rapped the door with his staff. Khrom greeted him and invited him in.

"Welcome to my humble home, Great Sorcerer."

"Captain Eric will be with you soon."

As he waited, the sorcerer felt something tugging on the bottom of his robe. Tyree rushed to grab the small wolf. Gaul placed his hand on the boy's head.

"I know you. You are the one called Tyree."

"Yes, Great Sorcerer."

"One day you shall be a king!"

"Thank you, Great Sorcerer."

"Forgive me, Sorcerer Gaul. I didn't expect you so soon," Captain Eric said.

"I arrived at the appointed time. I assume all is ready."

The sorcerer flipped over the hourglass.

"The wedding will begin when the last of the sand has passed."

Jal prepared to walk with Freeya through the hall to the place of the ceremony. He waited outside the queen's chamber, while Khrom and the rest of the men entered the hall. He was the first of the men to witness the radiant beauty of Freeya and her wedding party.

Khrom waited impatiently for his bride. Gaul escorted Queen Dora into the hall. Soon the invited guests filled the hall. Captain Eric embraced Khrom.

"I am full of joy for you on this day Khrom. I go now to be with your mother."

"I love you, Captain," Khrom said as a tear ran over his cheek.

"You have been a good father to me."

Captain Eric walked briskly to the head table. He passed the sorcerer and nodded his head in respect.

"Come next to me, Eric!"

"As you command, My Queen!" responded Eric.

Eric felt the hand of the woman he loved clutching his own. Four trumpets announced the arrival of Princess Freeya. Sharonn led the procession. She held a large straw basket filled with colorful mums.

"Our daughter is quite beautiful," Eric said.

"Yes she is, Eric."

Behind his little sister, Khrom saw a wondrous sight—Freeya dressed in her shimmering white gown. With her every step Khrom's heart beat faster.

Freeya clutched Jal's arm. He walked proudly with this young woman he considered to be one of his daughters. Behind Freeya walked Jasmine in her regal beauty. Many of the young soldiers turned their eyes from the bride to focus on the Nubian beauty.

Jal placed Freeya's arm onto Khrom's. Freeya knew she had completed one journey and was about to embark on another. A hush fell over the hall when the sorcerer approached. Jasmine cried when he placed his hands over the couple.

"I have come to join this couple with the blessing of my father, the God Odin."

The sorcerer placed a special potion into a goblet of wine. Both Freeya and Khrom drank from the goblet. Freeya felt a warm flush within her, as did Khrom.

The Sorcerer Gaul began to speak. "Princess Freeya, will you love this man beyond all things and care for him and all children that you shall bear for him?"

"Yes, I love Khrom above all things."

"By the power of Odin and the Norse Gods, I pronounce you husband and wife."

Khrom felt Freeya's warm lips merging with his own.... After a brief moment she parted from her new husband and embraced Jal. "I am happy for you, my daughter." Jasmine hugged her sister and kissed her cheek. Dora kissed her son and his bride.

"Hail, Prince Khrom! Hail, Princess Freeya!" shouted Captain Eric and the guests.

After a brief respite and a goblet or two of mead, the guests departed to the courtyard to join with the villagers awaiting the Coronation.

Two aristocrats stood in a tower overlooking the courtyard. One was quite portly, while the other had a slim frame. The thinner man began to speak.

"I could slay Prince Khrom from here with my bow, Balda."

"You sound like a fool, Svine. Be patient my friend, when the time is right we shall prevail. If you were to slay him now we would be hunted down and hung from the wall."

"The time has come for your coronation, Your Highness," announced the sorcerer.

Trumpets blared as Jasmine and General Jal ascended the ramp to the platform in the center of the courtyard. The crowd cheered when they saw Queen Dora being escorted by Captain Eric. Sharonn and Tyree held hands and skipped up the ramp behind their parents. Freeya took a deep breath and stepped from the hall onto the cobblestones of the courtyard. She held the arm of her new husband for support.

Khrom reveled in the sounds of trumpets and the cheering of his subjects. This would be a day he would remember for a very long time. On this day he would be made king and he had just married the most beautiful woman in all the realms.

The couple climbed the ramp to the summit of the platform and kneeled together. The sorcerer faced the young prince and princess. He touched the top of each of their heads and motioned for the crowns to be brought forth. Queen Dora removed her crown while Captain Eric held the crown once worn by Khrom's father.

The Sorcerer Gaul began the Coronation. "Princess Freeya, Prince Khrom, on this day the Kingdoms of Nevau and Vall are to be as one. Both of you are to have equal power over this new realm. You are duty bound to serve and protect your people.

Be fair and honest in your judgments. Prince Khrom, Princess Freeya, as Rulers of this Kingdom do you agree to the words I have spoken?"

"Yes, Sorcerer Gaul!" Spoke Khrom and Freeya in unison.

"By the power granted me by the God Odin, Ruler of the Asgard, I proclaim you to be the rulers of this realm!"

Queen Dora placed her crown atop Freeya's head, while Captain Eric placed the crown of Vall onto Khrom's head. The new king and queen rose to face their cheering subjects.

Khrom addressed his people. "I thank you, my countrymen. Without your help this day would have not been possible. Like my father before me, I promise to be a fair and just king. Thank you once again."

Freeya began to speak. "Our kingdoms have become one. We have defeated our enemies. We no longer pay tribute to any tyrant. Our future lies within our own hands. My king and I will serve you as you have served us."

Captain Eric held up his hands and began to shout. "Long live our new king and queen!"

The captain lowered his hands to make an announcement. "I have found two bullocks that our friend the dragon has not taken. They await us in the cooking pit. All are welcome. Please join us in our feast of celebration!"

Eric turned to the party on the platform. "Dora and I wish your presence in the tower."

While the people of Vall feasted, the party climbed the stairs to the tower. The two aristocrats bowed before their new rulers and departed.

"Guard, we must not be disturbed!" Eric commanded.

Dora felt a rush within her. She was no longer bound by the duties of a queen. She held her daughter next to her. Her eyes were drawn to her captain's. She would love this man to the time of her death and beyond.

The sorcerer stood before Dora and Eric. Both bowed before him. He touched their heads with the tips of his fingers.

"Dora, do you love Eric above all things and promise to care for him and all his children?"

"Yes, I love Eric above all things."

"Eric, do you love Dora above all things, promise to care for her and protect her and her children?"

"Yes, I love Dora above all things."

"By the power of Odin and all the Norse Gods, I pronounce you husband and wife!"

"Thank you, Sorcerer Gaul!" spoke both Dora and Eric in unison.

"You are welcome. Please visit me in the spring."

"We shall, Sorcerer!" Dora said.

"Enjoy your feast. I must return now to my realm."

Nogard

Chapter 48   Struggle in a Distant Land

The once proud Kingdom of Nubia was void, replaced by a cruel occupation. The Nubian people had become slaves. The women of Nubia were forced to be concubines for their Arab conquerers, while the men were forced to work the salt flats of the great desert.

Death was common in this unforgiving place. Cracking whips forced the Nubians to pry huge blocks of salt from the bed of the desert. They loaded the salt into carts, which were hauled by oxen to distant lands to enrich their masters.

One Nubian, an eighteen-year old youth, detested his oppressors. Malica preferred death rather than to continue living as a slave. He remembered stories of how his prince had escaped with his young daughter. *Perhaps,* he thought, *if I can escape and find Prince Jal, he will lead an army to free Nubia.* He whispered to his companions in the darkness of the cold desert night. By dawn, he and three of his comrades had rubbed stones over their skin to create sores and bleeding over their bodies. They moaned as if they were victims of the plague.

The ruse succeeded. The overseers rushed to separate the diseased men from the rest of the slaves. When Malica heard the click of the lock releasing his bond, he struck. He rapped the chain that had once bound him around his oppressor's throat. He heard the muffled cries of the overseer as the chain squeezed out his life. Within in a short time he freed his countrymen. The guards were caught by surprise. They drew their swords in an effort to stop the revolt.

"Kill them all!" Malica screamed.

A hundred Nubians surged forward to slay their overseers with their bare hands. The blood of both Nubian and Arab stained the sand and salt of the unforgiving desert.

"To the mountains, my friends!" shouted Nimba, an older man who had once served in Jal's army. "We have struck a blow for freedom this day!"

"I will not join you, Nimba," Malica said. "I journey to find Prince Jal! One day he will lead us to victory."

"I wish you success," Nimba said. "Go where you must and find our prince. When you find him, tell him of our kingdom's plight. My thoughts go with you, my son."

Malica embraced his father then began the search to find his prince. He heard his father taking charge of the Nubians.

"Take their weapons; bring our dead and wounded!"

"What of their dead?"

"Leave them for the birds of death!"

Nimba looked at the bodies of his fellow Nubians. They had slain fifteen of their enemy and lost nearly thirty of their own. *It is far better to die as a warrior than a slave,* he thought.

The Nubians made for the protection of the mountains. From a hidden stronghold they hoped to begin a resistance movement to free their Kingdom.

Malica began his quest. He hid during the heat of the day from enemy patrols. He walked across the desert during the time of starlight. On the third night, the sand beneath his feet gave way to short grasses. In the distance he saw the shapes of palm trees. "The Nile is near," he murmured to himself when he heard the roar of water rushing over the cataracts. Climbing a dune overlooking the mighty river he saw a small boat with a sail beneath the mighty falls.

Malica descended the dune and entered the river. The sound of the roaring water masked his approach. The craft had been abandoned for the night. He severed the rope that tethered the boat using the sword he had taken from the guard, and climbed aboard. The current thrust the small vessel into the powerful river. With only his instincts to guide him, Malica began his desperate journey to find his prince.

Nogard

Chapter 49   The Inn of Nevau

The Kingdom of Vall lay within the grip of the long northern winter and a blanket of white spread from the eastern mountains to the vast western sea. The snow enveloped the scars of war, which had ravished this fertile land. Peasants honed their plows in anticipation of the spring planting.

Freeya and Khrom learned to govern from Queen Dora.

"Above all, remember your word is law the moment it is spoken. Think before you speak."

"Yes, Mother!" spoke Khrom, while Freeya nodded her head in agreement.

"I am ready to pass judgment!" Khrom proclaimed.

Khrom knew his first decision would please many, and anger the former nobles of King Copen. An older peasant entered the hall followed by a noble. The peasant bowed before his new king and queen.

"Your Highness, I plead for justice. Sir Balda has threatened to force me and my family from our home."

"Why?" Khrom asked.

"I owe him a debt from the time of King Copen. I could not pay. My grain was taken to pay tribute to Raggnor."

"Balda, step before my throne!" Khrom commanded.

"Yes, Your Highness."

"Is it true you are going to throw a man and his family into the cold, for a debt made during the reign of Copen?"

"A debt is a debt, Highness."

Khrom turned to council with his queen. After a brief time he turned to face Balda.

"All debts made during the reign of King Copen are now void! No man, woman or child shall be thrown into the cold!"

"Thank you! Thank you!" cried the peasant.

"Balda, while the soldiers and peasants fought to free our kingdom from Raggnor and the Troblin armies, you and Copen's supporters went into hiding. It is you and your fellow nobles who owe a debt to the people of Vall. All of your lands and titles are now property of the realm!" Khrom proclaimed angrily.

"You are still a brigand! You will never be the king Copen was!"

"This is true! I will be a much greater king than he! Balda, speak not another word or I will have you hung from the castle wall!"

Balda realized he had spoken out of turn. He shuddered when he thought of the noose being placed over his head. His hand touched his throat.

"Forgive me, Highness. I spoke in haste."

After Balda departed, Captain Eric spoke. "Your decision was just, Khrom, but I fear you have made powerful enemies."

"Captain, they were my enemies before my proclamation!"

"I stand with my husband," Freeya said.

"I agree with you, Khrom," Dora said. "However, next time try not to make quite as bold a change. A canceling of the peasant's debt would have been enough for now."

"Yes, Mother."

Jasmine and Jal had taken up residence in the partly reconstructed castle of Nevau. Jasmine had relinquished the throne of the Kreigg to the ambassador. She moved to Nevau to be with the peasants rebuilding their castle.

Jal felt the presence of someone searching for him. He joined his daughter in the tower. He looked in vain and saw only the endless expanse of snow surrounding Nevau.

Jasmine looked into her father's eyes.

"You are troubled, Father!"

"Yes! Someone searches for me. I know not who or why."

"Ask the Sorcerer Gaul, Father. We are to meet with him in

the Kreigg fortress in two days, when he will send Kee's sister dragons to their realm. We are to join Freeya and Khrom here. They will take us to the fortress."

Jal ran his fingers through his beard and pondered how Freeya and Khrom could cross the expanse of snow.

Khrom spoke to his coachman. "My queen and I must travel to Nevau and on to the Kreigg fortress. Do you know a way to cross the snow?"

"Yes, Sire. Many years have passed since the time of the great winter storm. A stranger from the north and his woman came to Vall in a carriage without wheels. He called the craft, which glided across the snow, a sleigh. The sleigh was pulled by two pair of animals he called reindeer."

"What happened to the man, his woman and their reindeer? Do you know where the sleigh is now?"

"The snow melted and they have lived among us since this time." The coachman paused. "The reindeer fed many hungry people. The sleigh lies below the hay in the stable, where I hid it from King Copen."

"Can you drive this craft over the snow with a team of horses?"

"Of course. After I made changes to the sleigh, I used to take your mother and father on rides through the wood."

The coachman had the sleigh pulled from beneath the hay and cleaned for the journey. He inspected the craft and found it to be sound. At dawn the coachman harnessed two large horses to the sleigh. He sipped a drink of hot mead. Freeya and her husband nestled into a covering of sheepskins. She witnessed the steam rising from the bodies of the large horses. The red faced driver cracked his whip in the air and with a sudden lurch the runners glided over the hard packed snow. The horses had little difficulty pulling the sleigh.

Khrom saw a fox and a pair of red deer, as they raced past a stand of pines. In the distance he saw the silver coats of wolves bounding over the white terrain. He looked at his queen buried within the sheepskins.

"I love you, Freeya," Khrom said softly.

"I know," Freeya replied.

In the valley of the swine, Kee touched his muzzle to each of his sisters. He knew the females would soon be returned to the realm of their birth. Kee wished to return with them, but he respected the sorcerer's wishes and agreed to remain behind. The dragons had feasted the night before on a wild boar and an ibex, which had fallen from the cliff face. Kee knew there would be little time for a final farewell at the cave of lights. A tear welled in his eye, as he knew their time together was growing shorter.

For the final time they ascended together, above the steam laden valley of the swine. Their massive shadows fell upon the expanse of snow. The dragons instinctively flew toward the fortress of the Kreigg.

Freeya saw the flight of dragons flying over the sled. In her excitement she stood to wave in the moving sleigh and tumbled into a high drift. Khrom laughed before giving his command to the coachman.

"Halt! Stop the sleigh! Our queen is stuck in a snow drift."

Freeya tried to scream for help, but her mouth was filled with snow.

She spit out the snow. "Stop laughing, Khrom. I could have been hurt."

"I can't help myself. Let me pull you free."

Freeya waited until Khrom was inches from her. She grabbed a glob of snow and shoved it into his face. Khrom responded by pushing snow into Freeya's. The two grabbed one another and began rolling and laughing in the drift.

The coachman returned to his horses. After a short time he was joined by the red faced royal couple. The horses made steady progress throughout the remainder of the day and evening. The coachman saw a wisp of smoke rising from a structure near the snow covered road.

"We are near Nevau, Your Highness. I will tell these peasants we will be spending the night."

"Tell them we are travelers. Ask them if we can stay the night. We do not wish to force ourselves upon them," Freeya said.

Khrom escorted Freeya into the lodge, while the coachman and the innkeeper boarded the horses. Freeya felt the warmth and heard the flames consuming logs in the hearth. She saw a big woman tending the fire. The woman placed a large fowl onto an iron rod and began to cook it over hot coals at the edge of the fire.

"Welcome to my Inn; my name is Helen. We are having swan this night."

"My name is Freeya, and this is my husband. Pardon me, Helen. Aren't swans the property of the king?"

"Provisions are hard to come by and His Majesty has many more important things to be concerned with. Besides, Vall is quite a distance from here. Where do you journey from?"

"Vall!" Khrom replied.

"Oh!"

Khrom controlled his urge to laugh, as he did not wish to embarrass his host further. "I am confident our king and queen have many more important things to be concerned with," Khrom said.

The coachman and the innkeeper entered the lodge. Helen set a large wooden table. Soon everyone began to dine on the swan and drink goblets of mead. The coachman turned to Khrom. "This fowl is delicious, Your Highness."

"Yes, it is," Khrom replied. "You are an excellent cook, Helen!"

"Thank you, Your Majesty," Helen said trying to hide her embarrassment.

"I wish to build an inn near Vall," the coachman said.

"You will need a wife," the Innkeeper said.

"I have a sister," Helen responded. Everyone began to laugh and drink. That night they slept near the fire in the hearth, while the cold north wind battered the lodge.

Freeya saw the sleeping form of her husband. She touched her lips to his and whispered. "I love you, My King."

"I know," Khrom replied.

At dawn the wind abated. The sun reflected off the snow creating a blinding glare. The innkeeper and the coachman harnessed the horses. Helen gave her guests wooden snow glasses. Their eyes soon adjusted to the slits in the bark lenses.

𝔑ogard

Chapter 50   Return to 𝔑ogard

Once more the sleigh lurched forward to continue the journey across the expanse of white. By mid morning they arrived at the gate to Nevau. Jasmine had watched their approach from the tower and she met them, with her father, at the entrance.

"Join us, Jasmine, the sleigh is fun," Freeya said.

"Please join us, General!" Khrom said.

The horses adjusted to the additional weight. Jal sat next to the coachman while Jasmine squeezed between Freeya and Khrom. Freeya gave Jal her snow glasses. Both sisters laughed and talked excitedly.

The sleigh entered the Pass of Lund and by midday the frontier of the Kreigg. Jal saw a unicorn with its rider streaking across the frozen terrain.

The horses halted in front of the Kreigg fortress where the ambassador met the arriving royalty. He wore a crown upon his head, as Jasmine had proclaimed him to be the King of the Kreigg. "We must hurry, Your Highness. The Sorcerer Gaul waits."

Kee and his sisters stood by the cave's entrance. The sorcerer waited for the portal to open into the cave of lights. Freeya ran up the ramp ahead of the rest of the party. She saw Kee and his sisters near the caves entrance.

"Kee! Kee! I come to be with you."

The Black Dragon turned from his sisters to see Freeya running towards him. Freeya felt both his sadness and joy over his sisters' return to Nogard, the realm of their birth. She touched his massive head and felt the wetness of his tears. The dragons began a moaning sound, as the time grew nearer.

The back of the cave turned orange, as the wall of stone began to part. When the portal appeared a dazzling array of lights beckoned to the female dragons. The sorcerer held his necklace of power and aimed his turquoise pendant at the first of the females. In turn each of the dragons turned blue and shrunk rapidly to a fraction of their original size. They did not hesitate to enter the cave and join with the radiant lights. In a twinkling they became one with the lights which transported them through time and stone to Nogard.

The female dragons green color and massive size returned as they departed the cave and entered the Realm of the Dragons. At first they would live in a cave with their mother. They would tell her of Kee and his sacrifice. They would fly over rugged peaks and valleys that dragons love. In time they would mate and raise young of their own, knowing they would never see their brother again.

Freeya and Kee shed tears together. She felt her friend's sorrow and pain. Khrom hurried to be with his bride. He had seen the female dragons entering the lights and the cave returning to stone. Khrom held Freeya's left hand while she stroked the head of the dragon with her right.

The sorcerer turned his attention to Kee. The dragon read his thoughts and agreed to fulfill his obligation. In the morning he would return to the glacier.

Jal approached the sorcerer. "Sorcerer, may I ask a question?"

"Does it concern your dreams?"

"Yes."

"The one who seeks you is your countryman. He desperately needs your help. Do not seek him, he will find you. That is all I know, General."

The unicorn Thor pranced in place waiting for his master. The sorcerer spoke to his friends. "My work here is complete. I must return to my realm." He mounted his steed. With a single bound Thor leaped from the plateau. The unicorn's feet barely kissed the surface of the snow. Thor's feet danced as he raced over the white terrain. The sorcerer knew he would soon be in the warmth of his castle.

Kee spent the night in the care of the Kreigg dragon handlers. His tears subsided as he accepted his fate.

Jasmine declined an invitation from the newly crowned King of the Kreigg to spend the night. They began their journey to Nevau at dusk. At first a bright moon reflected off the white surface as they entered the pass of Lund. A dark cloud passed between the moon and the earth. Suddenly they were caught in a snow squall.

"I fear we are lost," the coachman said.

"Make for the shelter of the pines!" Jal said.

"Yes, General."

Upon entering the protection of the conifers, Khrom felt the wind subsiding. He left the sleigh to cut pine boughs to form a shelter for the night. In the dim light he saw a trail of blood in the snow. He walked cautiously forward. He heard many large creatures rushing through the pines. At the end of the trail he saw the body of a partially eaten deer. A branch snapped behind him. Khrom turned to face the threat.

He saw his beautiful queen standing beside a large male wolf. "Do not be frightened, My King. The wolves will escort us to Nevau."

The large wolf departed to rejoin his pack, while Khrom followed Freeya to the sleigh.

Khrom faced the coachman. "Follow the wolves lead. They will show us the way to Nevau."

The wolves howled, then ran ahead of the nervous horses pulling the sleigh.

"Why were the wolves in the pines?" Jal asked.

"We entered their realm in the darkness," Freeya answered.

The wind abated, as the dark cloud departed from the moon. Jal saw the wolves bounding effortlessly through the snow in the lunar light. In the distance he made out the flicker of a torch in the tower of Nevau. He pointed to the torch. The coachman guided his team toward the light. The wolves howled as one, before turning toward their home in the wood.

"We will soon be in Nevau, Majesties!" the coachman said.

Jasmine gave a sigh when the sleigh crossed the drawbridge. Two peasants assisted the coachman with the horses and the sleigh when they entered the courtyard.

Khrom felt the heat of a roaring fire when he entered the rebuilt hall of Nevau. He saw several peasants and their families gathered within the hall. Freeya joined her husband.

"People of Nevau gather round! I wish to present to you my king and husband, Khrom. I am his queen. Together we are the Sovereigns of the Combined Kingdoms of Nevau and Vall."

The peasants cheered, some cried. A woman fell to her knees before Freeya.

"You have given us hope! We rebuild the castle and live in its hall until it is completed."

Freeya looked into the woman's eyes. "My king thanks you for all that you have done here. You may live in this hall for as long as you have need."

Jasmine and her father entered the hall.

"Freeya, stay with me in our old chamber."

"What of Khrom and your father?"

"My father and Khrom can stay in the hall this night. Please, it is only one night and I will not see you for a very long time."

"Go with your sister, Freeya," Khrom said. "I wish to be with the citizens of Nevau this night."

"Thank you, Khrom."

Freeya followed her sister up the stairs to her former chamber above the hall. She noticed the invaders had inflicted little damage to the chamber. Jasmine started a fire within the small hearth. The young women talked and laughed through the night. They spoke of men and their many adventures. They held one another when they shared their tragedies.

"My father has a recurring dream. I fear we will be returning to the land of my birth in the coming year."

"Oh Jasmine, your kingdom is ruled by an evil tyrant."

"Yes, I know this. My father wishes to free our people."

Khrom met with the peasants. They told him of their plans to sow the fields of Nevau in the spring and help the Kreigg plant their wheat. After many long discussions, Khrom and his people slumbered on the floor of the hall.

Nogard

Epilogue

The long winter night surrendered to the brief time of sunlight. Kee lifted from the Kreigg Fortress to begin his journey to the Realm of Gaul. He maintained a course, which would take him over the castle of Nevau. From the air he saw Nevau covered by a mantle of white.

Freeya heard the sound of massive wings beating a cadence. She dressed quickly and ran to the courtyard. Kee eclipsed the morning sun. He flew low over the castle and saw Freeya waving to him. A single tear fell from his eye. He beat his wings to regain the heights needed to reach the glacier, where Kee joined once more with the great body of ice and snow. As before, he shut down five of his six hearts. He would remain in this tomb of ice until summoned by the Sorcerer Gaul.

Freeya and Khrom returned to Vall. Throughout the winter the young king and queen ruled under the guidance of Dora. Freeya often thought of her sister and the words she spoke. *"I will be returning to the land of my birth. My father wishes to free his people."* Freeya knew Jasmine would ask for her and the dragon's help in her quest to free the people of Nubia. She did not mention her conversation with Jasmine to her husband.

Khrom was consumed by two loves. The love he had for his kingdom's people and the love he felt for his beautiful queen. Khrom held Freeya's hand in the tower one morning and scanned the endless snow, which isolated Vall from the rest of the earth. A time of peace reigned over his Kingdom. Only the wolves and their prey remained active beyond the walls of Vall.

In the castle of Nevau, Jasmine waited for the return of spring. She saw the anguish in her father's face and shared his pain. She had resigned herself to support her father no matter what the outcome. Jasmine noticed the days growing longer and the cold of the night starting to abate. The time for her quest was nearing.

Jal's dreams continued. He waited in anticipation for the unknown stranger to find him. Every day he would climb the tower to scan the horizon for the one who sought him. One morning he noticed droplets forming on the daggers of ice above him.

"The time for the stranger grows near," he murmured.

On the morning of his second day on the river, Malica saw what appeared to be a large log floating in front of him. To his horror, the log turned and opened a massive maw filled with dagger sized teeth. The tenseness of his body relaxed when the crocodile dove into the murky Nile to feed on a large school of perch. He lay on the bottom of the boat when he saw a band of horsemen on the shore. That night he passed a giant monolith from ancient Egypt.

"I will find you, My Prince, or I shall die in the trying," Malica pledged, as his boat drifted into the unknown perils that lie before him.

Author Robert Conard

Robert Conard was born in Columbus, Ohio in November, 1939. He is a Navy veteran who served on a destroyer as a gunner's mate during the Cuban Missile Crisis.

At the age of ten, his grandfather read *The Iliad* to him by lantern light in a small town in southern Ohio that had yet to receive electricity. He has been hooked on the classics ever since.

Bob is an avid fisherman, and has written several periodicals for the New England Fisherman. He has also written several short stories—*Sharks' Soup* being the most famous.

He currently lives with his wife Priscilla in Guilford, Connecticut.

Made in the USA
Middletown, DE
28 December 2015